DEAD
WEST

BOOKS BY MATT GOLDMAN

Gone to Dust

Broken Ice

The Shallows

Dead West

MATT GOLDMAN

DEAD WEST

FORGE®

A Tom Doherty Associates Book / New York

This is a work of fiction. All of the characters, organizations, and events portrayed in this novel are either products of the author's imagination or are used fictitiously.

A Forge Book
Published by Tom Doherty Associates
120 Broadway
New York, NY 10271

www.tor-forge.com

Forge® is a registered trademark of Macmillan Publishing Group, LLC.

The Library of Congress Cataloging-in-Publication Data is available upon request.

ISBN 978-1-250-19134-2 (hardcover)
ISBN 978-1-250-19135-9 (ebook)

Our books may be purchased in bulk for promotional, educational, or business use. Please contact your local bookseller or the Macmillan Corporate and Premium Sales Department at 1-800-221-7945, extension 5442, or by email at MacmillanSpecialMarkets@macmillan.com.

First Edition: June 2020

Printed in the United States of America

0 9 8 7 6 5 4 3 2 1

For my wife, Michele
Who is loving, intelligent,
Beautiful(ly) challenging
Always kind
How lucky I am
She married down.

DEAD WEST

1

Beverly Mayer sat tall, strong, and upright. Her blue eyes sparkled. A pair of reading glasses hung around her neck from a gold chain. Her gray hair appeared long but was twisted and folded on top of her head like a challah. She wore a soft pink suit of thick wool. It looked European and expensive. She sat next to her husband of sixty-seven years. I know because that's how she introduced him. "This is Arthur, my husband of sixty-seven years."

Arthur Mayer did not speak. He rode shotgun in a vehicle called marriage. He slumped shrunken in his suit made of brown herringbone tweed. His neck was too small for his white dress shirt—the shirt didn't touch his neck the way Saturn's rings don't touch Saturn. His lower jaw jutted forward. Heavy black-framed spectacles crept down his nose. A fingerprint marred the left lens. Arthur Mayer's eyes had shrunk, too, small and green like lima beans. A Band-Aid covered something on his forehead, as if his skin had worn thin in one spot and needed reinforcement. He clutched a black metal cane in his right hand and made no eye contact. But Arthur Mayer had great hair. Thick and silver and combed meticulously. It appeared he hadn't lost a strand since the Great Depression. I couldn't take my eyes off it.

"Are you listening to me, Mr. Shapiro?" said Beverly Mayer. She put a smile under her nose and said, "Mr. Shapiro?"

"Yes," I said. "I'm listening. Go ahead."

Beverly Mayer said, "Our grandson's fiancée died last week. Heart failure, they say. Imagine that. A twenty-eight-year-old who hadn't been sick a day in her life. Poor Ebben is devastated. We're already concerned about what he's doing with his trust fund out there in Hollywood. And now this girl, Juliana, goes and dies. It's bound to lead to imprudent decision making. For heaven's sake, the principal from which Ebben's trust fund grew was earned over 150 years ago. We will not sit idly and watch him squander a fortune like his father did."

"Any foul play suspected in his fiancée's death?"

We sat in the Mayers' cavernous living room on St. Paul's Summit Avenue. The mansion was built by Frederick C. Fallhauser, lumber baron and grandfather of Beverly Mayer. It had 33,000 square feet of mahogany floors, oak-paneled walls, carved wooden ceiling beams, and leaded glass windows. It's the kind of place that, after the Mayers die, will have a gift shop and velvet ropes steering people to a gift shop that sells tickets for tours and commemorative coffee table books.

Beverly said, "The police didn't suspect foul play. Apparently, the girl had one of those eating disorders. I suppose they all do out there in Hollywood. Maybe she starved herself to death. But why she died is not really the point. The point is we'd like to know what business dealings Ebben has got himself into. He's having an open house tonight to celebrate Juliana's life. I asked if Ebben meant a funeral. He said no, a celebration. I don't know what that is. Regardless, Arthur and I would like you to be there."

"In Los Angeles? Tonight?"

"Yes. It's only 7:00 A.M. there. You have plenty of time to make it."

I looked at Arthur to see if he agreed but got nothing. He might have been sleeping with his eyes open. I said, "All right, well, I suppose I can get on a plane to Los Angeles and find out how Ebben is spending his money. But you do realize once he received the trust fund, it's his. He can do whatever he wants with it. You have no recourse against your grandson."

"We have no legal recourse," said Beverly Mayer. "That I understand. But Arthur and I are still the heads of this family, and families are like small countries with their own rules and penalties when a member steps out of line. The good news for Ebben is he's our only grandchild. That makes him a wealthy man. The bad news for Ebben is he's our only grandchild. Our eyes are on him alone. Do you have children, Mr. Shapiro?"

The house smelled of wax and varnish. A radiator knocked and clanged. The old wooden floors creaked. I felt my early childhood in the air but had no idea why.

I said, "Yes. I have a daughter."

"And how old is she?"

"She's ten months old."

"Oh my," said Beverly Mayer. "You started late. Young wife?"

"No." That was true on two counts: the baby's mother was my age and she wasn't my wife. To explain how Evelyn Stahl-Shapiro came into this world would take too many minutes and looks of disapproval from the woman who thought families are like nation-states.

"Well, good for you," said Beverly Mayer. "You're in for quite a ride."

"I'm enjoying it already."

"Now," said Beverly Mayer, "what I'm about to tell you I've already told to Mr. Ellegaard, but since you're the one going to Los Angeles, he advised I repeat it to you. He said you might pick up on something he missed."

Ellegaard was my business partner at Stone Arch Investigations. My tall, stoic, morally upright Scandinavian—a mandatory fixture in any Minnesota enterprise.

"Ebben received $50 million on his thirtieth birthday. Before that he behaved quite respectably. Brown University then an MBA at Wharton. He worked two years as an investment banker for Piper in New York City then returned home to work in private equity. He did everything he could to educate himself about money. But six months before his thirty-fifth birthday, he quit his job, let his hair grow, and stopped wearing suits and ties. Somehow he met a girl named Juliana Marquez, fell in love, and got engaged. They flew all over the world, taking meetings in Los Angeles and New York and London and Beijing of all places. When I ask what he's up to, he says some nonsense about exploring new opportunities."

"You think he's lying?"

"Only by omission," said Beverly Mayer. She straightened her long spine. "What I fear Ebben's not telling us is he's getting involved in the motion picture business. And I happen to know something about that business and how they prey on good people with money. My older sister, Grace, may she rest in peace, was quite beautiful and married a powerful agent at the William Morris Agency in New York. It was his job to find funding for films, and I heard him boast several times, quite coarsely, about getting fools to open their wallets because they so badly wanted to participate in show business. He used to say, 'The key is to get them spending. Invite them to parties with beautiful people. They'll feel lucky to be there even though they paid every dime for that party.' Then he would laugh and puff on his cigar. It's that cigar smoke that killed my sister. Vulgar habit. Vulgar man."

I looked to Arthur Mayer who had yet to make eye contact with me. He moved, so I knew he wasn't stuffed. I said, "I can go to Los Angeles, Mrs. Mayer, but you might get better results hiring a private detective there."

"No," she said without hesitation. "I trust you. I trust Mr. Ellegaard. I've spoken to half a dozen people who sing your praises. People I've known for over half a century. People I trust. If you're smart enough to solve the Duluth Murders, you're smart enough to figure out Los Angeles. If you need help when you're there, then hire away. We will spare no expense."

"Just to make sure I understand: You will spare no expense to confirm your grandson, Ebben, is investing in show business? Because that's easy to find out. You could probably pick up the phone and ask him. I bet he tells you the truth."

"I have asked him, Mr. Shapiro. And he has denied it."

"I thought you said he lied by omission."

"Well, it's not a direct denial. He just keeps saying something about new opportunities."

"Maybe because it's too hard to explain. Maybe he's investing in virtual reality, augmented reality, or artificial intelligence." Beverly Mayer responded with the same blank expression as her husband's. I said, "Or maybe Ebben's new opportunity isn't about business. Maybe it's about love."

"Oh, dear," said Beverly Mayer. "Young people no longer need love. The world today offers love's advantages à la carte. No need to buy the whole shebang to get the few things you want."

That got a response from Arthur Mayer. His eyes swung toward his wife then he exhaled what sounded close to, "Huh?"

Beverly Mayer ignored her husband of sixty-seven years. She reached to the side table, grabbed an envelope, and handed it to me. On it, she had typed MR. SHAPIRO with an actual typewriter. "Here is Ebben's address in Los Angeles. He's rented a house for the winter. We've also included a check for $25,000. That should cover your travel expenses and fee."

"That's quite generous. Thank you."

"Arthur and I won't live forever, and the money will eventually go to Ebben anyway. We are more than willing to leave him a little less to straighten out that boy."

Arthur Mayer sighed, either to communicate he agreed or to remind me he was alive.

I stepped out of the Mayer mansion and into mid-January. A perfect winter day. Three degrees, no wind, and bright sunshine in a sky so blue it'd make the ocean green with envy. I put sunglasses on my face and walked down to Summit Avenue where I'd parked my hockey mom mobile. I had planned on replacing the Volvo station wagon with something less maternal, but since Evelyn was born, it had become too damn practical.

A large man sat in my passenger seat. He wore a 5-XL parka, fur-lined aviator hat, sunglasses, and a scarf wrapped around his face. The rest of him was in there somewhere. I sat behind the wheel and said, "Why'd you turn off the car? Get a little heat in here and you wouldn't have to wear everything you own from the big and tall man's shop."

"I like being bundled up," said Jameson White, his voice muffled under his scarf. "Can't do that when the heat's on. Get too sweaty."

"All right if I turn the heat on while we're driving?"

The big man nodded. I started the car. He pulled the aviator hat from his head. His big Afro hit the car's ceiling. Jameson White was six foot seven inches tall—his hair didn't have much room. He unwrapped his scarf, revealing a beard he'd grown since leaving his job. A temporary leave, I hoped. I pulled onto Summit Avenue.

Jameson said, "What took you so long in there?" I handed Jameson the envelope from Beverly Mayer. He read, "*Mr. Shapiro.* We going to visit your dad?"

"No. We're going to Los Angeles."

2

A couple years ago, I took a hunting arrow in the shoulder and would have bled out if a medical examiner hadn't been on-site and had the good sense to cauterize my wound. Still, I needed surgery and a week in the hospital. But I was working the case of a missing seventeen-year-old girl and couldn't take a week. So my ex-wife hired a private nurse to tend to me twenty-four/seven to clean my wound, change my bandages, and make sure I didn't miss a dose of antibiotics.

That nurse's name was Jameson White. The best trauma nurse—correction: nurse practitioner—in Minnesota.

When I met Jameson, he had a booming laugh and all the charm and twinkle his six-foot-seven-inch frame could hold. He's a great talker—I'm a decent listener. We became friends.

He was fascinated by my work and offered to help if we needed him. Once in a while, we did. Private investigators sometimes hire distractors to divert the attention of their subjects. It's usually a pretty man or woman, but in certain situations a six-foot-seven-inch-tall black man with a giant Afro worked beautifully. Especially a man full of charm, social grace, and intelligence. You couldn't take your eyes off Jameson. His physical immensity drew you to him and his charisma kept you there.

I didn't know anything about Jameson's private life other than what he'd told me. He was single. He followed a woman to Minnesota. It didn't work out but I never asked why.

Jameson played offensive line in the Canadian Football League for the Montreal Alouettes. Played his college ball at UCLA and knew Los Angeles. Knew it well because he spent his summers driving a cab after football practice. I'd never been to that town and needed local expertise I could trust. That was one reason I invited Jameson White to join me in Los Angeles.

The second reason—the big reason—was because a year earlier, a gunman entered a middle school, killed fourteen students, three teachers, and wounded ten others. All because one of the teachers refused him a second Tinder date. The first victims were rushed to Jameson White's ER. He worked until every child and teacher who could be saved had been saved. He saw too many of them die. Thirty-some hours of saving and losing people, mostly children. Then he went home. Next day he returned to work and did so the day after that. For five months Jameson White worked his shifts without complaint. Then he fell apart.

Now, he sat in my passenger seat as I drove away from the Mayer mansion and headed west on Summit Avenue. Car exhaust

MATT GOLDMAN

condensed out of tailpipes like clouds, swirled in the automobiles' wakes then vanished. The January sun bounced off yesterday's three fresh inches of snow. The town lay frozen white and clean.

Jameson said, "Los Angeles? Why would we go to Los Angeles?"

I told Jameson about Beverly Mayer and her grandson, Ebben, and Ebben's dead fiancée, Juliana, and said, "You want to go see Ellegaard with me or should I drop you off so you can pack?"

"I don't know. I haven't decided if I'm going." Jameson folded his arms and looked out the passenger window.

Leaving Jameson behind wasn't an option. Not since his breakdown. An old teammate of his was an assistant coach at UCLA. The two of them had remained close friends. I called the guy last night and told him I might be coming out for a job. If I brought Jameson, would he be able to spend some time with the former giant of joviality? He said he'd take Jameson the whole visit. He'd bring him to work. Have Jameson teach those kids how to use their hands and feet. I thought that might do Jameson some good, although I wasn't ready to part with him the whole visit.

I also wanted to get Jameson out of town on the anniversary of the school shooting. He didn't need to relive that. It's bad enough every subsequent mass shooting in the country dragged him back down. That's something he'd have to manage for the rest of his life.

We stopped at the Mississippi River. Evaporate froze above the open water—it looked like steam. I turned right then jogged northeast, on and off East River Parkway. The big man still stared out his window, arms folded.

I said, "I called your buddy August last night. Told him we might be coming out to L.A. He sounded pretty excited."

Jameson said, "You told August I might be coming out?"

"He wants to take you to practice to learn the young'un linemen a thing or two."

"I get it. You want to hand me off so you don't have to babysit me anymore."

Seven months ago, I got a call from a doctor in Jameson's ER. The doctor said Jameson hadn't showed up to work in two days, and the ER staff had discovered Seconal missing from the lock-up. I drove straight to Jameson's place and knocked on the front door. No answer. I picked the lock and found him wearing his usual gray sweatpants and sweatshirt, drinking Redbreast, eating Pop-Tarts, and watching *The Price Is Right*. The bottle of Seconal was on the coffee table.

"I see my Irish whiskey habit has rubbed off on you." He turned his head and showed me his glassy eyes. "How many of those did you take?"

Jameson White said, "Not enough."

I have kept him close ever since.

I pulled into the parking structure at Riverplace and said, "Guess you're coming with me to see Ellegaard."

"I like Ellegaard," said Jameson. "More than you."

"You know that's not true. You like us the same."

Jameson sighed. "Yeah, I do."

I drove down a level toward my parking spot, though I hardly needed a reserved space. The Saint Anthony Main area boomed in the eighties and nineties, but now it had more vacancies than tenants. I said, "I'm not babysitting you, Jameson. If you want to kill yourself, I sure as hell can't stop you. But sometimes a guy needs a friend. I'm honored to be that friend. And I thought you could use some warm weather and a walk on the beach and to visit your old campus and football buddy. That wouldn't be so painful, would it?"

Jameson shook his head.

"Plus, I don't know that town. Traffic's supposed to be a nightmare. Thought maybe you could help me find my way around town."

Jameson White turned his big face toward me. "I got to fly first class. I don't fit in coach."

"I'll ride up there with you. I heard you can eat all the almonds you want. Come on. Let's go see Ellegaard. After that, I'll drop you at home to pack and we'll head to the airport."

"Heh," said Jameson, a hint of a smile in his voice, "pack. You don't got to pack for L.A. All you need is a T-shirt, pair of shorts, and flip-flops. Pack. Such a Minnesota boy."

"No shit. That's why I need you."

3

Kenji Thao greeted us at the reception desk. He first came to Stone Arch Investigations as an intern from Harding High School. A handsome kid with kind eyes, a broad nose, and a big smile. He combed his thick black hair like young Elvis Presley and wore a wisp of unripe facial hair. He'd carved out a personal style of white shirts under suit vests. A pocket watch rested in one of the vest's pockets fastened to a chain that ran across to the other pocket. I'd seen the actual watch once. Kenji's only defect was he stood five feet ten inches tall, defying the Hmong stereotype of being short. I don't care for it when people who are supposed to be short are taller than me. I blame hormone-infused milk of which I drank none because I'm lactose-intolerant.

"Hey boss," said Kenji. "You going to California?"

"We are." I handed him the envelope minus the check.

"What up, Jameson?"

Jameson nodded. "Kenji."

"Please book us a flight leaving this afternoon, a nice rental car but not a convertible because I have delicate skin, and two rooms at a good hotel near the address in here."

Jameson said, "And I got to fly first class. I don't fit in coach."

Kenji looked at me for approval. I gave it.

We walked toward Ellegaard's office. Kenji said, "You want a seat in first class, Nils, or are you small enough to ride on Jameson's lap?"

Anders Ellegaard sat at his desk reviewing a document, a highlighter in hand. Sunlight poured in through the window in the stone wall. Ellegaard squinted in the bright light. He kept his eyes on his work and said, "How did Beverly Mayer behave?"

"Her face smiled but the rest of her didn't. You should come to Los Angeles with us."

"Wish I could. Maisy and Olivia both have hockey tournaments this weekend. Molly and I have to divide and conquer. I'd send Annika with you if she wasn't on vacation." Annika Brydolf was our junior investigator. She'd taken her two kids to Florida—her first vacation in over ten years. Ellegaard looked up. He and Jameson exchanged nods. Ellegaard had approved paying Jameson's way in return for him playing tour guide. Truth is, Ellegaard would have approved it even if Jameson had never been to Los Angeles. He loved the big guy just as much as I did.

Ellegaard smiled an easy smile. He had crow's-feet around his eyes. I met him when we were both cadets at the Minneapolis Police Academy. Nineteen years later, he looked the same other than those crow's-feet. And lines in his forehead. He looked like a boy with a man's markings. I wondered if I'd always see him like that—if I were incapable of seeing him as a forty-one-year-old.

I placed the check on his desk. "Seems like a lot of money for almost no work. How well do you know Beverly Mayer?"

Ellegaard looked up and said, "Not well. But my parents know Beverly and Arthur's son and his wife. Not that they run in the same social circle. My mother decorated their lake home, and they became friends. My parents spend weekends up in Brainerd with them."

"Beverly said something about Ebben's father squandering his trust fund."

"He didn't squander it. He started a foundation to narrow the achievement gap in Minnesota schools."

"Wow. Beverly Mayer is a piece of work."

"Not a nice woman by all accounts. Her son doesn't talk to her."

"What's her grandson, Ebben, like?"

"I asked around before I sent you to the Mayers. I haven't heard a bad thing about Ebben. Not from business associates. Not from family. Not from ex-girlfriends. He's respected and well-liked. And if he's investing in entertainment projects, no one cares other than Beverly Mayer. This job should be a paid vacation. Might as well enjoy it."

Paid vacations, like free lunches, exist in the land of unicorns and once-in-a-lifetime investment opportunities. I said, "Did you hear Ebben's fiancée died last week?"

"Yeah," said Ellegaard. "His parents are concerned about him. I think Beverly's just concerned about the money."

Kenji Thao stuck his head into Ellegaard's office. "Do you want to fly at 1:21 or 3:10?"

I turned to Jameson, "What do you think, boss?"

Jameson said, "1:21. The 3:10 would put us on the ground around 5:00 Pacific time. Los Angeles is a parking lot at 5:00."

"Local knowledge. Can't beat it."

"Kind of just common sense, but whatever."

I dropped Jameson at home to pack his T-shirts, shorts, and flip-flops and went home to do the same.

She had put the DO NOT DISTURB sign on the condo door to let me know the baby was napping. We had stolen the DO NOT DISTURB sign from the Fairmont Hotel in the Canadian Rockies. I asked her to marry me during that trip while hiking a trail high above the emerald-colored Lake Louise. It was mid-July, sunny, and warm. We trekked over what remained of an avalanche flow, which, the previous winter, had taken out thousands of pine trees. The avalanche had ripped the trees out by their roots and snapped them into bits. But the ice and snow captured and preserved the trees, keeping them fresh and green and fragrant like Christmas, even months after they'd been torn from the soil. I had planned on proposing at dinner, but the avalanche flow proved too picturesque and smelled like what I'd want heaven to smell like. So much beauty in the aftermath of destruction. It was just too damn symbolic of our romance. I had the ring with me because I didn't feel safe leaving it in the hotel room. She said yes, and we continued up the trail, me with one wet knee.

I removed my shoes in the hall, turned the door handle like

a safecracker, then tiptoed into the foyer. My fiancée sat on the couch, half under a wool throw, typing away on her laptop. She'd left work early to spend the afternoon with Evelyn Stahl-Shapiro. She had never wanted a baby, but in March we'd marry and that would officially make Gabriella Nuñez Evelyn's step-mother. That thrilled Gabriella.

I looked at the baby monitor on the end table. Evelyn slept under her quilt. I wanted to go get her, but Gabriella thought we should let her sleep because Evelyn had a cold and needed the rest. She sucked a pacifier in her mouth and held one in each hand. I didn't think it was a big deal that Evelyn still used a pacifier at ten months old, but Micaela and Gabriella wanted it gone. That was another beautiful gem in the aftermath of destruction. Micaela Stahl, my ex-wife, Evelyn's mother, had embraced Gabriella Nuñez not only as my fiancée, but as Evelyn's soon-to-be stepmother.

The aftermath of my failed marriage had spent its energy like a tsunami after an earthquake. It destroyed everything in its path. But it was over, and the seas had grown calm. Gabriella had to fight through insecurity and convention to trust that I had let go of Micaela. She'd succeeded. It's what happens when you fall in love with a skilled cop—she knows when you're lying and she knows when you're telling the truth. Gabriella, even though she sometimes doubted it, understood I was emotionally free and clear to love her. And with each passing month, Gabriella's trust grew to match what she knew. I loved her. Only her.

We all lug around baggage. Mine was I had been married to Micaela. Years after our divorce, we'd fall in and out of bed together. The physical part of our relationship lived while the emotional part died. We held on to it like Evelyn held on to her pacifiers. We didn't think Micaela could get pregnant so we did nothing to prevent the possibility. Then without telling me, Micaela took clomiphene and got pregnant at forty years old. The baby certified the death of our romantic relationship. It was as if Micaela and I were meant to have a baby together. Nothing more.

I'd met Gabriella when we were in our early twenties, both cadets at the Minneapolis Police Academy with Ellegaard. Micaela had known her for years—the two had always liked each other. That made for an unconventional but functional family. Micaela and Gabriella read the same parenting books and bored me with the same conversations about sleep training and diet and waiting lists for preschools.

I sat on the couch next to Gabriella, wriggled my way under the blanket, and kissed her.

Her dark eyes shined. Her black hair fell straight to the middle of her back. She said, "Thank you."

"Come to Los Angeles with us."

"The job is on?"

I nodded. "You can drive down to San Diego to see your family. Or maybe they'll come up for a few days."

Gabriella said, "Wish I could. But you'll be back soon."

"Yes, I will. With a perfect farmer's tan."

"Ooh. I can't wait."

We stared at the baby monitor and watched Evelyn sleep. It was weekday winter quiet. Windows shut and we were probably the only souls in the building. We just sat there staring at and listening to Evelyn breathe. Little moments. Take 'em when they come.

4

Jameson White and I touched down in Los Angeles. I turned on my phone. First up: a text from Beverly Mayer. I didn't know she could text. I should have insisted on combat pay.

Dear Mr. Shapiro, this is Beverly Mayer. Ebben just received autopsy results for his fiancée, Juliana. She died of heart failure. Most likely from an overdose of diet pills. Death ruled an accident. I thought you should know. —*Beverly Mayer*

I texted back that we'd just landed in Los Angeles, thanked her for the information, and hoped to hell I wouldn't hear from her again.

Jameson White stared out the window. "Man," he said, "it's the light."

"What are you talking about?"

"The light in Los Angeles is different. All bright and diffused. Doesn't make a lot of shadows."

I looked out the window. The light did look different, at least from Minnesota light. Like there were two suns and they were both white.

We stepped out of the Jetway and into Terminal 2 of LAX. It was trendy-restaurant loud and box-store bright. We followed our fellow passengers past Ford's Filling Station, The Farmer's Market, Barney's Beanery, and a Spanx store. We passed security, and an escalator-conveyor belted us toward baggage claim and dumped us onto the ground floor where a thicket of limo drivers stood in ill-fitting suits. Each had a luggage cart and a name on a tablet.

The pilot had said it was sixty-five degrees in Los Angeles, but when we stepped outside, sixty-five degrees felt like ninety in comparison to what we'd just left. The air smelled like exhaust. A massive herd of travelers pushed carts and wheeled luggage. Some dressed in garb from their country of origin. They clustered in familial units, multiple generations stuck to each luggage-laden cart like burrs on a toy poodle.

I felt like an immigrant getting off a steamship in 1885. Uniformed police officers walked from car to car in an effort to get traffic moving, but it stayed put. Jameson led me into a crosswalk, and cars stopped as if we were a couple of baby ducks. That got us to a median where we boarded a rental car shuttle.

The shuttle turned into the rental lot on a street called Interceptor. I said, "Interceptor is the best street name I've ever seen."

"Yeah," said Jameson, "it's pretty good. Just don't comment on all the street names. This is Los Angeles. There are a lot of 'em."

We rented a white Land Rover Discovery. Jameson insisted on driving. I didn't object.

I had never seen anything like Los Angeles. Heavy traffic on a weekday afternoon, passing strip mall after strip mall after strip mall, each with a packed parking lot and single sign listing the businesses within, as if it were a menu. Yoga studios, tanning salons, donut shops, laundromats, coffee shops, taco stands, sushi restaurants, phone repair shops, dry cleaners, juice shops, smoke shops, tax accountants, nail salons, cryotherapy places (whatever those are), pet grooming, and marijuana dispensaries. The signs didn't stop and neither did the strip malls, all sided in stucco painted white, yellow, beige, or pink.

Sunglasses were mandatory, as if the whole city was controlled by a dimmer switch, but the opposite of that—a brightener switch. And it was cranked up as high as it could go. We passed over a freeway with eight lanes on each side. Traffic crawled in both directions.

"That's the 405," said Jameson. "We're not taking that. I know a shortcut."

Jameson's shortcut took us on a fifteen-minute ride through more signage and lights and cardboard-carrying panhandlers followed by five minutes of brown hills and oil fields studded with pendulating pumps followed by twenty minutes of more signs, lights, and panhandlers. I saw no pedestrians. Not one. The panhandlers didn't count—they weren't walking, just standing at stoplights, their sad story written on a piece of dead box. *Homeless. Veteran. God bless. Kids to feed.*

After almost an hour (some shortcut) of slogging through all that, Jameson turned out of traffic and into a dead still neighborhood. The change was abrupt, like going from a rock concert to a library. The neighborhood had large homes, old streetlamps, sidewalks, and big fat leaved-out trees.

I said, "Where are we?"

"Hancock Park."

"Never heard of that town."

"It's not a town. It's a neighborhood. Bunch of UCLA boosters live in this hood. Had parties at their houses for players and alumni. I ate some delicious hors d'oeuvres in some of these houses." Jameson pulled over and parked along the curb. He pointed to a massive home. "That's the house Ebben's renting. Thought you might want to see it in the daylight before the celebration of the dead woman tonight."

The house was two and a half stories tall, hugged by lush landscaping, and sided in stucco painted the color of coffee with milk. Spanish tiles covered the roof. The house had no shutters, which looked strange. There were a few cars in the driveway. I glanced at the clock on the dash. The celebration didn't start for a couple hours.

Jameson said, "That ain't right."

"What ain't right?"

"The gardener."

"What's wrong with him?"

"He's using a broom and a rake. No real gardener in L.A. would do that. He lowered his voice an octave and got theatrical. "The leaf blower is all powerful! The leaf blower is God! Behold the beauty of the leaf blower and bend the knee!"

I let that hang a moment then said, "You feeling all right, buddy?"

Jameson said, "Plus the guy's white. You're more likely to see a white rhino in this neighborhood than a white gardener. If you ask me, he's playing lookout for Ebben or he's working for someone else who's keeping an eye on Ebben."

Either Jameson had started our trip with a useful dose of local knowledge or my big friend was losing his mind. I said, "How far is our hotel from here?"

"Five minutes. Kenji did us right."

Five minutes later, Jameson White and I checked into The Line Hotel on Wilshire Boulevard. We'd traveled about a mile from ritzy Hancock Park to Koreatown. Still a lot of signs, but most were in Korean, which, thanks to my ignorance of the language, was a relief from the onslaught of information. There, I did see a few pedestrians. They, like the signs, were mostly Korean, too.

We stood in line to check in. Jameson said, "Damn. This is a hipster hotel."

He was right. The people inside The Line Hotel were mostly young. Beards, topknots, and tattoos aplenty. We have hipsters in Minnesota, but they're not allowed in nice hotels. Jameson and I retired to our separate rooms to nap for the night ahead.

5

At 6:30 P.M. Jameson drove off to see his friend August, and I walked the mile from the hotel to Ebben's house.

A path of red brick led me to the house. I smelled lilac, gardenia, and rosemary. The only place you'd experience those scents in January back home would be in a candle shop at the mall. Floods lit the yard. A few trees had dropped their leaves but most hadn't. Roses bloomed from beds of dirt carved from a deep green lawn. The blades of grass were thin and the yard smelled of manure. Music blared from inside the house and a helicopter roared somewhere overhead.

I approached a large wooden door and entered a foyer of terracotta tiles and Mission-style sconces, the lightbulbs trying their best behind mica panes to illuminate the deceased. Or at least a poster-sized photograph of Ebben Mayer's dead fiancée that sat on an easel. A woman of about thirty, dark eyes and brown skin, wearing a white cotton dress. She looked peaceful. Serene. Content. A placard on the bottom of the photo read: JULIANA, WE LOVE YOU FOREVER.

Her eyes had a rare combination of wisdom and innocence, as if she'd learned the meaning of life without the burden of experience. I was there to investigate Ebben. Juliana was just a fact associated with Ebben. Like his address or hair color, what kind of car he drove. But in one photograph she transformed herself from fact to tragedy.

I'd seen those eyes somewhere before. Not on Juliana—I'd never met her, of that I was sure. Not in the mirror. The tiny bit of wisdom I'd acquired came from an abundance of experience— I'm a slow learner. Not in my ex-wife—she's too ambitious. Not in Gabriella—she's seen too much as a cop. Then I understood. I'd seen Juliana's eyes in Ellegaard. Ellegaard's were blue, not brown, set in a white face under blond hair as opposed to Juliana's brown skin under black hair. But Ellegaard's eyes had the same wisdom as Juliana's, as if they were somehow born knowing.

I peeled myself away from Juliana's wise eyes and left the foyer. A few people gathered in the living room under a beamed ceiling. I walked through as if I knew where I was going and followed the music through the kitchen and into a large, oak-paneled den. A crowd lingered in clumps of twos and threes. Most of the women wore their hair long, even those in their fifties and sixties. Most everyone wore jeans. It all looked casual and easy yet expensive.

A woman approached. Early thirties with long, wavy black

hair parted down the middle, olive skin, a black turtleneck, faded jeans, stop-sign-red lips, a black Converse All Star on her left foot and a boot cast on her right. She sipped from a glass of red wine. She had dark eyes and a tiny square jaw which she used to say, "And I know you from where?"

I said, "Here, I think. I don't think we've met before."

"But I know you. You're an actor, right?"

"I'm not."

"Director?"

"Sorry."

"Agent?"

"Of chaos, maybe, but no."

"Okay, this is weird. I don't think I know people and not know them," she said, burying the assumption that if I were famous, she knew me. She extended her hand. "Brit."

I shook it. "Nils."

"What do you do, Nils?"

"I'm a private detective."

Brit laughed. "Fuck! I love that!"

"And you?"

"Writer. Ebben is producing my movie. *For the People*." She talked fast like the nasty side-effect disclaimers at the end of a pharmaceutical commercial. "Maybe you've heard of it? It was in Deadline on Monday. Small budget, indie. Six mil. It's about this young idealistic political campaign staffer who gets kidnapped by one of the politician's major donors. He takes her to his rape chamber. It's totally fucked up and decorated like a little girl's room with a white, wrought-iron bed. He rapes her then binds her to the bed, but before he can return for another round, she frees her hands enough to twist one of the bed's iron metal balls off the bedpost. He comes back, and when he's going at her, she brings the iron ball down on his head and kills him. Then she drives his body up to her family cottage and rows it out to the middle of the lake and drops him with the anchor wrapped around his body."

I said, "Sounds empowering."

"Yeah," said Brit, "and that's just the first ten minutes of the movie. Turns out the politician she's working for used to be a defense attorney and he got all these scumbags off on technicalities. So she breaks into his files and finds all the rapists and starts killing them one by one, all while pretending to be an innocent young staffer."

"And let me guess—the fish in the lake her cottage is on start getting really big."

"Ha ha. We're still trying to lock down an A-list director and will have to take it to the festivals to get distribution but we'll get it because Kate Lennon is attached as the lead role."

I didn't know what most of that meant, but I knew who Kate Lennon was. I'd seen her in dramas and comedies—she's one of those rare actors who can do anything and you believe they're the character while simultaneously knowing they're a big movie star. It's quite a trick. I also just got confirmation of Beverly Mayer's suspicion. Ebben was investing in show business. I was free to leave. If there was a red-eye to Minneapolis, I could make it home by breakfast. But I had the hotel for the night, and Jameson was visiting his friend, and I wanted to meet the man who had earned the love of Juliana's wise, innocent eyes.

I said, "What?"

"What do you mean, 'what'?"

"Well, for one, Brit, what is Deadline?"

"Seriously?"

"Seriously. This is my first visit to Los Angeles. I know nothing."

"Deadline Hollywood Daily is a website. That's where everyone goes for show business news." I could barely understand her—she talked auctioneer fast. "Too bad you didn't see the article. My picture was in there and I'm one of those people who photographs better than I look. Even though half my head was shaved in the picture. I was going through a phase. I have to get new headshots but it's so fucking boring, all the Sativa in the bong can't get me to do it. Who does your headshots?"

"JCPenney."

"Oh, I fucking love it. *Love* it." Her expression didn't change when she said, "Were you close with Juliana?"

"No," I said. "I never met her. I'm a family friend of the Mayers. Came to pay my respects." I looked down at her boot cast. "Your shoes don't match."

"Yeah. I had to get bunion surgery. No more high heels for me."

"Just as well. High heels don't fool anyone."

"Guys like them."

"Not me. I see heels and I think there's a woman with short legs trying to make them look long. I wonder what else she's hiding. Have you seen Ebben?"

"He's out back. I think he's about to make a speech."

"Thanks. Are you in here because you don't want to hear it?"

Bunion Brit took a deep breath to fill her bellows and rapid fired: "Ebben loved Juliana so much. Waiting for him to talk about her feels like waiting for a car crash. No way I'm joining the crowd of ghouls out there for that." She held her wineglass to the light and used her thumb to wipe the lip print off the rim. "Like you know it's going to be devastating and you want a front-row seat to see every molecule of pain on Ebben's face. I hate that side of human nature. Loathe it. I mean, where the fuck does that come from? Sometimes I hate people so much. Here we are, the dominant species. No real threat to our existence so we're hell-bent on destroying ourselves. I mean, I'll go out there to hear Ebben, but not until he starts and I will stand in the back. And I took an Ativan fifteen minutes ago to get through it. Want one?"

"No, I'm good. Thanks."

"Hey, I've been kicking around a TV idea about a woman P.I. set in L.A. She's a struggling actress. Just can't catch a break. But she's got mad chops. Hollywood won't give her a chance but we see how fucking brilliant she is on her cases because she's always transforming herself into different characters for her investigations. One second she's a hooker, the next she's a soccer mom. I'm thinking she has a roommate who works as a costumer and maybe a neighbor who works in hair and makeup. So she's got all the tools of transformation right there. Kind of like *Fletch* meets *Alias* because she can kick ass. She's a fucking star, but she won't play the game. She's like, too principled."

So much for writers being quiet and opaque. Maybe Hollywood writers are different. Maybe they're always trying to sell their next project, even if they're talking to a private investigator from Minnesota. I said, "I might watch that TV show."

"I know, right? Maybe we could grab coffee so I can pick your brain about private investigation. What it's really like and all that. If I get it on the air, you'd get a consulting fee. Six figures and all you'd have to do is—"

"Brit," said a man, "we should head into the backyard." His hair was impossibly black, so dense it could suck a planet out of its orbit. And it was too full—I hoped it was a wig because if it wasn't, who knew what kind of medical hocus-pocus he'd endured. "We should be out there when Ebben starts."

Bunion Brit said, "Thom Burke, this is Nils. Nils is a family friend of the Mayers. Thom is Ebben's line producer."

I nodded as if I knew what that was. Thom Burke and I shook hands and exchanged nice-to-meet-yous. He looked fifty-five trying to pass for thirty-five. His efforts succeeded like new paint on a two-hundred-year-old house. One side of the foundation had sunk, the windows hung askew, and the roofline sagged. But when he looked in the mirror, he must have only seen the new paint and thought, *I look fantastic. I'm fooling them all.* Otherwise, how the hell do you go out in public like that?

We exchanged greetings and Bunion Brit said, "Nils is a private investigator."

"Really?" said Thom. "Are you here because the game is afoot?" He laughed at his stupid joke.

I said, "Nope. Just a family friend from Minnesota. Paying my respects."

"Nils and I are going to have coffee and chat about my *Morgan Who?* project." She turned to me and said, "*Morgan Who?* is the title I'm thinking of because Hollywood is like, *Who* the hell is she? And when she's in disguise it's like, *Who* is that? And her name is Morgan so—"

"But there was that show *Samantha Who?*" said Thom. "They might bump on that."

"Fuck," said Bunion Brit. "That stupid amnesia show? Who gives a shit about that? Want to go out back with us, Nils?"

I said, "Yes, please," and followed Bunion Brit and The Picture of Dorian Gray into the backyard. The patio was crowded and loud. A jazz trio—piano, bass, and drums—performed on a portable stage. The marijuana cloud overhead was so big it probably showed up on Doppler radar. Some people were bundled up as if it were thirty degrees, not sixty. One woman wore a full-length, down Patagonia frock you wouldn't see in Minnesota unless the temperature had dipped below zero. She sat on sleek patio furniture near a blazing firepit.

Brit introduced me to Sebastiano and Debra. Sebastiano, I learned, was Ebben's agent and set himself apart from the crowd by wearing a suit. He was tall, maybe six foot three, dark-skinned with short-cropped hair and the chiseled face of a model in one of those cologne ads you see in magazines at the doctor's office. His cheekbones looked painted-on. He said a quick hello without smiling. He looked like he had the weight of the world on his shoulders.

Debra, I learned, was Ebben's manager. She was about forty years old and heavyset but also tall. At least six feet. A round face, classically pretty, with blue eyes behind octagonal eyeglasses made of bright pink plastic. I guessed they had some big designer's name on them and ran four figures. Although if you had told me Walmart sold them in the toy department, I would have believed you. Debra wore dangly earrings of green jade. They must have hypnotized me because I never saw Ebben walk onto the stage and take the mic. I just heard:

"Thank you, everyone, for coming."

I broke free from my earring-induced trance to see Ebben Mayer standing at the microphone. He was tall and thin with sandy, windswept hair. Old Levi's and a moss-colored quarter-zip sweater. He appeared casual, confident, and kind. It's hard for someone to make that impression without opening his mouth but he did. He took a deep breath and said, "Oh boy, this is the hardest part of the evening." He took a moment to gather himself. No one in the backyard said a word. "I . . . I, uh . . ." He cried a bit.

Sebastiano the agent looked at Debra the manager. She responded with a slight head nod then worked her way through the crowd, stepped up on stage, and squeezed Ebben's left hand. Then he raised his right hand, which clutched a twenty-four-ounce energy drink. The can looked like an outfit the band Metallica would wear. Ebben took a gulp then said, "Okay. I can do this. I need to do this. *We* need to do this."

A few words of encouragement from the crowd. Ebben started to say something about Juliana, and a torrent of emotion overwhelmed me. I felt light-headed. My vision blurred. I sat down on the brick wall of a planting bed. Bunion Brit limped over to me, put a hand on my back, and said, "Are you all right?"

I nodded. But I wasn't all right because I'd just realized that Juliana Marquez had been murdered.

6

That's how it happens. I feel it before I understand it. The inaccessible part of my brain makes calculations but it can only communicate the results with emotion. Then I have to wait for my conscious brain to catch up, to understand what part of me already knows. It's like I've been given a sealed envelope. I received the envelope because what's inside is important. It just takes me a while to figure out how to open it.

That's what happened when Ebben began to talk. An emotional beacon told me Juliana Marquez was murdered. But I had no idea why.

Ebben said, "What gives me the most comfort, I suppose, is that everyone who knew Juliana loved her. I'm not going through this alone. And my suffering can't compare to that of the Marquez family." Ebben indicated a Latino family who occupied half of the backyard. Two or three dozen people. You could see the progression of the American Dream in the generations. The oldest weathered and worn from sun and manual labor. The younger generations standing erect in expensive clothing and with less fatigue in their eyes. "On Monday we all attended a funeral at Saint Charles Borromeo Catholic Church. And there we mourned our loss of Juliana. But tonight, I want to celebrate her most beautiful soul."

Ebben shut his eyes to gather himself. He took another sip from his oil drum of energy drink. "It's hard to celebrate while feeling such terrible loss. To know Juliana won't be a wife, a mother. That she won't continue to spread her love. To know we will no longer be the beneficiaries of her beauty, inside and out."

I glanced at my newfound friends. Bunion Brit the writer, Thom the line producer, Sebastiano the agent, Debra the manager. All filled with reverence. None filled with emotion.

"I was so looking forward to Juliana meeting my family. My mother and father would have loved her. My grandparents, too. It is possible my grandmother, the self-appointed matriarch of our family, some might say the Don of our family even though we have no Italian blood in our veins . . . It is possible that the great and powerful and outspoken Beverly Mayer would not have said one nice thing about Juliana—it simply isn't in her nature. But . . . but nor would she have said one negative thing about Juliana because that was not within the realm of possibility. For anyone.

"A lot of my business associates are here tonight. It's important that you know something. Juliana begged me not to mention this before, and I honored her wish. But I can no longer do that. The Creative Collective was Juliana's idea. She inspired me to fund and foster exceptional films and television shows by letting the creators work unencumbered . . ."

There it was again. This time, straight from Ebben's mouth. He'd invested in show business by founding The Creative Collective, whatever that was. I'd Google "The Creative Collective" later, then I'd have plenty of information for Beverly Mayer.

Ebben continued speaking. I drifted away from my newfound acquaintances and made my way behind the stage to see the faces who had come to celebrate Juliana Marquez. I didn't know who or what I was looking for other than something or someone who didn't seem to fit. That's hard in a city you don't know, where people work in an industry you don't understand.

The faces looked more diverse than what you'd typically see in Minnesota. Still, no one looked out of place. All of the eyes conveyed similar expressions of sorrow, empathy, and solemnity.

Except for one.

The owner of the eye stood over a long table filled with platters of finger foods. Shaved head, barrel chested, ample bellied, and wearing an eye patch. He piled his plate high while Ebben recounted the story of how he and Juliana met. His eye on the food. Even the caterers had stopped working out of respect for Ebben's speech. But this guy acted as if he'd arrived at an all-you-can-eat buffet fifteen minutes before closing time.

Ebben said, "Tomorrow, Juliana's family and I will start the process of spreading Juliana's ashes." He set down his big energy drink and picked up a rectangular wooden box that looked like what would house an expensive bottle of whiskey. "She loved to kayak the Channel Islands, so we'll take some there. She loved to hike Runyon Canyon, so some will go there. She said Dodger

Stadium had the greatest feel of community anywhere in Los Angeles, so come April, we'll sit in the bleachers and drop a little over the outfield wall and onto the field. A good portion of her ashes will stay in the Marquez home so she can be with the family she loved and who loved her.

"She was so excited to visit Minnesota. We had planned on going in the spring to canoe the Boundary Waters. She would have loved it, so I'll take some of Juliana's ashes there." Ebben paused and pushed the hair out of his eyes. He gathered himself and said, "For everyone who's come tonight, please celebrate Juliana and never, ever forget her. I know you won't. It's impossible."

Ebben nodded to indicate he'd finished, stepped off the stage, and disappeared into the family Marquez. They huddled around and swallowed him up. I found Bunion Brit the red-lipped writer and said I'd meet her for coffee tomorrow to discuss the realities of being a private investigator. I gave her my card and told her I was staying at The Line Hotel. She promised to text me the when and where. I looked around the gathering of celebrants one last time and walked back through the house and into the front foyer.

Juliana Marquez had not moved. She rested on her easel and looked at me with omniscient, innocent eyes. I looked back hard for thirty seconds or ten minutes. I had no idea. I stared back until my conscious brain told me what the unreachable part of my brain already knew—how Juliana was killed.

7

I about-faced it back into the house, found the kitchen, and opened the refrigerator. There they were, a couple dozen cans, double stacked in neat rows. I returned to the backyard. Ebben was surrounded. I waited for an opportunity and, when one presented itself, I approached.

I said, "I'm sorry, Ebben. What a terrible loss."

"Thank you." He looked at me for a moment, waiting for recognition, but it didn't come. "Are you a friend of Juliana's?"

"No." I handed him my card.

He nodded. "Who sent you?"

"You know."

He almost smiled. "My grandmother is a proactive person who lets nothing fall through the cracks."

I shrugged. "You are kind to put it that way. She sent me because she wanted to know if you're investing your trust fund in show business. It took me five seconds to learn that you are. But there's something else I'd like to discuss with you. I know it's a bad time, but it's urgent."

Ebben smiled. "You're not going to pitch me a project, are you?"

"I don't even know what that means."

We walked into the house and upstairs to his office. He shut the door. I said, "I know this may sound insane, but Juliana's death may not have been an accident."

Ebben didn't look surprised. He said, "I'm listening. . . ."

The bookshelves were filled with what I assumed were scripts, their titles written in Sharpie on their spines. *Deep Harbor, Fucking Forty, The Bennetts, Lake Lundquist, The Archers of Omaha, Bunk Bed Brothers.* A big iMac sat on a walnut desk and a sixty-inch TV clung to the wall. A couch faced the TV. A walnut coffee table matched the desk, which had a chair for Ebben and a couple chairs on the opposite side for guests. That's where we sat.

I said, "And of more immediate concern, I believe your life may be in danger."

Ebben blinked hard a couple times. "Explain that, please."

"Your grandmother informed me the medical examiner determined Juliana's death was caused by an overdose of diet pills."

"Yes."

"Did she take diet pills?"

"Sometimes, although the pathology report is a little more complicated than what I told my grandmother. Juliana died of a combination of diet pills and a congenital heart defect that had gone undetected in routine physicals. They say she might have felt it in her forties or fifties, but she had no idea of the problem. The diet pills increased her blood pressure and pulse rate over a prolonged period of time, and her heart gave out."

I nodded, but must have looked dubious.

Ebben said, "You don't believe the autopsy results?"

"I do. A diet pill overdose probably means a caffeine overdose."

"It does. That's indicated in the report."

"Did Juliana drink coffee?"

"No."

"How about your energy drinks?"

"No. She thought they were disgusting."

"Did she ingest any other forms of caffeine?"

Ebben shook his head. "She only took the diet pills when she couldn't find time to exercise. So not often. Juliana was the most wonderful person I've ever known, but she wasn't perfect. She had body image issues."

"Was she anorexic?"

"Not at all. But a lot of people in her family are overweight. Juliana was determined not to let that happen to her. She ate clean. She exercised regularly except when her teaching schedule made that impossible." He looked down. When he looked back up, he had tears in his eyes. "Hey, I got a houseful of people. I should get back downstairs."

I said, "I understand. But think about this: unlike Juliana, you consume a great deal of caffeine. You downed a twenty-four-ounce can of it just while talking about Juliana a few minutes ago."

"I know. I have a problem. I'm trying to kick it." He managed a weak smile then quoted the movie *Airplane!* "Looks like I picked the wrong week to stop sniffing glue."

I smiled. "Great movie."

"The fourteen-year-old me wouldn't have survived without it." His smile faded and so did Ebben Mayer.

I said, "I checked out your refrigerator. It's full of those energy drinks."

"Like I said—"

"I'm not judging you. I'm pointing out that if someone wanted to kill you, a caffeine overdose would most likely be attributed to the cans in your recycling bin."

"Why would anyone want to kill me?"

"That's the next question. The question I'm asking now is: Is it possible Juliana consumed something meant for you?"

"Like what?"

"Could've been anything. A glass of water, a cookie, salad dressing. A teaspoon of pure caffeine powder can send a person into cardiac arrest."

"How do you know that?"

I said, "Did some research for a case I was working on a decade ago. As little as two of those twenty-four-ounce cans you drink have killed kids."

"Jesus."

"How much did Juliana weigh?"

Ebben shrugged. "I don't know. A hundred and twenty-five pounds maybe. Oh, man. I wish we wouldn't have cremated Juliana's body."

Did Ebben wish Juliana hadn't been cremated? I couldn't tell. I didn't know him well enough. He was well-spoken and had a self-assuredness that often belongs to those born into money—

they're entitled to money so they're entitled to everything. But I found him low-key and unassuming and there was just something decent about the guy. I've met a handful of people who I put in the *intrinsically good* category. Like Ellegaard. They must have the same complexities and complications everyone has, but only goodness surfaces. So far, Ebben seemed to be one of those rare gems.

I said, "Cremation isn't always a problem. Forensic scientists can test the ashes. But in this case, it may not matter because if the ashes test for caffeine, the diet pill cause of death is still possible. I'll make some calls, but I don't think they can isolate the source of caffeine."

"So that's it?" said Ebben. "Someone may have killed Juliana and gotten away with it? We don't go to the police? We don't say anything?"

"You can go to the police if you want. Explain to them what I've explained to you. But I shouldn't. I'm a licensed private investigator in one state. Minnesota."

Ebben nodded. I saw concern in his eyes, but somehow he grew even more gentle and kind and said, "What do you suggest for my safety?"

"That's why I'm talking to you. If someone was trying to kill you, chances are they'll try again. Unless their objective in killing you was somehow achieved by killing Juliana. Did anyone have a problem with you two marrying?"

Ebben shook his head. "There were no jealous exes. No one would want to stop our marriage."

"What about family members?"

Ebben thought about that and took his time doing it. A shadow of stubble seemed to have emerged on his jaw in the time between his speech in the backyard and our chat in his home office. He rubbed a thumb across his chin and said, "No one in Juliana's family, I'm sure. They were thrilled about our marriage. And no one in my family had even met her. Besides, no one in my family would try to kill me. And according to your theory, I was the target."

"Yes. And still may be. I suggest you leave town for a while. Go back to Minnesota. Or go to someplace warm. But leave town. As a precaution if nothing else."

Ebben Mayer's eyes drifted away. He said, "I understand your theory, but I don't believe anyone has a reason to kill me."

"All right. That's cool. Just thought I'd share it with you."

Ebben seemed genuinely dumbfounded. He was tired. It showed in his eyes and in his slumped shoulders. He said, "I need to get back downstairs." He stood. "I'll call you if I think of someone out there who might have a grudge against me." He pulled out the business card I'd handed him in the backyard. "Is your cell on here?"

"Yeah. By the way, what's The Creative Collective you mentioned?"

He shut his eyes. He didn't want to explain it. But when he opened them, he was kind. "Normally, a writer writes a script, a director makes the movie, actors act in the movie. And there are all sorts of businesspeople involved. Non-creative producers. Studio executives and distribution people, network executives if it's television. And they all have something to say about the creative work. Sometimes it's valuable—there are some creatively intelligent executives out there—but often it detracts from the creators' vision and voice. Someone pulls a thread here and a thread there, and the whole fabric falls apart.

"The idea of the Creative Collective is to directly fund artists. I put no creative restraints on them other than budgetary. I think that will lead to exceptional work. We'll make money in the process, but if we don't, that's okay, too. It's about creating a body of work we can all be proud of."

I thought about that then said, "So you're cutting a lot of people out of the process."

"We're cutting a lot of fat out of the process."

"Fat that may not be thrilled about being cut out."

Ebben nodded. "Probably not too happy at all." He shrugged. "But it's to protect the work."

Ebben walked me downstairs and to the front door. He looked at my card and said, "I'll call you, Nils, if I think of anything. And even though my grandmother sent you, I'm glad you came and I'm happy to know you." He smiled, then looked down again at my card. "Why does your name look familiar?"

"Nils Shapiro is a common name."

He laughed. Then, "Oh, I know. A couple summers ago, I had an intern from the University of Minnesota. She showed me an article about you in the *StarTribune*. You solved the murder in Edina with the vacuum cleaner dust."

"Yeah. Nothing like a clever murder to help a detective get a rep."

Ebben said, "We tried to option your story. But if I remember right, you declined."

"Oh, that was you? Then yes. You remember right."

He produced his business card as if he were a magician pulling it out of thin air. "Call me if you change your mind."

I took the card, turned to leave, then stopped. "Hey, Ebben, there was a bald guy here tonight. A tough, Eastern European type. A patch over one eye. Spent a lot of time around the food. Any idea who he is?"

Ebben shook his head. "None."

"You may want to check into that. And hey, do you know your gardener?"

"What?"

"Do you personally know your gardener?"

"No. I'm just renting the house for six months. I say hello to whoever's doing the yard. That's about it."

"Latino or white?"

"Latino."

"There was a white guy working on your yard this afternoon. You may want to check into that, too."

I left Ebben scratching his jaw and stepped outside. I smelled eucalyptus. Los Angeles has some good smells.

8

I jumped in a Lyft and headed out to meet Jameson White and his friend who coached at UCLA. I called Gabriella from the car. It was our first night apart since our engagement, and I missed her. I felt grateful for the longing and told her so. She said she preferred her men evasive and withholding. I filled her in on my evening. She told me I'd done my job and to get my ass back to Minnesota. I appreciated her directness.

The car dropped me at a place in Beverly Hills called Honor Bar. It was a long, narrow wooden room with a bar on the left and high-top tables on the right. The clientele looked upscale but not obnoxiously so. The two giant men were not hard to spot. Jameson sat across a high-top from a six-and-a-half-foot-tall guy with dark, neatly combed hair and a baby face. Jameson introduced him as August Willingham the Third.

I shook the giant's hand and said, "Do you go by Gus?"

He said, "I do not. You can call me August or you can call me Three. But I do not appreciate Gus. Or Auggie."

"Glad I asked."

Jameson said, "We ordered you a cucumber martini, fried chicken sandwich, and French fries. I don't want to hear a complaint out of you, Shap, because even though Beverly Hills has lots of big-name fancy-ass restaurants, this joint is its finest."

"I'm not complaining."

"That's right, you're not. Now I got to hit the head. If the fries come, keep your mitts off mine and eat your own."

"I think he's talking to you, August."

"Yeah, he's talking to me. But I make no promises."

Jameson got up off his stool and said, "You touch 'em, you buy 'em," and headed toward the back of the bar.

I said, "How's he doing?"

August Willingham the Third shook his head. "Jameson's broken. I've never seen him like this. Even when we lost the Rose Bowl, he found something positive to say with his big smile and big laugh. Now he's either discontent or angry or mute. My old buddy hasn't made an appearance yet."

"Has he talked to you about the shooting?"

"Barely. I've tried to get him to open up, but it's not coming. And Jameson White is not a man who holds things in. At least he wasn't. I roomed with him for four years. I know more about the man than any person should."

"I know almost nothing about him other than he played college ball here and professionally in Montreal and that he ended up following a woman to Minneapolis and it didn't work out."

"Yeah. Joline. Wonderful woman."

"What happened?"

"Brain tumor."

"Oh, man."

"It was sad. But Jameson powered through somehow."

"What about family?"

A waiter in his thirties with a pencil mustache brought our sandwiches and drinks. He set them on the table with a toothpaste commercial smile and told us to enjoy.

August said, "Jameson lost both parents in his twenties. He had one brother. He was killed in Afghanistan. Jameson powered through all that, too. But the school shooting, him trying to help save those kids, there's no powering through that. I'm concerned."

"Maybe spending time with you on a football field in the warm sunshine will help."

"Maybe. But there's no shortcuts on this one. Sorry if I sound like a know-it-all. I have a PhD in psychology. Took thirteen years of off-seasons, but I got it. Thirteen years in the Jets locker room with the name *Dr. Freud* written on my locker. I took a lot of shit for getting that degree, but it'll help make me one hell of a coach."

"Can I call you Dr. Freud?"

"You may not." August smiled.

Jameson appeared, sat on his stool, and said, "Let's eat, boys." He took a bite of his sandwich and shut his eyes. His face displayed a moment of peace. He swallowed then said, "That means stop talking about me. I'm just going through some shit." August and I shared a quick glance. "I saw that. Seriously. Don't worry about me. Just treated a couple dozen kids Swiss-cheesed by semi-automatic gunfire. Watched 'em die while I was holding their hands because their parents couldn't get there in time."

August and I both bit into our sandwiches. Jameson was talking. Finally. I don't know what triggered it. Maybe it was the combination of his oldest and newest friends sitting at the same table. Or the atmosphere. Or the cucumber martinis, which were sweet, spiced with sliced jalapeño, and potent. We focused on our food, which was as good as Jameson had claimed, and waited for the big man to pick it back up.

"The parents." Jameson shook his head. "No offense to your avocation, Three, but all the psychologists on the planet couldn't have helped those poor people. Not on that day anyway. Nothing personal. Morphine wouldn't have helped 'em either. Otherwise, I would've loaded up a syringe in each hand and jumped 'em the moment they set foot in the ER."

Our sandwiches were cut into thirds. Jameson finished two-thirds and half his fries before he spoke again. "I'm getting me another one of these chicken sandwiches. I will tell you that much."

August flagged a waiter. "Nils?" I shook my head. August ordered two more sandwiches and two more martinis, but Jameson didn't say another word about the shooting. August talked about how today's offensive linemen don't know how to run-block like they used to because the game has become so pass intensive. He blathered on as a gaggle of Beverly Hills fortysomething women crowded around the bar trying to look like twentysomethings.

Jameson said, "This bar is full of women, and I bet there ain't more than four natural breasts in here." He wasn't gregarious, buoyant Jameson, but it was something.

My phone buzzed. The caller ID showed a 612 area code. Minnesota. I didn't recognize the number, but it was after 11:00 P.M. there so it might have been important. I took the call and walked toward the back where it was more quiet.

"Nils."

I had no idea who it was. "Yes?"

"It's Ebben Mayer. Someone just tried to run me off the road."

9

I asked Ebben Mayer if he was okay.

He said, "For the moment, yes."

"Did you call the police?"

"No. I don't want to do that."

I asked why.

He said police reports are public records and he didn't want the incident to find its way into the entertainment industry trades. That would be bad for business. "I hit a boulder. A tow truck is on its way. Any chance you can pick me up? I'm up on Mulholland Drive. I'll text you my location."

Mulholland Drive snakes across the top of the Hollywood Hills, which divide the Los Angeles basin from the San Fernando Valley. Chances are you've seen Mulholland Drive before, if not in a movie or TV show, then on a car commercial as the featured car hugs hairpin turns. I learned all this from my tour guides, August and Jameson, as we drove up Coldwater Canyon out of Beverly Hills. I told them I suspected Juliana Marquez was murdered and I suspected that the caffeine she ingested was intended for Ebben Mayer.

We headed east on Mulholland, and Jameson said, "I knew that gardener was fishy! What'd I tell you? A white gardener in Hancock Park. That's got bullshit written all over it. So, what did the police say when you told them?"

I sat in the back seat of August's Chevy Tahoe. We made eye contact via the rearview mirror. I'd hoped Jameson would get involved in the case, not because he was a master sleuth but to give him a sense of purpose. Something to distract him from that horror-filled day in the ER.

I said, "I didn't tell the police."

"What?" said Jameson. "Why not?"

"Because I have nothing more than a suspicion. And I called my M.E. buddy, Dr. Meltzer, back in Minnesota. The forensics people can probably detect a caffeine overdose from cremated remains, but they can't tell if it came from diet pills or caffeine powder or twenty-five cups of coffee."

"So you're just going to let somebody get away with it?! You are turning your back on justice, Nils Shapiro. Never thought I'd see the day."

"What do you think I should do?"

"Are you kidding me? Is that a serious question?"

August caught my eyes in the rearview mirror and gave me the faintest nod.

I said, "Yeah, it's a serious question. I don't know any LAPD. And I'm not licensed here."

"Don't know any LAPD?! Not licensed! Since when does Nils Shapiro give a shit about networking and playing by the rules?! Hell, the reason I met you is because you disobeyed doctors' orders and left the hospital the same day you had surgery. I'm talking hours after! They wanted you to stay a whole week. And St. Paul PD hated your guts for stepping on their turf. But a seventeen-year-old girl was missing so you let none of that shit get in your way. You lied to the police. You broke into buildings. You did what it took 'cause you were the real deal, Shap! The operative word there is *were*. What the hell are you now?"

Jameson had a point. A year ago, I wouldn't have let Los Angeles and the lack of a PI license dissuade me from following my gut on a suspected murder. A year ago, if a rich old lady in St. Paul had handed me a fat check to fly to warm weather just to find out if her grandson was investing in show business, I would have yawned and walked away. But yesterday, I viewed the job as easy and safe and lucrative. What made yesterday different than a year ago? The answer is simple: Gabriella Nuñez and Evelyn Stahl-Shapiro.

I don't talk tough or get in fights. I rarely carry my gun. Two stiff drinks and I need a nap. But I've been a justice freak driven by an intrinsic need to find the truth. I don't know why. I don't have an origin story that explains my motivation. I was just born that way. My drive has taken its toll on my finances, quality of life, safety, and personal relationships. But it gave me an identity. Something to hold on to while the rest of life passed me by.

Then the rest of life stopped passing me by. I fell in love with Gabriella Nuñez, and she reciprocated. And Evelyn was born and evoked something in me beyond love. Beyond purpose. Something akin to the meaning of life. Gabriella and Evelyn became my identity. Truth and justice yielded with quiet dignity.

"Well?" said Jameson. "You got an answer for me, Shap? What the hell are you now?"

Jameson White and I had never had a spat. We'd had disagreements about the Minnesota Twins' starting rotation, the value of jam bands, and the accuracy of weather predictions, but those were laugh-filled disputes and ended in one of us buying the other a beer. But on that drive up Coldwater Canyon, Jameson White tried to pick a fight with me. A real fight. I didn't engage. If I had, I'd have to tell him the reason I'd lost my investigative drive because I had something worth living for, putting my life in sharp contrast to his. I'd also have to tell him there was no difference in me abandoning justice and him abandoning his emergency room patients. No way I was going to take that shot at my friend.

I said, "What the hell am I now? That's a good question, Jameson. I'll have to think about it and get back to you."

"You do that. But I will not hold my breath." The car grew quiet for a few minutes as we each continued the conversation in our minds. Then Jameson said, "Mulholland Drive. Best place in town to murder someone, other than Griffith Park. Griffith Park's got more bodies in it than the Mall of America on Black Friday."

The valley was to our left. The Los Angeles basin to our right. At night, you could see both sections of the city were an almost perfect grid, its streets running north/south and east/west. The glowing matrix looked like a giant computer motherboard with information traveling from one part of the system to another. Only it wasn't information. It was steady strings of cars, white lines of headlights moving in one direction, red lines of taillights moving in the opposite direction.

We found Ebben's Lexus LX pulled over near Outpost Drive. At least I assumed it was his because it had Minnesota plates and was crunched into a boulder, the front passenger side wheel broken at the axle. But I didn't see Ebben Mayer.

"Where is he?" said Jameson.

We got out of the car. Two Porsche 911s sped by, motors revving, a red one on the tail of a yellow one. They roared around the curve and disappeared, their upshifting engines fading into the night awash in city light.

August said, "I think it's time to call the police."

"No. Please."

I got down on my hands and knees and shined my phone's flashlight under the SUV. Ebben Mayer lay on his stomach. "It's safe to come out. I brought muscle."

Ebben crawled out from under his car. He was covered in a beige dust that Los Angeles seemed to be made of. He looked up at Jameson and August but said nothing.

I said, "If you're scared enough to hide under your car, Ebben, you should call the police."

"No."

"You sure? There might be tire marks on the road. They could help us find out who did this."

He shook his head as the tow truck driver pulled up next to us. Ebben had the car towed to Lexus of Beverly Hills, and August drove the four of us down Outpost Drive, then we ended up on Hollywood Boulevard, where double-decker buses ferried tourists past famous movie theaters and discount shoe warehouses. Grown men and women dressed as superheroes and posed for pictures with people who thought that kind of thing was fun. We continued down the hill toward Hancock Park, and Jameson pointed out iconic restaurants and movie studios like Sunset Gower and Paramount and Raleigh.

He showed me where famous movie scenes had been filmed, and I wondered why Ebben felt so strongly against getting the police involved. The reason could be what he'd told me, that he didn't want the publicity. Or the reason could have been more complicated than that. Maybe he had something to hide. Maybe he'd slipped Juliana the caffeine overdose. Or maybe he had something completely different to hide, like what was in his bloodstream when he may or may not have been run off the road.

I said, "What's that store?"

Ebben said, "House of Spies?"

"Yeah."

"It's a store for James Bond wannabes. They sell tracking devices and equipment to bug rooms and spy on people. Cuff links that are cameras. Kind of creepy but it's been there for a long time."

"I wouldn't mind a bow tie that's a camera."

"That's the place to shop for one."

We arrived at Ebben's. The big boys were hungry again, so we ordered pizza and another delivery service brought a six-pack of Shock Top, Jameson's beer of choice. Ebben went upstairs to change out of his dusty clothes, and I said, "Turn on your bullshit detectors, gentlemen. I like Ebben Mayer. I'm worried that will skew my judgment."

Over pizza and beer, Ebben explained that he and Juliana used to pick up late-night In-N-Out Burger, drive up to Mulholland, and eat while overlooking the city. He said his stomach wasn't up for a burger, but he felt the need to go up and look over the city to feel connected to her. "After being around all those people at the celebration this evening," he said, "it felt like a way to be alone with Juliana. I hadn't planned on it. I was just driving around when I got the idea and took Laurel Canyon up to Mulholland. A couple minutes later I noticed an SUV behind me."

I said, "Bigger than your Lexus?"

"About the same, I think. I saw mostly headlights, and it was right on my ass. It did look kind of square, like a Jeep. Didn't matter if I tapped my brakes or sped up. The son of a bitch stayed on my tail. I wanted to pull over, but all the turnouts were taken. Then it bumped me. Bumped me hard. I tried to outrun him, but he stayed on me. All the way to Outpost. I knew there was a big spot to pull over there because that's where we'd hike Runyon Canyon. So I jerked off the road and into the parking area, but I couldn't stop before hitting the boulder. I thought whoever was in the SUV would come back for me so I crawled under the car and hoped, if they did come, they would think I ran into the canyon."

Jameson said, "But no one came?"

"No." Ebben sipped his beer. I looked at his hand to see if it shook. Steady, steady, steady. "Nils, can you protect me?" He said it calmly, as if he'd asked me to paint his house.

Jameson stifled a laugh.

Ebben said, "What?"

"Shap can't protect you. He can't protect anyone. Look at him. He's all puny and weak."

I said, "Hey. That's a matter of perspective."

"Then how 'bout this perspective? You can still buy your shirts in the boys' department."

"For your information, Jameson, I stopped buying my shirts in the boys' department when I was twenty-five."

August Willingham the Third laughed hard.

Jameson said, "I can protect you, Ebben. But I don't work cheap."

Ebben looked at me, and I looked at August. He nodded without making eye contact, and I passed it on to Ebben. Ebben said, "So you'd move in here? Go to business meetings and things with me?"

"If that's the job, no problem. I got you covered."

10

August drove me back to the hotel to get Jameson's stuff. Ten-thirty on a weeknight and Wilshire Boulevard was packed with cars. Where in the hell was everyone going? August said other than rush hour, L.A. traffic made no sense. It could slow to a crawl any time day or night, then it would free up for no apparent reason. Then jam up again for no reason. There were just too many cars and not enough lanes, which seemed impossible because, as far as I could see, Los Angeles was mostly made out of streets. It's what impressed (or unimpressed) me most. The lack of green space. Even in tree-lined Hancock Park, the streets were wide and the lawns were tiny. And if there was a park in Hancock Park, I hadn't seen it.

August said, "I like the idea of Jameson keeping an eye on

Ebben. It'll give him a sense of purpose. Much more than hanging out with me at practice. He knows that's a charity move. Busy work. But protecting Ebben is a real responsibility. My question is: Is it dangerous?"

"I don't know if it's dangerous. I do know if someone really wanted to hurt Ebben tonight they could have. Seemed pretty remote up on Mulholland. All they would have had to do was stop, walk back and they could have accomplished their goal. Either someone's trying to scare him or he made it up."

"Why would someone try to scare him?"

"Well, he can't owe anyone money. He has plenty of that. Maybe someone blames him for Juliana's death. Maybe someone just wants him to leave Los Angeles because they don't like his Creative Collective."

"Why would he make up a story about being run off Mulholland?"

"I have no idea. He doesn't seem like the type who is desperate for attention."

"And that thing with the white gardener. And the eye patch guy. And Juliana's caffeine overdose. Those aren't made-up."

"No," I said. "Those are real."

We arrived at The Line Hotel. I'd agreed to move into Ebben's along with Jameson. I had no idea what we were signing up for or if we'd want to get out of it, so I didn't check out of the hotel. August Willingham the Third went up to Jameson's room to get his bag. I went to my room to get mine. I opened my room door and saw a sheet of paper lying on the floor. A handwritten note.

I'm in the hotel bar. Please come see me when you get this. –Brit

Bunion Brit. I'd said I'd meet her for coffee tomorrow. Showing up at my hotel felt pushy and forward. It was late. And how did she know what room I was in? Some high-end hotel this was. I grabbed my bag, went back downstairs, scanned the hotel bar, and saw her sitting at a table for two.

I found August in the lobby, explained the situation, handed him my bag, and told him I'd get a ride back to Ebben's within the hour.

Bunion Brit's painted red lips drank red wine. When she saw me, she set down her glass and stood. "Nils."

"How'd you know what room I was in?"

"I can't tell you that. Someone would get in trouble."

"You're going to have to tell me or this conversation is over."

She gave me a *that's not fair* look but my expression didn't budge. She sighed and rapid fired, "For fuck's sake. A friend of mine works here. He or she is an actor who owes me a fucking favor. He or she put the note under the door to repay that fucking favor. I don't actually know what room you're in because he or she wouldn't tell me. They just delivered the message. Satisfied?"

"Yes. So what was wrong with meeting ten hours from now like we're supposed to?"

"Oh, we're still meeting then. But the guy I'm seeing insists on joining us so this is a pre-meeting."

"Is the guy you're seeing named Ebben Mayer?"

Bunion Brit gave me a dead cold stare. It felt uncomfortable so I looked around the bar. There was an abundance of attractive people, as if I'd been popped into a modeling agency or a beer commercial.

Bunion Brit said, "Are you implying the only way Ebben

would produce my movie is if I slept with him? That a woman writer isn't good enough to have her work produced on the merits of the work as opposed to the merits of her body?"

"No," I said, "I'm implying something doesn't feel right to me about Ebben Mayer and about how Juliana died and I'm wondering if he was cheating on his fiancée. I was just taking a shot in the dark. It rarely works but you never know." She didn't want to get off her high horse and that was all right with me. She could ride away any time she pleased. "So why are you here now? What did you call it?"

"A pre-meeting."

"I've never heard of a pre-meeting."

"It's a meeting to prepare for a meeting."

"And why do we need it?"

"Because the guy I'm seeing insists on coming to our meeting and I want to discuss some things with him not around."

"So if you hadn't told him about our meeting, we wouldn't need this pre-meeting."

"Exactly."

"Hmm . . ."

"Hmm, what?"

"Is that why there's so much traffic in this town? Everyone's going to meetings *and* pre-meetings?"

"You're kind of being an asshole right now."

"It's late. I get cranky when I'm tired. And I can't sleep in tomorrow because I have to meet some writer for coffee."

"Now you're totally being an asshole."

"Although I'm getting a sense I should cancel that meeting."

"You will not. The guy I'm seeing—"

"You mean your boyfriend?"

Brit twisted up her mouth and swung her eyes to the far right to think. She swung them back toward me and said, "No. We date, but I don't consider him my boyfriend. Anyway. It's Thom." She lifted her eyebrows as if to say, *You know, Thom.*

I said, "Thom?"

"You met him tonight."

"Oh, right. The guy with the light-sucking hair."

"He dyes it."

"You sure it's not press-on?"

"Yes. It's his hair. Just dyed."

"Isn't Thom a little old for you?"

"He's twenty years older than me. He's sweet, and I like mature men. I always have. I'm an old soul. Even when I was in my twenties, I dated—"

"Stop."

Bunion Brit's forehead wrinkled. "Excuse me?"

I lowered my voice. "Not now, but when I tell you, look behind you. A bald man with an eye patch just entered the lobby."

"So?"

"I saw him at Juliana's celebration tonight. Ebben has no idea who he is. But the dude doesn't look friendly."

Bunion Brit nodded. "Can I look?"

"Please."

Bunion Brit turned and looked. The barrel-chested eye patch spoke to the clerk at the front desk. In about thirty seconds he'd search the bar. I said, "We need a way out of here."

Brit turned back to me and said, "Follow me." She set a twenty on the table and walked toward the back of the bar. She opened a door labeled BREAK ROOM 86 and we stepped into a bar that looked like 1986. Vintage stereo speakers. Old boom boxes atop the wall of liquor. Vinyl hung on the wall. The place was full of hipsters sipping cocktails and microbrews. Brit limped toward the bartender, a young man with a Brad Pitt head on a print model physique. "Dustin, is there a back way out of here?"

Dustin said, "Yeah, but I can't take you out that way. I could get fired."

"I'm not fucking around, Dustin. This is serious."

"Oh shit, Brit. Jesus. It never ends with you. But now you owe me one."

"Fine."

He made a subtle motion with his head. We followed him behind the bar, through a swinging door and into a room full of liquor. Beer kegs sat in glass-doored refrigerators, connected by a mass of tubes like Intensive Care patients. Dustin pointed, "That door leads to outside. Get out of here. Hurry up."

I pushed the door open and we stepped into an alley behind the Line Hotel. Bunion Brit kept hobbling so I followed. We walked a block west on Wilshire Boulevard then entered BCD Tofu House, a Korean restaurant that looked like a humongous Denny's, only the pancakes and the clientele were thinner.

Bunion Brit said, "You really have no idea who that eye patch guy is?"

"None."

"He looks Russian."

"I bet he's from somewhere in that neighborhood. He's been keeping that eye on Ebben. Like the gardener."

"What gardener? What are you talking about?"

"And I'm guessing he followed August and me here."

"Shit. What do we do?"

What do *we* do? What do *I* do? I was free to walk away. And if my only choice was to chase down a rabbit hole to find out who murdered Juliana Marquez or go home, I would have gone home. But the shaved-head was different. He was a threat. I couldn't walk away from a threat.

I said, "What we do is find out who he is."

"And how are we supposed to do that, ask him?"

"You really do know nothing about private investigators."

"Fuck you, Shapiro." She said it with a smile.

We walked back to the Line Hotel. Bunion Brit played lookout in the lobby while I questioned the valets and dispensed hundred-dollar bills. The valets told me the eye patch spoke in a heavy Russian-sounding accent and drove a Mercedes G550. I spent another hundred to have them bring Brit's Audi Q5 two cars behind the Mercedes SUV when the eye patch requested his car. It was an easy transaction—the valets didn't blink.

I was in a town where almost everything and everyone was for sale. Good to know.

11

The valets worked like a synchronized swim team. First the eye patch's Mercedes G550 followed by a Tesla followed by Bunion Brit's Audi Q5. Our valet got out of the car and held open the door. I started toward it.

"I'm driving," said Brit.

"You're in a boot cast."

"I'm a great left-foot driver. I practiced for a month before the surgery. And out-of-towners don't know how to drive in L.A. You fuck up everything. I'm driving."

Brit could've been right about that, so I headed toward the passenger side. She drove well, although every stoplight, lane change, and left turn catalyzed a chain of profanity so long that the chains ran together to form their own language.

The eye patch drove hard and fast as if he was late to an appointment.

Brit said, "Fucking Eastern Europeans. They think Wilshire Boulevard is the Indy 500. So do the Persians and Israelis. And the Italians. But get behind an Asian and you might as well be walking."

"Huh," I said, "I expected people in Hollywood to be more politically correct."

"Only in our work. In real life we're a bunch of assholes like everyone else."

I said, "Get right behind him. But just for a few seconds." Brit checked her mirrors then jerked the Audi out of our lane and hit the gas. I said, "Don't slip behind him until you can do it smoothly."

"Don't tell me how to drive."

"I'm not telling you how to drive. I'm telling you how to tail. It's one less thing we'll have to discuss at our coffee in the morning. That is, if we're done with our pre-meeting."

"Our pre-meeting hasn't even started yet. What are you doing?"

"Getting his plate."

"So are we done with this guy?"

"Not yet. Let's see where he's going."

Brit dropped back and let a car slip in between us. The Mercedes moved into the right lane and turned right on Wilton. She said, "He's headed north. If he turns left on Third, we'd better warn Ebben."

"We're close to his neighborhood?"

"Very."

I called Jameson. He answered on the second ring. "Where the hell are you? I was thinking about getting worried."

"Stay on the phone and turn out all the lights in the house."

"What's going on?"

"The eye patch might be headed your way. We're tailing him right now."

Brit said, "He's turning onto Third."

Jameson said, "Who's that?"

"It's Brit. She works with Ebben."

"Nils Shapiro," said Jameson, "I'm disappointed in you. You're a betrothed man."

Brit swatted me with her right hand and said, "Don't tell him I work with Ebben. Tell him I'm a writer who has a project with Ebben."

"Jameson, get those lights turned off and get in the basement."

Brit laughed. "What?"

"Houses in California don't have basements."

"No basements? A house without a basement is like a trailer with no wheels. Just turn out the lights, Jameson, stay on the phone, and keep away from the windows. Is Ebben with you?"

"Yep. All the lights on the main floor are off. We're headed upstairs."

Brit said, "The bald guy is taking a right on Van Ness."

I said, "That means nothing to me."

"He's turning into Ebben's neighborhood."

We followed the Mercedes up a long block, an extra-wide street lined with large homes. I said, "Jameson. You upstairs?"

"Yes, sir."

"Let me know what room you're in. In case I have to call the police."

I heard Jameson ask Ebben what room they were in. Ebben said they were in his office.

"Hold on," said Bunion Brit. "He should have turned on First. If he crosses Beverly, he's not going to Ebben's."

"Hold tight, Jameson."

We stopped at a light. Beverly Boulevard. Cars whipped by as if they were on a freeway. I asked what the dark space was on our left. Brit said it was the park in Hancock Park. The park was small, the size of three or four house lots, and it was surrounded by a high, wrought-iron fence, gated and locked with a chain.

I said, "They don't let people in the parks here?"

"Not at night. They'd be full of homeless and drug dealers."

The light turned green. The Mercedes crossed Beverly, and so did we.

I said, "Jameson, I don't think he's headed your way. Wait a few minutes, and I'll give you the okay to turn the lights back on."

When the eye patch turned left on Santa Monica Boulevard, Brit said we were headed west again. I asked her to tell me more about Ebben's Creative Collective. She said it was a dream come true for artists. Complete creative freedom. Not a lot of money up front, but if the TV show or film succeeded, everyone would share in the profits, which could be substantial. That's always been theoretically true for writers, actors, and directors, she said, but in Ebben's collective, everyone meant everyone. Set designers and makeup artists and editors and camera operators and the sound department. Even production assistants and the people who drove the actors to and from set.

I said, "This must have been tried before."

"It has," said Brit. "But things have changed. Today, distribution isn't a hurdle. You don't have to find someone willing to distribute to movie theaters and you don't have to convince theaters to show the movie."

I said, "Because of streaming?"

"Exactly. Ebben doesn't care if our movies end up in theaters. I mean, he'll rent a theater and run a film a few times so we qualify for the Oscars, but he believes the public movie theater experience is dead. And it is for most people over forty. It's not like he's going to make a superhero movie. Ebben likes small stories. And even if every art house theater in the country shows a film, that's nothing compared to digital distribution, which gets it in people's homes. That's where the real viewership is. We don't need suits for funding and we don't need them for distribution. No one can tell us what to do. Or what not to do."

"Who's us?"

"Ebben and everyone involved in the Creative Collective's productions. Like me."

"What about Ebben's agent and manger? Sebastiano and Debra? How do they fit in?"

Brit remained two cars behind the Mercedes. It was almost midnight, and traffic had eased. We passed a Rolls-Royce and Bentley dealership. The Mercedes moved into the right lane. Brit slipped back to the third car behind the shaved-head and also drifted into the right lane.

I said, "You're a natural tail."

"Sounds like a pickup line."

"It's not."

"You spend a lot of time behind the wheel in this town. You learn how to drive."

"Tell me about Sebastiano and Debra."

"They get their commissions but that's it."

"What do you mean, that's it? That's good, right?"

"No. Agents want packaging fees and managers usually get executive producer credits and fees and points. Agents and managers get rich off clients like Ebben. But not with The Creative Collective. If Ebben pays himself 100 grand to EP a project, Sebastiano and Debra each get 10 grand. Even if Ebben makes a movie for 10 million and it rakes in 100 million. That's 90 million of profit. But Sebastiano gets 10,000. Debra gets 10,000. That's a slap in the face to them."

I pointed to a building on my right. "Is that *the* Troubadour?"

"Yep."

"As in James Taylor, Linda Ronstadt, and The Eagles?"

"In the early seventies it was quite the place to be. Goddamn that fucker never signals his turns. Looks like we're headed up Doheny."

The Mercedes turned right at the light. The cars in front of us went straight, which put us directly behind the eye patch's boxy SUV. Brit hung back. We said nothing for a minute and kept our eyes on the Mercedes. When it looked like it'd turn right on Sunset Boulevard, Brit sped up. We passed more rock-n-roll history: The Roxy and Whisky a Go Go and The Viper Room. A couple blocks later, the Mercedes turned left on Sunset Plaza and sped up into the hills.

"Okay," said Brit. "This is a little weird."

The road grew narrow and winding. "Let him get a curve or two ahead, and hope we get lucky. But there's a good chance we'll lose him."

"Hold on. I think I know where he's going."

"Where?"

The road twisted out of sight every half block. Houses sat so close to the street you could almost reach out the car window and ring a doorbell. I thought, *How do they drive these hills when it snows?* Then I remembered it doesn't snow. Ever. Brit turned off her lights and slowed to a crawl.

I said, "What are you doing?"

She pulled over to the curb and said, "Look. In front of the green house on the left. The one with carriage lights on the garage."

I could see the Mercedes's silhouette fifty feet ahead. It, too, was pulled over with its lights off. "How'd you spot that?"

"I had a feeling it might be there."

"Based on?"

"I know who lives in that green house."

"Sebastiano or Debra?"

Bunion Brit shook her head. "No. Me."

12

Brit said, "Why would that Russian dude go to *my* house?"

"Maybe he didn't follow August and me to the hotel. Maybe he followed you. And he's still looking for you."

"I'm a writer. I'm not involved in anything. What would he want with me?"

"You owe anyone money?"

"No. I don't even have credit card debt."

"Romantic entanglements?"

"None," said Bunion Brit. "I've been seeing someone over a year. I was married in my late twenties. That ended amicably. I haven't had a jealous boyfriend since eighth grade."

"Well. We can sit here and wait until he leaves. Or, we can

turn around and spend the night at Ebben's. I'm sure he has room, and at least you'll have company."

Brit ran it around in her brain and started her Audi. She backed into a driveway then started down the hill.

Ebben assigned bedrooms, I said good night to Jameson, and slept seven solid hours in a four-poster canopy bed fit for a princess. At eight o'clock, I was the only one awake. I stepped outside. No gardeners. No boxy Mercedes SUVs parked on the block. Nothing. I mapped coffee and walked a couple blocks to Larchmont Boulevard where I had my choice of half a dozen coffee places on one adorable block.

I summoned a Lyft and commanded it to take me to Lexus of Beverly Hills. The service waiting area looked more like a hotel lobby than a car dealership. Half a dozen service advisors stood behind white counters with white computer monitors showing their white teeth. I approached a young man who said, "Good morning, sir. How may I help you?" He spoke with an accent. I couldn't tell if it was European or African or South American or Middle Eastern, but it sounded like it belonged in Beverly Hills.

I said, "Hey, I got into a little accident last night, and they towed my car here."

"What name would that be under?"

"Mayer. M-A-Y-E-R. Ebben."

"Just one moment." The man typed on his white keyboard. A white keyboard in an auto service center. I once had a Mac with a white keyboard. It lived in my living room and showed more dirt than a white bulldozer. "Yes, your car came in last night. A mechanic should be able to look at it today."

"Great. Is it accessible? I can't find my wallet and think I might have left it in the car."

"One moment. I'll check." The young man stepped out from behind the counter and disappeared into the service center. A young woman approached and asked if I'd like anything to drink. Coffee? Water? I said no thank you, and she drifted into the waiting area to ask the next customer, a woman whose hair, skin, and clothing shouted forty while her eyes whispered seventy. She wore yoga pants and a skintight top to highlight swells and curves that did not belong on a woman of seventy. Perhaps she was in the service center to get her personal fluids topped off.

The young man returned and said, "Sir, the car is accessible. I just need to see some ID to let you have a look inside."

I smiled. "That's why I'm here. I left it in the car."

The young man acknowledged our dilemma with a crooked smile and said, "Come on. You look trustworthy to me."

He led me into a giant garage that looked like "the garage of the future" in a science fiction movie. The place was too clean. The cars. The floor. The people working on the cars. Ebben's Lexus sat in the back corner. They hadn't put it on the lift yet. I opened the driver's side door, leaned inside, and made a big fuss about searching the floor near the gas and brake pedals. Nothing. Then I crawled in farther and bent over the center console to search the floor of the passenger side. I reached into my pocket, pulled out my wallet, then sat up. I got out of the car. "Found it. Thanks."

I walked around to the front of the car and looked at the broken axle. "Man, I haven't seen it in the light before. Not good."

Then I walked around to the back of the car to see what I'd come to see. The back bumper had no dents, no scratches. It looked factory fresh. Maybe Ebben didn't get rammed by the SUV. Maybe he just got a tap. Maybe the SUV never existed.

Bunion Brit called to tell me Ebben and Jameson volunteered to drive her to meet me for coffee. She asked where I was. I told her Beverly Hills. Half an hour later, we sat in Joan's on Third, a chatty-loud place full of white tile and a surplus of good-looking people.

Jameson had left with Ebben to bodyguard him during a series of meetings with broadcast networks. Ebben said something about never being more in need of a bodyguard. I had no idea what he was talking about.

I saved a table while Brit ordered. She returned carrying a number on a stick and said our coffee and food would be delivered soon. I was about to ask if "the guy she was seeing" would be joining us when a voice said:

"Sorry I'm late. The 405 was a clusterfuck." Sebastiano, Ebben's tall, handsome, dark-skinned agent stood in contrast to the white tile. "Did you order for me?"

Brit said, "I ordered for everyone."

"I bet all the bubbles will have bubbled out of Thom's Perrier by the time he gets here. Son of a bitch is too cheap to valet."

Brit said, "Lay off. You know it has nothing to do with money."

Sebastiano looked at me and said, "Thom claims he won't valet because they always fart in his car. But that's only because they know he doesn't tip for shit."

I said, "Who's Thom?"

"Brit's boyfriend."

"He's not my boyfriend," said Brit. "He's just the guy I'm seeing. And it's a new car. He wants to keep it that way."

Sebastiano said, "It's a Subaru Outback," with a derogatory headshake.

"Sorry I'm late," said a woman. I looked up and saw Debra, Ebben's manager, moving her big-boned body in our direction, her octagonal bright-pink plastic glasses leading the way. "Someone better have died on the 405 to fuck it up like that. I'm not kidding. There'd better be chalk outlines on the fucking pavement." She looked at Brit. "Did you order for me?"

"Yes."

"Almond milk decaf cap?" Brit nodded. "Dry?" Brit nodded.

Brit, Sebastiano the agent, and Debra the manager continued to discuss what was and wasn't about to be brought to our number on a stick when I realized Brit and I had never had our premeeting, a concept I mocked only yesterday but that now seemed like it would've been time well spent. I thought I was having coffee with Brit and her boyfriend or whatever she called him. But now Ebben's agent and manager were there.

"Hey, guys." I looked up. Thom Burke wore red Converse All Stars, ripped jeans, a wrinkly yellow Oxford with a navy sweater draped over his shoulders. He looked like an Abercrombie & Fitch model doing an AARP campaign. His black hair had no sheen—it ate light. He said, "Found a meter on the next block. Nils, glad you could make it."

I gave Brit a *what the hell?* look but we were interrupted by a server bringing our food. Conversation began with where everyone ate last night and what they watched on TV and what they thought of it. Both Sebastiano and Debra had seen the "overnights," which I learned were television ratings from major markets. The "nationals" would come in the afternoon. This mattered because everyone had a friend, client, loved one, or bank account involved in one of the shows that would or would not be renewed. It was as if people back home met for coffee every day to discuss the share price of Target, 3M, Best Buy, Medtronic, and General Mills because a tick up or tick down meant they could buy a new house or file for unemployment.

I tried to make eye contact with Brit but she avoided me. I'd agreed to this meeting to answer her questions about the day-to-day reality of being a private detective. But this gathering seemed to be about something entirely different, and I had no idea what.

The conversation turned when Sebastiano and Debra peppered me with questions about my personal life. Was I married? Did I have kids? Have I lived anywhere other than Minnesota? They both gushed about Minneapolis, praising the Guthrie Theater, Prince, the LGBTQ community, Macalester and Carleton Colleges. They had big smiles on their faces and didn't mention Minnesota's winter, so I figured I was being buttered up for something. Debra's the one who divulged what it was.

"So Nils," she said, "we can't tell you how thrilled we are that you're optioning your story to Ebben. And with Brit attached to write, it's a team of superstars."

I looked at Brit, who did not hang her head in shame. Or look away. Or behave in any decent way whatsoever. She just smiled and said, "I'm so flattered to be a part of this."

I said, "Hold on. What are you talking about?"

They all looked at each other with genuine or manufactured confusion. Then Sebastiano said, "I'm sorry, Nils. We thought Ebben had spoken to you about this."

"Ebben said he'd like to option the rights to a case I investigated, but I didn't agree to anything. Or give him any indication I'm interested. Did he tell you I did?"

Debra said, "Ebben said he thought we could make a deal. If you sign on, we can sell this. We'll start with premium cable, Amazon, Netflix, Hulu, Apple, maybe YouTube TV. Pretty sure we'll end up at one of those places. But if not, basic cable is easy. I'm thinking TNT for sure but I know BBC America is looking for just this kind of thing. And they're on the rise."

"I have questions."

"Of course you do," said Sebastiano. "That's why you asked for this meeting, right?"

"First of all, I didn't ask for this meeting. I thought I was having coffee with Brit."

"And Thom," said Brit. "I told you about Thom."

"Yes. Brit and Thom."

Sebastiano said, "I represent Brit and Ebben. I have to be here."

"And I manage both," said Debra. "So I have to be here."

"Fine. Great. Everyone's supposed to be here. Except Ebben's not here. And doesn't The Creative Collective exclude agents and managers?"

"Only as profit participants," said Sebastiano. "And not all of Ebben's projects run through The Collective. He first showed me the article about you before The Collective was formed, so it's considered preexisting business."

"All right. Whatever that means. But why do you even need

my story? There's plenty of public information out there about the dust murder in Edina. Make up your own private detective."

"Can't do it," said Thom.

"Why not?"

"We won't be able to sell it if we can't say it was based on actual events. We need an article and a personal way in. You're that personal way in. With you, we have a sale. Without you, we don't."

"And the best part," said Debra, "is you don't have to do anything because you already did it. You solved the case. Just pop your head into the writers' room once in a while and visit the set. It's show business. It's fun."

It didn't sound fun. My cell rang. Ebben. I excused myself and stepped outside onto Third Street. Traffic whipped back and forth. Drivers changed lanes as frequently as Minnesota meteorologists changed weather forecasts. No one honked. Traffic flowed. No matter what lofty dreams these people were chasing in Los Angeles, they all seemed to have achieved the status of accomplished driver.

Ebben asked where I was and said he'd be there in half an hour to pick me up. He needed me to attend the rest of the day's meetings with him. I asked where Jameson was and heard "I'm right here. On the Bluetooth. I got something I gotta do so it's your turn to play bodyguard."

I said, "Are you going to tell me what you're up to?"

"I am not."

"Any sign of a gray Mercedes SUV?"

"Nope. And I've been checking for tails. Just the way you taught me. Even took Riverside Drive back from ABC instead of the 101. Nice and curvy. No place to hide. Haven't seen a thing."

"You're going to earn your junior detective shield yet."

"Damn right I am. Waze says we'll be there in twenty-seven minutes. See you then."

I hung up with Jameson and Ebben, turned back toward the restaurant, and found someone standing in my way.

"Hey, buddy, who are you?" The shaved-head with the eye patch stood about five foot nine, barrel chested and big bellied. He wore a black leather sport coat over a red T-shirt, black jeans, and Italian-looking loafers sans socks. He spoke in a heavy, Eastern European accent, like Count Chocula. "I ask you a question, buddy. Who are you?"

13

"My name is Nils Shapiro. I'm visiting from Minnesota."

"I know Minnesota, buddy. The Vikings. I learned do not bet on Vikings. They break your heart and your wallet. No?"

"You know the Vikings all right."

"So buddy, why you visit here?" He pulled a pack of Marlboros from his jacket pocket, fished out a cigarette, and stuck it in his lips. "You want smoke? I give to you if you want."

"No thanks. Don't smoke."

"Fucking Americans. No smoke. No drink. Go to gym every day and wait month for parking spot because you be too lazy to walk block. You should live life."

"Maybe you need to see more of America before you judge the country as a whole. We got plenty of drunk smokers who only get off the couch to grab another Bud and refill their bowl of Doritos. And those are the classy ones who eat their Doritos out of bowls."

"I like Cool Ranch Doritos. But the orange dust I do not like on my steering wheel."

"You're more American than you think."

He smoked with an affable grin between inhales and exhales. He was having a good time. His one eye squinted in the sunlight. He said, "I like you, buddy. You fucking funny as shit. Why you leave the Vikings? For sunshine? The beautiful women? You go surfing? Ride the board on the wave? Or maybe want to be famous on the TV? Why you here, buddy?"

I have been asked this question a thousand times in the line of duty, and I've lied almost every time. It's part of the job. But when Brit asked me what I did, I told her the truth. Mostly, anyway. I don't know why—it just felt like the right move. Maybe it had something to do with being an outsider. A stranger in the strangest land. The truth gave me an anchor to keep me from drifting off into make-believe. I said, "I'm a private detective. I have a client in Minnesota who asked me to come out here and check on one of her investments."

He laughed. "You are private detective? For reals?"

"For reals."

"Why you tell me? Do you not want to be, what do you say? Undercover?"

"Sometimes, I do, yeah. But right now, I don't give a shit."

His smile went away. "Don't fuck with me, buddy. I'm not person to fuck with."

The sun bounced white and hot off the buildings and pavement. Every car that whizzed by gleamed as if it had just been shot out of a car wash.

"I'm not fucking with you." I took out my wallet. "Here's my driver's license. Nils Shapiro. See? Minnesota. And here's my PI license."

He smiled. "Okay. All right. You private detective. Like Sherlock Holmes. That's what you say. Even though I could make phone call and have Minnesota driver license and private detective license in two hours, I believe you."

"Thank you."

"You got honest face."

"I know. It gets me in trouble."

"Ha! With women, right? You get in trouble with women?"

I smiled and nodded. "You know what I'm talking about."

"Eh," he shrugged. "I try. So, buddy, I need something from you. The people you eat breakfast and drink the coffee with, you have to give them message."

"No problem."

"You tell them, *No Kate Lennon.*" He pointed at me with his cigarette.

I said, "You don't like Kate Lennon?"

"I love Kate Lennon. Best actress in Hollywood. Hot at box office. I say bravo for Kate Lennon in *Easy Enough* and *The Daughter. New York Love*, I did not believe her. But I blame script. I can write better script than that. I have one in car if you want to read. Russian tragedy. Will make you cry. But the point, buddy, is tell your friends no movie with Kate Lennon. Find new A-lister."

I've never dropped acid, but if I had to guess what hallucinations might come of it, this conversation would be one of them.

I was working hard to suppress a laugh when the shaved-head stuck a finger under his eye patch, scratched whatever was in there, and said:

"This is not joke, buddy. One pretty girl is dead. No one else needs to be dead. So tell your friends. Find new actress."

One pretty girl is dead? That changed the tone of our little chat. I said, "I'll go inside and tell them right now."

"I like you, buddy. I don't want to hurt your family."

I stared something cold in his eye and may have even lost my Minnesota Nice smile. "Can I tell them who gave me the message? Your name? Someone you work for?"

"Nah, buddy. I do my job in shadows. Saving name for when I make it big time."

"All right, but I don't see many shadows around here. Too much sun. Everywhere you look. Nothing but sun."

"Welcome to Los Angeles, buddy. And fuck this place you are eating. Get hot dog at Pink's. You wait in line, but it be best." He turned and walked away.

I went inside having no idea what to do with the eye patch's message. I intended to relay it—I saw no reason not to—but I had no footing with these people. I didn't understand half the words that came out of their mouths. I was in a joke or a nightmare or both. The one-eyed son of a bitch had just threatened Gabriella and Evelyn whether he knew it or not.

Ebben seemed the most relevant person to hear the message. Brit wrote the movie, but he funded it. And he wouldn't be there for another fifteen minutes.

When I sat back down, Brit, Thom, Sebastiano, and Debra had reverted to opining about TV shows and which actors shined in their roles, which directors had heat on them (their words, not mine), and which of the shows would continue for another season. They talked about show business the way Minnesotans talk about the weather. Show business was their collective experience, what bonded them, what created the foundation of their community. Maybe that was unfair. Maybe people in the shoe business talk the same about what styles are selling and which cobblers are in demand. But it didn't feel unfair. Their conversations felt more live-to-work than work-to-live.

That I understood. Living to work had been the sad reality of my life. How the meaningless task of hunting an unfaithful husband with a telephoto lens could create meaning in my life. Or the illusion of meaning.

My fiancée and baby daughter rescued me from that. They gave my life mass. Made it real. I could feel them in my heart and in my gut. I woke in the middle of the night and sensed them next to me even when they were two thousand miles away. I wondered if that made my job superfluous, obsolete for all it has provided other than a paycheck.

"Nils? Are you with us?"

I popped out of my head and into Joan's on Third. "Sorry?"

Brit said, "You're from flyover country. How do you think people there would respond to a show about a rogue group of doctors who are like Robin Hoods of medicine? By day they're in private practice catering to the rich who come in complaining about all sorts of bullshit ailments. The rogue doctors write them scrips for the expensive drugs, but give them placebos and give the real drugs to those who can't afford it."

I said, "Are they doctors or pharmacists?"

Brit looked at Sebastiano, Debra, and Thom, and said, "Fuck. He's right. Unless they have their own pharmacy in the doctor's office, the rich patients would get the scrips filled at their local CVS or wherever."

Sebastiano said, "Maybe there's a pharmacist in the group. The way Robin Hood had Friar Tuck but instead of a friar he or she is a pharmacist."

Debra, dead serious, "That could work. I'd buy that. That would definitely work."

Thom said, "Is there a way to do it with doctors providing services for the poor instead of prescription drugs? Because basically stealing medicine from the rich and giving it to the poor is insurance fraud and, even more importantly, none of the pharmaceutical companies would advertise on the show. Do we want to walk away from that revenue?"

Sebastiano folded his arms over his chest and gave that a good think. I wondered if they assumed I'd decided to sell them the rights to my story or if their attention span was so short they had simply moved on to the next idea.

Ebben Mayer walked up to our table with a new number on a new stick, and I told the table about my conversation with the eye patch. Drop Kate Lennon. No need for someone else to die.

Thom the line producer said, "I'm calling the police."

Ebben said, "No. If you call the police, they'll file a report and we'll have to tell our insurance company. The production could lose its insurance, then we lose the production. And we can't lose the production. This movie is the cornerstone of The Creative Collective. The script is fantastic—thank you, Brit. We have a major star. We—"

Sebastiano said, "But Ebben. Making a movie is not worth risking anyone's personal safety. When someone dies on a movie set, careers are ruined."

Debra said, "Okay, hold up. This conversation cannot leave this table. Not a word. If it gets back to Kate, she could withdraw from the movie. That would be worse than losing production insurance."

Brit said, "I can't believe this is happening. I finally get a movie greenlit and some crazy fucking Russian dude is trying to intimidate us into shutting it down. Unfuckingbelievable. I turned down twenty-two episodes on *NCIS* to focus on this movie. Do you know how much money I walked away from?"

Ebben said, "We're making *For the People*. With Kate Lennon. And I wasn't going to share this yet but I think you all need to hear it. I got a call from Ava St. Clair's agent on my drive over. Ava loves the script and wants to direct. She wants to be part of The Creative Collective. She's rearranging her schedule so we can go into preproduction in March. Now we have a huge star and a huge director. The deal's going to make. Ava doesn't care about up-front money.

"If we lose this project it would be like Netflix losing *House of Cards* before *House of Cards* got off the ground. *House of Cards* had all the elements to make Netflix the gold standard of original content. Just like *For the People* will make us the gold standard. We can't lose it."

Thom said, "But we can't have thugs threatening us. We have to call the police."

"No," said Ebben. He looked like he wanted to shout but instead spoke more quietly to prove his point. "If word gets out about this, I don't care who leaked it, everyone at this table is fired. I'm sorry to be so punitive but you need to know how serious I am. I will find new representation. I will find a new line producer. And Brit, I'll find a new scribe for on-set rewrites."

Thom reached over and placed his hand on top of Brit's. It was the first sign I'd seen of their so-called seeing each other.

Sebastiano and Debra stared hard at Thom, who held up his free hand in surrender and said, "Got it. No police."

Ebben said, "And Nils. You don't have anything vested in this, but please. I'm begging you. Keep this quiet."

I felt my phone vibrate but kept my eyes up. Sebastiano and Debra had everything to gain from derailing The Creative Collective. It threatened their business model, which appeared to be their life. I looked at Ebben and nodded. "I won't say a word." Then I glanced at my phone. It was a text from Ellegaard. *Ran the plates on gray Mercedes SUV. Call me.*

14

Ebben stayed in the restaurant while I waited for his car at the valet. There was a line that included to-be-car-seated children so I took the opportunity to return Ellegaard's call. He told me the gray Mercedes was registered to Vasily Zaytzev in Sherman Oaks and that he'd text me the address. I told him what I'd learned about Ebben Mayer and what was new with Jameson, and that I hoped to be on a plane back to Minneapolis that night. I just needed to check out Vasily Zaytzev. Not out of duty but out of conscience. Or at least something nagging at it.

A hand yanked away my valet ticket. I turned and saw Sebastiano standing tall and broad-shouldered, his angular face tilted just so to catch the sunlight. His eyes were cloaked behind sunglasses, which, like his expression, looked curated. He said, "Let me pay for this."

"Nice way to cut in line."

Sebastiano smiled. He placed a hand on my shoulder and said, "So I hear you're a friend of the Mayers."

"Some of them."

"And you came out from Minnesota to pay your respects."

"Guilty."

"Even though you'd never met Ebben before."

"All true."

"*And* you just happen to be a private detective."

"You have good sources."

"So is this a personal or professional visit?"

"Little of both. I'm sure you know how hard it is to leave work at the office."

"Can I give you some friendly advice?"

"If it's really friendly."

"Go back to Minnesota. It's safer there." The valet returned. Sebastiano handed him both our tickets, and the valet ran down the street. Sebastiano said, "Let me tell you how this town works. The valet is going to bring my car first. That's because Ebben's rental is a Lexus and my car is a Porsche. Status matters. Perception matters even more. And the perception is that I'm a partner at the ACI Agency and you're a hick from the Midwest sticking his nose in where it doesn't belong. The only value you have in Los Angeles is to rent yourself out as a passenger for the carpool lane."

The sun felt hot on my pale skin. I stepped into the shade of the valet's patio umbrella and said, "Wow. You're like a cartoon villain."

Sebastiano smiled his white-toothed smile. "I can live with that."

"And a raging asshole."

"I can live with that, too." Sebastiano looked at his phone. "Excuse me. I have to take this." He held the phone to his face and said, "Tell me," and walked down toward the adjacent storefront. He just kept walking, his back to me as if I'd never existed. I was thinking about chasing him down to scold him for his bad manners when the valet pulled up in a bright blue Porsche Panamera, got out, looked at me, and held open the door. I tipped the valet a five, got in Sebastiano's Porsche, and drove away.

I adjusted the seat way up and aligned the mirrors—safety first when stealing a car—and pulled into traffic. Nice ride, although I would've gotten a stick. Probably too much traffic in L.A. to drive a stick. Your right hand would be on the shift lever so often your oat milk latte would get cold. The Porsche's nav showed a hospital a few blocks away. Cedars-Sinai. I took a few turns, made the tires squeal once, and found a lovely parking spot marked EMERGENCY VEHICLE ONLY. I turned on the flasher in case parking control wasn't paying attention, adjusted the seat even farther forward, turned on the seat heater to high, found a country music station, cranked it up, and turned off the car. I got out and locked it because I'm nice, then walked away with the keys in my pocket and texted Ebben. Ten minutes later, he picked me up outside a windowless monolith called the Beverly Center. I got in the car, and he asked me what was going on.

I said, "Where's Jameson?"

"I don't know. He said something came up and he had to go. What happened? Why didn't you get the car from the valet?"

"Did Jameson say he was going to see August?"

"No. He didn't say anything."

"Strange."

Ebben said, "Why didn't you pick up the car?"

I said, "Your agent, Sebastiano, has some issues."

"I know," said Ebben. "That's what makes him a good agent."

"We had a not-so-great conversation while waiting for the cars."

"Is that why you walked away?"

"I didn't walk away."

Ebben said, "Yes, you did. I got the car."

"You got the car, but I didn't walk away."

"I'm confused."

His cell rang. I saw Sebastiano's name pop up on the car's screen. Ebben pushed a button on the steering wheel and said, "Hey, Sebastiano. What's up?"

Sebastiano's voice came through loud and clear on the car's speakers. "Is that motherfucker with you?"

"What motherfucker?"

"Nils Shapiro."

Ebben said a tentative, "Yes . . ."

"Where's my car, Shapiro?"

Ebben said, "What's he talking about?"

I said, "It's at Cedars-Sinai."

Sebastiano said, "Where at Cedars-Sinai?"

"In a no-parking zone."

"You fucking asshole. You stole my car."

I glanced at Ebben. His eyes smiled.

Sebastiano said, "Are the keys in it?"

"No. I have the keys."

"Well, what fucking good is that going to do me?!"

I said, "You may find this hard to believe, but I wasn't thinking about what was good for you."

"That car cannot be towed!" said Sebastiano. "It will ruin the transmission!"

"Well," I said, "you shouldn't have threatened me."

"I did not threaten you. I just suggested you go back to the middle of nowhere."

I said, "How's your pal Vasily Zaytzev?"

"Who?"

"Uh huh. Listen, Sebastiano. We'll drop the keys at your office after our meeting." I turned to Ebben. "Where are we going?"

Ebben said, "Fox. It's ten minutes from Sebastiano's office."

"Hear that, Sebastiano? You'll have them in an hour or two. Then you can find a pal to drive you to the impound lot."

"Ebben," said Sebastiano, "we'll talk later."

Ebben said, "Sorry about all this." But he wasn't sorry. He had a kid's mischievous joy in his eyes.

Sebastiano said, "Yep," and hung up.

Ebben asked me what was going on, and I told him about my exchange with Sebastiano at the valet stand and that I kind of stole his car. "You shouldn't have done that." Then he laughed. "But it's pretty awesome you did."

"Why do you work with that guy?"

Ebben lifted a devil-worship-themed energy drink can from the cup holder. He took a sip and said, "He's powerful. He can get me any meeting I want. He can team me up with the best writers, actors, and directors. Studios love him. He makes things happen. Who's that Russian you mentioned?"

"Vasily Zaytzev is the name of the eye patch who threatened us." He nodded and said nothing. "Vasily's words were, 'One pretty girl is dead. No one else needs to be dead.' He was at Juliana's memorial or celebration or whatever you want to call it, so it was an easy threat to make whether or not he had something to do with her death."

Ebben said, "That's worrisome."

"The other thing is I got the plates of the Mercedes SUV he drove to Brit's house last night. It may also be the same SUV that forced you off Mulholland Drive. I had my partner, Ellegaard, run the plates. That's how I got Vasily's name. I also got his address. I'll grab Jameson this afternoon and we'll go say hello. See if we can learn anything more."

Ebben kept his eyes on the road. "Thank you."

"One more thing. Are you comfortable with me telling your grandmother about The Creative Collective?"

"Sure. I don't care."

"Why didn't you tell her?"

"The honest answer is I don't like her all that much. She's not a nice person. Treats my father like shit. Hates my mother. I don't want her in my life."

"Can't blame you for that."

"But tell her this because it's the truth: I put $1 million of my own money into The Creative Collective. That's it. The rest I've raised both domestically and abroad. I won't bore you with a lot of details, but basically fifty percent of the collective's profits will go back to investors and fifty percent will go to production participants. The reason that's attractive to investors is our upfront costs are low because the big salaries—actors, directors, writers—are working for scale."

"For scale?"

"The minimum amount required by union contracts. Those involved in the production will make their money on the back end if there's back-end profit. Just like the investors. And we're much more likely to see a back-end profit because, like I said, our upfront costs are low. Also, our accounting is legitimate. Make a deal for back-end profit with a studio, they'll make sure they never show a profit. Ever. They'll repave the entire studio lot with diamonds and charge it off to your production before they pay a cent of profit participation. But our books will be wide open. Is any of this making sense?"

I said, "Low upfront costs. Everyone makes money if the project makes money. It's all out in the open and legit."

"You got it. I used a prospectus to raise money. I'll give you one. Between what I've just told you and the prospectus, that should convince my grandmother I'm behaving prudently. Get her off my back and get her off yours."

I said, "I like the sound of that."

"You know," said Ebben, "you grow up in Minnesota with a dream to make good movies and TV shows. That's it. Some quality work you can be proud of. Work that people will still watch when you're long dead. You get born into a family that makes you luckier than winning the lottery. You educate yourself about money, work with money, study people who have and who have lost money. Then you study film. From its beginning. My grandmother didn't tell you I have a second degree in film, did she? That's because she doesn't know. I have an MFA, and she has no idea. But go ahead and tell her that, too, because I don't give a damn about her anymore."

Ebben Mayer was on a roll. Something about riding in cars gets people talking. Maybe that's why powerful people pull up in limos and tell people to get in. If I ever become powerful I'll give it a try.

Ebben said, "I have worked hard to be where I am right now. Since I was sixteen years old. Studied hard and got into good schools. Made my own money as an investment banker and in private equity. Serious money. I could have done this without my trust fund. In fact, I have done this without my trust fund. I had seven figures in the bank. My trust fund is a safety net and that's not nothing, I know. But still. I've earned this opportunity. I'm not going to let some thug take it away from me."

Ebben shifted into the turning lane to take a left on Pico Boulevard. The actual turn would not happen until the light turned green then red then green then red then green one more time.

I said, "But isn't the show business industry vested in keeping the status quo? Change scares people. Makes them do stupid things. The Creative Collective is like a nature conservancy that swoops in and buys up a bunch of land, taking it away from hunters and developers. You've threatened their way of life. And now one of them might be threatening you."

Ebben said, "But why would they? I've greenlit one low-budget film. I've cut out the middleman and the bankers, so to speak, but so what? It happens every day. *Blair Witch Project*, *Napoleon Dynamite*, *El Mariachi*, and thousands of other projects were made outside the system. They didn't change the industry, and I won't change the industry. Upfront money has always had the loudest voice and it always will. Anyone who's threatened by what I'm doing isn't thinking clearly."

My phone buzzed. It was August Willingham the Third. I answered.

"Hey, Shap. Is Jameson with you?"

"No. I was hoping he was with you."

"He should have showed up to practice half an hour ago. Shit."

"Did you try calling him?"

"Of course. His phone goes straight to voicemail. Doesn't even ring."

"All right. If he doesn't show up in an hour, we'll go look for him."

"In L.A.? I wouldn't even know where to start."

I had to admit, neither did I.

15

Security wasn't expecting me to attend Ebben's meeting, so it took a few phone calls to get past the guard gate at Fox. Then I sat in on Ebben's get-together. Three executives all under the age of thirty seemed thrilled to meet him. One confused Minneapolis with Indianapolis, a common mistake if you've never lived more than five miles from an ocean. Another just wanted to talk about Bunion Brit's movie *For the People*, gushed about taking the fight for equality to the next level. And the third said nothing and took notes, as if what they were discussing was important enough to be documented. When it was over, business cards were handed out like mints at a halitosis convention, then we drove to a glass tower in Century City to drop off Sebastiano's keys.

Ebben idled in the delivery area, and I approached a security desk in the lobby. Half a dozen navy-jacketed security guards wearing matching white shirts and red neckties stood behind a white marble monolith. They looked like underwear models and wore earpieces. A guard with a crew cut asked me to sign in. I said I wasn't going in. I just needed to drop off some car keys for one of the building's tenants. Then I felt a hand on my shoulder.

"It's time you and me have a talk." I didn't have to turn around to know it was Sebastiano. "My office. Ebben will be back to pick you up in an hour."

I could have refused and walked away, but sometimes I feel like a dentist. My job involves picking and probing and, when I find something rotten, I feel obligated to drill into it.

The security guard handed me a card on a lanyard and said, "You'll need that to get upstairs. And I have to see your ID."

I showed the security guard my ID. He said, "Thank you, Mr. Shapiro. And please sign in."

So I did. Name: *Jim Rockford*. Date: January 16. Time: 12:47.

The card on the lanyard allowed me to pass through a revolving door. Banks don't have this much security. Art museums that house $50 million paintings don't. Over-the-top security is a statement of self-importance, as if foreign spies are lurking about, waiting to steal that stupid Robin Hood doctor show idea.

We passed two assistants to enter Sebastiano's office. One mentioned Sebastiano's personal trainer asking to move 8:00 to 8:30 and the other said something about a screening tomorrow night on the Warner Bros. lot. Sebastiano responded to both and we entered his office. A lot of glass and steel and two separate seating areas, one upholstered in brown and white cowhide, the other in black and white cowhide, providing plenty of meeting space and both oriented toward a billboard-sized TV. Sebastiano had a stand-up desk because type A's never sit, and a *Fast and the Furious* pinball machine to show that, even with all this success, he was still a kid at heart.

We sat on the brown and white cowhide, and a different assistant, not one of the two who sat out front, entered pushing a cart of food and beverages. Sandwiches and salads and cans and bottles. Some labels read gluten free, others dairy free, others vegan, and others paleo. The assistant asked if we wanted anything else, Sebastiano deferred to me, and I said, "Does he usually eat this much?"

The assistant noted Sebastiano's smile, parroted it, then excused herself and left.

I said, "Well-trained kid."

Sebastiano said, "That kid was top of her class at Harvard."

"Huh. I would have figured a Harvard grad would get a more lofty job than sandwich pusher."

Sebastiano smiled. "She just started working here. In three months, she'll cover my desk. In a year, she'll make agent. In five, she'll make partner and pull down seven figures before she's thirty. But we're not here to talk about her. We're here to talk about you. That was a bold move taking my car. I respect bold moves."

"I'm not after your respect."

He eyed the sandwiches but left them where they were. He said, "Ebben Mayer has let you into his inner circle. That doesn't happen often. I won't insult you by blowing a bunch of smoke up your ass so I'll cut right to it. Ebben is one of my most important clients. That means I make his business my business. That includes his personal life. I don't know exactly why he's let you in or exactly how you fit in, but you do, so here you are and here we are. We're going to be in each other's lives now so we need to get along."

I helped myself to a turkey sandwich and said, "I'm visiting. There's a six-thirty flight I'm hoping to be on this evening. Then you'll never see me again."

"Why would you go back to Minnesota if Ebben wants you here? No offense, but everything is happening in Los Angeles. What's happening in Minnesota?"

"I heard you say 'no offense,' but 'what's happening in Minnesota?' is offensive. Saying 'no offense' doesn't make it not offensive."

"Yeah well, I'm not just talking shit—I'm from the Midwest. Danville, Illinois. Got a need-based scholarship to the University of Illinois. Then law school at Loyola. Worked as an AUSA in the Southern District of New York. That's Manhattan. I lived in New York City. They wanted me to move to D.C. and slot me into DOJ, but I wanted to make some money so I came out here and worked my way up to all this."

Did I ask for his résumé? Was I supposed to be impressed? Is that how everyone in Hollywood talks? I said, "This is a good turkey sandwich. Do you mind if I take another one for later?"

"Take all you want. The point I'm making, Nils, is I've lived in Illinois. I've also lived in New York and now I live in Los Angeles. I know what the coasts have to offer. I think you should spend more time out here and see how you feel about it."

Huh. A few hours ago he told me to go back to Minnesota. Maybe these free sandwiches weren't because Ebben brought me into his inner circle. Maybe Sebastiano wanted me in his. The big powerful agent and cheekbone show-off was trying to ingratiate himself, and in my experience, that meant he was afraid of me discovering something about him, something he didn't want Ebben to know. He thought he could wine and dine me so I'd look the other way, but his efforts had the opposite effect. I wanted to look more closely.

I said, "Isn't Ebben's Creative Collective taking significant business from you?"

"I see it as one step back and two steps forward."

"So one step forward?"

"Show business has been changing since we gathered around the fire in caves to hear stories. It's always attracted the best and brightest storytellers. But even the smartest creatives can't run a business. And under the glitz and glamour, this is a business like any other business. You have to make more money than you spend, otherwise you go poof. So the creatives will always need people like me."

Sebastiano reached over and grabbed a salad marked *paleo*. "Doesn't matter if their work is on the stage or in movie theaters or on TV or on the internet or beamed directly into people's brains. Studios might go away. Networks might go away. Non-writing producers might go away. Hell, even publicity and advertising might go away. But if the creators are the bricks in the wall, then I'm the mortar. I connect the bricks to one another. I make them into something strong and durable that has purpose. Without me, they're just a pile of bricks. With me, they can stand together for eternity."

I swallowed a mouthful of turkey sandwich. "You don't have much of a self-esteem problem, do you?"

Sebastiano smiled. "I don't have much of an anything problem."

"But you have a me problem. That's why I'm here."

"The reason you're here is because you're not a problem. You were a potential problem but we've handled that. When you leave, you'll be an asset for me, and I'll be an asset for you."

"All right. Can I ask a question?"

"That's why we're here. Get to know each other a little better."

"Did you kill Juliana Marquez?"

"What?" No delay. No exaggerated facial expressions.

"She died of a caffeine overdose."

"I know. From diet pills."

"She took diet pills. But she wasn't dangerous about it. I think she ingested a lethal dose of caffeine unsuspectingly. I think someone mixed caffeine powder into some food or drink and she consumed it."

Sebastiano's giant office was dead quiet. Unnaturally quiet. The interior walls were probably insulated to give the master agent and brick mortar the silence his genius demanded. He thought about what I'd said then took a sip of bubbly water. "Why would anyone want to kill Juliana?"

"They didn't want to kill Juliana."

"Now I'm really confused."

"They wanted to kill Ebben." I kept my eyes on Sebastiano. He held my stare for a good five seconds then looked away, stood, and walked over to a bowl of fruit on the credenza behind his desk. He picked up the whole bowl and returned with it, set it on the coffee table, and chose an apple.

Sebastiano cupped the apple in his hands the way a baseball pitcher cups the ball. "I understand you know nothing about show business. You couldn't unless you worked in it. But don't let your imagination get the best of you. Show business is rife with misbehavior. On every level. It's often ignored, or worse, celebrated. And there are real victims, especially when it comes to sexual misconduct and gender discrimination and racism. Not a lot of senior agency partners with skin my color. For all the liberal grandstanding at awards shows, we got plenty of inequalities of our own."

He nipped at the apple, chewed, and swallowed. "But we're not the mob. People in this business don't get murdered for business reasons. Some get murdered in crimes of passion, but that happens in every town in every community in every subculture whether it's religion or business or whatever. Murder motivated by business just does not happen in Hollywood."

I said, "That's a hard-to-believe generalization."

"I know. You're right. But the truth is, all of us who do this know on some level we're lucky to be here. Don't get me wrong. People are smart and work hard. But still. Working in show business is like playing with house money. Look at this office. It's ridiculous. I'm a kid from Danville, Illinois. From the wrong side of the tracks. And every single day I have a moment where I think, *I'm the luckiest son of a bitch in the world*. We all do. From studio heads down to production assistants fetching donuts at two A.M.

"You know, there's a saying in this town: there's no such thing as a show business emergency. And it's true. Because the stakes just aren't that high. They never are. Everyone runs around like chickens with their heads cut off because we create the illusion that what we're doing is important, but none of it is. Worst-case scenario is a movie gets shelved. So what? Or a TV show shuts down production for a week or two. Drop in the bucket.

"My point is, there's nothing worth killing anyone over. Hollywood is high school with money. That's all. A game."

Sebastiano took a big bite of apple, sat back, and waited for me to respond. He'd just fed me a big, fat lie. Not that I knew anything about show business, but his *there are no stakes therefore there is no murder* theory was complete bullshit. Every day, people manufacture stakes over seemingly nothing. Some asshole didn't get a second Tinder date with a teacher, so he killed a bunch of kids in her middle school. A mother kills a teenage girl so her daughter can get a spot on a cheerleading squad. Road rage. Disrespect. A fix.

I looked at the smug cheekbones and said, "So you're telling me it's impossible someone intended to kill Ebben with a caffeine overdose."

"I'm telling you it's unlikely show business motivated someone to make an attempt on Ebben's life."

"Did I say show business was the motivation?"

Sebastiano took a sip of bubbly water and shook his head. His phone dinged. He looked at the screen. "Hey, sorry, I got to cut this short. Thanks for the talk. Here's my card. My cell's on the back. I'm available twenty-four/seven. Whatever you need." I took the card and shoved it in my front pocket. The office door opened, and one of Sebastiano's assistants entered. "Derek here will show you out."

Sebastiano stood and extended his hand. I took it. Firm steady grip. I looked him in the eye and said, "Thanks for lunch."

"Anytime."

I gave him an I-know-that's-not-true smile and walked out with Derek. Just as we stepped out of Sebastiano's office, I saw the other assistant use her phone to snap a picture of her computer screen. I pretended not to notice by asking Derek where he was from and how long he lived in L.A. and what his long-term goals were. We passed assistant after assistant outside other offices as he answered my questions. None of them were taking pictures of their computer screens. We rounded a corner and I said, "My keys!" I darted back around the corner and saw Sebastiano's other assistant holding her phone in front of her computer screen. Again, I pretended not to notice, turned around, and said, "My bad. Didn't drive."

Derek walked me to the elevator, reminded me to return my badge to security, then sent me down twenty floors. The navy blazers shot me warm smiles. I tossed my card on the marble slab. The crew cut said, "We'll need you to sign out." I went to the sheet, wrote down my departure time, and started to turn away then stopped. I looked down at the sign-in sheet again. Date: January 16. I said, "Son of a bitch."

The guard said, "Something the matter, sir?"

"No. Sorry." But something was the matter. January 16 was the anniversary of the school shooting, and Jameson White's first step into darkness. And I had no idea where he was.

16

I got back in the car with Ebben. He took one look at my face and said, "Sorry. I didn't know he was going to ambush you."

I said I didn't care about Sebastiano and told Ebben about Jameson White—the school shooting one year ago, Jameson's work in the ER, his breakdown, and why I invited him to Los Angeles. I had known the anniversary was coming up, but I'd lost track of days, and now Jameson was missing.

Ebben said, "Are you going to call the police? Or do you have to wait forty-eight hours?"

"The forty-eight-hour thing isn't true. Just on TV shows. But I don't want to get the police involved yet. A police report could reflect poorly on Jameson's mental state and jeopardize his return to nursing. Maybe if I knew someone at LAPD I could trust, but I don't know anyone in the department period."

"So what do we do?" said Ebben.

That's the effect Jameson has on a person. Ebben had known him less than a day and asked what do *we* do. I said, "We make some calls."

"All right. Should we head back toward the house or do we have another destination?"

"Are we close to Westwood?"

"Very close, yeah."

"There."

Ebben put the car in drive. I called August, got his address, and told him I'd be there in fifteen minutes. Then I called Ellegaard. He suggested I call my fiancée. I knew he meant for investigative reasons, but it felt personal. God, I missed Gabriella. The past twenty-four hours reminded me of the mess my life had been before her. I was either chasing something or missing something and, regardless of who I was with, I was alone. When I was married to Micaela, I was alone. When I dated someone, I was alone. It wasn't anyone's fault—I just hadn't found a real connection.

Then Gabriella, who had been in plain sight for almost twenty years, revealed herself. Like Kansas to Dorothy. Now that I'd found her, I couldn't stand being away from her.

Gabriella Nuñez was a deputy chief of the Minneapolis Police Department and MPD's representative on the Joint Terrorism Task Force. She loved Jameson. She promised to call me back as soon as she had some information.

By the time we got to Westwood, I knew the general vicinity

of Jameson's cell phone even though it was turned off. Gabriella wouldn't tell me exactly how, but she'd update me with both Jameson's phone location and credit card usage. That was the good news. The bad news was Jameson was downtown. Or at least his phone was.

Just after we hung up I got a call from a number I didn't recognize. 818 area code. I answered it and put it on speaker.

"Hey, buddy. How are you, buddy?" It was my friend the Cyclops. Ebben's forehead scrunched.

"I've had better days, Vasily. How about you?"

"Hey, buddy. How you know my name?"

"I'll tell you if you tell me how you got my phone number."

"Don't be joking. Anyone can get phone number. But not anyone can get name from face."

"Maybe I recognized you. Maybe you're famous."

"Sometime you piss me off, buddy."

"Can't please everybody."

"You are Nils Shapiro, no?"

"I told you my name earlier. I showed you my ID."

"I mad with you, Nils Shapiro. I mad because I read on the Deadline that Ava St. Clair will direct movie with Kate Lennon. I told you no Kate Lennon. I told you at your face. Fuck you, buddy. Fuck you so many times. Now we have big problem."

"Problems are no good, Vasily. Let's talk about it. But face-to-face. How about I come visit you on Weddington Street in Sherman Oaks?" There was a long pause. I said, "What's going on, Vasily? You checking the closets? Maybe I'm in the backyard. I should tell you, dogs love me. Can't remember the last time a dog barked at me."

Ebben gave me a raised eyebrow. I shrugged.

Vasily spoke. He sounded out of breath. "I kill you, Nils Shapiro."

"Don't worry, Vasily. I'm not at your house."

"I not believe anything you say."

"Let me ask you something. Do you lease that gray G550 or did you buy it? Kind of like the looks of that thing although you can't drive for shit."

"Fuck you, buddy. You know my house. You know my car. Fuck you, fuck you, fuck you."

"Relax, Vasily. I can't be at your house because I can't be two places at once. And right now I'm at the police station holding my phone up on speaker."

He hung up.

Ebben said, "What are you doing?"

"Keeping our one-eyed friend off balance. I don't know if this guy's a real threat or not and—"

"You don't know if he's a real threat? He just said he was going to kill you."

Traffic on Westwood Boulevard had come to a complete stop. I could see black smoke up and to the right. A police officer directed traffic going in our direction onto the opposite side of the street where we used one of their lanes to steer clear of a pickup truck engulfed in flames. The whole thing. Like a campfire gone bad.

I said, "What the hell is going on?"

Ebben was nonchalant and matter-of-fact. "Car fire."

"What? Cars don't just catch on fire in Minnesota. At least I've never seen one."

"Me neither, but they happen here. Not sure why."

"This is a weird town."

"It's different. But I like it. I used to visit cities like London and Paris and think, *Wow, the whole world is here.* They either live there or are visiting and feel lucky to be there. That's what it's like here. New York and Los Angeles are the United States' London or Paris or Tokyo or Shanghai or Rome. Los Angeles is truly an international city. Traffic sucks and cars burst into flames and sometimes it doesn't rain for months and the earth quakes but when you're here, you're at the center of something. The place makes me feel alive. Like I can do anything."

"Other than drive faster than five miles per hour, but I get your point."

August Willingham the Third lived in a high-rise on Wilshire Boulevard. We parked in visitor parking and approached a doorman who was expecting us. The doorman led us through a lobby that had more chandeliers than France, and rode the elevator with us in case we'd never learned how to push a button. We got out on the twenty-first floor and he led us to August, who stood in his open doorway.

His condo faced the ocean. We walked to the floor-to-ceiling windows and August pointed out the 405 freeway then Santa Monica and Venice. He said it was a clear day, though it didn't look that clear to me. In the haze, he identified Catalina Island twenty-five miles off the coast. I had only known Catalina as a salad dressing.

The condo was open and modern and everything was white including a grand piano, its lid propped open like a Venus fly-trap. Whoever recommended his interior decorator should serve time. I said, "What a dump."

August said, "It's an investment," as if he were apologizing. "My mom is a wealth manager. Thirteen years in the NFL and

I sent every paycheck to her. She put me on a strict allowance. While other guys were driving Ferraris and Lamborghinis, I drove an F150. They bought mansions. I lived in a one-bedroom apartment. I knew I had an assistant job waiting for me at UCLA, so we bought this early in my career."

He took us through the dining room and kitchen, down a hall and into a bedroom with a view of the L.A. basin like we'd seen from up on Mulholland. There were two crops of tall buildings. The close one was Century City where I'd just eaten a turkey sandwich with Sebastiano. The farther one was downtown Los Angeles, where according to my last update from Gabriella, Jameson's phone still was.

I turned to August and said, "Did Jameson have a connection to downtown when he attended UCLA?"

August said, "Not that I know of. It's possible he developed one during the summers he drove a cab, but his time was limited. We didn't have classes but we had two-a-day practices. I roomed with him. I knew when he wasn't on campus and those times were rare."

"What about relationships? Any old flames he might be visiting?"

He shook his head. "We prided ourselves on not getting in relationships back then. I know. It was immature, but we were kids. And it would have been impossible for Jameson to hide one from me. He dated, but no one steady."

My cell buzzed. I looked at the caller ID. Beverly Mayer. I excused myself and walked back to the ocean view where I told her Ebben invested $1 million as seed money to start The Creative Collective. The rest he raised from sources around the world. His first movie was about to go into preproduction. It would star

Kate Lennon, and Ava St. Clair was going to direct. I could send her information about those two people if she wanted to know who I was talking about. I added that Ebben was rocked by Juliana's death, but had chosen to press forward, taking meetings in an effort to find his second project. I guessed that working helped Ebben get through the days but any simpleton would have guessed that.

I did not tell her that most of what I'd learned she could have found on the internet. I did not tell her about my suspicion that Juliana was murdered and Ebben had been the intended victim. I did tell her Ebben was behaving like a well-mannered, financially responsible adult who had done his homework. When I was done talking, Beverly Mayer said nothing, but I heard her breathing into the phone.

I said, "Is there anything else you'd like me to look into, Mrs. Mayer?"

Beverly Mayer said, "No, Mr. Shapiro. You've been quite thorough. You have fulfilled your obligations and may return home at your convenience. Please come visit Arthur and me when you do." She hung up.

I walked back toward the other side of the condo and found Ebben and August in the kitchen. August held his iPhone, the screen facing me, *Jameson White* at the top of the display. The phone was on speaker and the microphone muted.

August said, "Got a call from Jameson about thirty seconds ago. Sounds like a butt dial. No one answered when I spoke."

I texted Gabriella: *Jameson's phone just butt-dialed us. Location?*

17

Half an hour later Gabriella called and said they'd located Jameson's phone just west of downtown Los Angeles at St. Vincent Medical Center. I phoned the hospital, but they wouldn't tell me whether or not they had a Jameson White registered. I relayed that back to Gabriella and she said she'd get on it.

Before hanging up, I walked back to the ocean view for some privacy. I said, "I don't think I'll make my flight tonight."

She said, "It's Jameson. Of course you won't. I wouldn't either."

"I love you so much."

I could hear her smile when she said, "How much?"

"More than pizza."

"Don't say it if you don't mean it."

"Oh, I mean it. And more than trout fishing. Because you're always in season."

"Stop it or I'll cry."

"More than not doing the dishes."

"You could be the next poet laureate. Find Jameson. And don't dillydally. Our bed misses you."

I drove with August and Ebben took his car. We passed the La Brea Tar Pits and the Line Hotel Jameson and I had checked into the day before. Then Koreatown turned into something poorer and more crowded. Old and run-down shops—most of the signs in Spanish. This, August explained, was a neighborhood of Los Angeles's working poor. The maids and gardeners and street vendors. A woman with four children crossed at the light. The people were tiny. August guessed they were Peruvian.

Each time I entered a new neighborhood in Los Angeles I felt like I'd entered a new city. Beverly Hills was different from Hancock Park which was different from Koreatown which was different from downtown.

We arrived at the hospital a few minutes after Ebben and divided forces. August and Ebben went to the emergency room. I went to hospital admissions and approached a man who sat on a stool behind a window of bulletproof glass. He was thin, and bespectacled in oversized wire-rim rectangles. He sat straight-backed and had an *I am the gatekeeper* sort of way about him. These attitudes aren't hard to overcome at hotels and health clubs and maître d' stands, but hospital workers see it all— it's tough to bullshit a hospital worker. It's better to let them throw their weight around to get their authority fix, let them get a full head of steam, then use their own momentum against them.

I said, "Excuse me, sir. A friend of mine is missing, and I'm wondering if he's been admitted to the hospital."

He lifted his chin, pulled back his shoulders, and spoke into a microphone. "Are you related to the man?" His voice came out tinny and small from a speaker in the glass.

"No. He and I are visiting from Minnesota." Let him know I'm in unfamiliar territory. Give him an extra boost of authority. "I'm worried about him hurting himself, and last I knew, he was in this part of town."

"I'm sorry, but I can't give out patient information to non-family members."

"I'm really worried about him. I'm not asking about his medical condition. I just want to know if he's here."

"Sir, HIPAA precludes me from sharing that information. Since he's missing, I suggest you go to the police."

"I understand." Acknowledge his authority. "Thank you. That's good advice." Ingratiate, ingratiate, ingratiate. "Where is the nearest police station?"

"It's on Sixth Street between Alvarado and Lucas."

"Is that walking distance?" I am helpless without him. Give him all the power.

"Yes, but I'd Lyft if I were you. It's not the best neighborhood."

I nodded, let my face fall and my shoulders droop. "Thanks. I've been up all night looking for him, so maybe I'll just rest here a bit before I head over." I was at his mercy like a young child to a parent. "And where's the chapel? I need to find a little strength before I go to the police."

I had respected his authority and shown gratitude for whatever mercy he bestowed upon me. And, by asking the location of the chapel, equated his power with the Almighty's. At least in his mind. He didn't have to fight the fight with me. The thin man with the rectangle wire-rims let his guard down.

His posture eased. His eyes smiled. He was vulnerable. "The chapel is just past the gift shop on the right."

"Thank you. You've been very helpful." He smiled a self-satisfied smile. I said, "Jameson White. Six foot seven. African American. Big Afro and beard."

The man behind the glass dropped his eyes, and I knew. He had seen Jameson. Los Angeles is a far more diverse city than Minneapolis, but there are only so many six-foot-seven black men with big Afros and beards. Most authoritative people crumble when they're on the other side of it. That's the card I played.

I said, "The FBI called in the last hour asking if Jameson White had been admitted to St. Vincent. You told them no." He said nothing. "You lied to a federal law enforcement agency."

"I did not. No one by that name has been admitted to this hospital."

"But he's here."

"I don't know that."

"A man fitting his description is here. You told federal officials he isn't."

"They didn't give me a description." I pulled out my phone. He said, "What are you doing?"

"Calling my colleagues at the FBI to tell them what you did."

"No." He took a deep breath. "Wait. Just wait." He picked up the phone then muted his microphone. I couldn't hear what he said behind the bulletproof glass. He hung up the phone and turned on the microphone. "Please have a seat. Someone will be right with you."

I took a seat and texted August and Ebben. If the man behind the glass had crossed me and called security, I'd need August and Ebben to threaten to call the FBI. But after waiting five minutes, I guessed the man hadn't called security. Even the worst rent-a-cops would have tossed me out within five minutes. I stopped worrying about what would happen to me and started worrying about Jameson. How did hospital admissions know of him if they hadn't admitted him? Had Jameson walked into the hospital, or had he been carried in? They don't admit dead people to hospitals.

I felt sick. Whatever happened to Jameson happened on my watch. I invited him to Los Angeles. I encouraged him to play bodyguard for Ebben. I let him out of my sight.

"Did you find him?" The voice belonged to August. But I didn't look at him.

My eyes were locked on a doctor walking toward me. A woman wearing a white coat, a stethoscope draped behind her neck. Chinese descent. Long hair pulled back and bunned behind her head. She had fierce cheekbones and an unreadable expression. My mouth felt like a sandlot. I could feel my heart beating.

The doctor said, "Are you the gentleman inquiring about Mr. White?" She spoke with a soft Chinese accent, as if it had faded to almost nothing.

Ebben and August stepped closer, standing on either side of me. Ebben put a hand on my shoulder and squeezed it.

I said, "Yes."

"I'm Dr. Li. Would you please come with me?"

18

Dr. Li had a matter-of-factness about her I found disconcerting. I wanted to flat-out ask about Jameson, but sensed she'd say nothing so I stood and dropped my hands at my sides like a child about to receive his punishment.

She said, "This way." She walked and I followed. Ebben and August started behind me, but Dr. Li stopped and turned toward them. "I'm sorry. Just this gentleman, please. You can wait here." August and Ebben sat.

Dr. Li led me past the admissions desk where wire-rims avoided eye contact, down the corridor, and into an elevator. My throat was tight and my palms sweaty. I shivered but my face felt flush. Dr. Li said nothing. The elevator opened on the third floor, and I followed her past a nursing station and several hospital rooms and into a small waiting area. She sat and indicated for me to do the same.

I sat.

She said, "Your name, please."

I swallowed. "Nils Shapiro."

"May I please see some identification?"

I dug my wallet out of my jeans and showed Dr. Li my driver's license. She looked at it too long, as if she was trying to memorize my address, then handed it back to me. She stared at me hard. "Jameson is in my office."

"Is he—"

"Okay? No. But he's safe."

"Why did you leave him? What if—"

"I've known Jameson over twenty years. He won't run off."

Jameson had never mentioned Dr. Li, but Jameson had never mentioned anyone. Most of what I knew I'd learned from August in the last twenty-four hours. I said, "You might know Jameson for twenty years, but if you haven't known him in the last year, then you don't know him at all."

"We've been in touch. The school shooting was all over the news. I had read the kids were brought to Jameson's hospital, so I reached out to him. We've talked almost every day since."

"Really? He never told me about you."

"Jameson is a very private person. I know him well."

"Maybe you used to. You haven't seen him hopeless. Day after day. Month after month. The old Jameson is gone."

"I don't believe that is true. He is in there. He just needs time."

"Time with you?"

"Yes."

"There are a lot of people in Minnesota who love that man. How do you even know him?"

"I don't need to prove myself to you. Or anyone else from Minnesota. Jameson values my friendship. That's why he's come to me."

Dr. Li was fast becoming my least favorite doctor. I didn't know if she and Jameson had a romantic relationship and I didn't want to know. He was about two feet taller and two hundred pounds heavier than her. Yet she acted like she was in charge of him. And in charge of me, for that matter.

I said, "Did you know Jameson was visiting Los Angeles?"

"I did not. I was making my rounds when he texted that he was in the lobby. And that it was the anniversary of the shooting. He didn't want to be alone."

"He wasn't alone. I didn't leave him alone. He was working with me. Engaged in something. He was doing better. Then he just disappeared. You're telling me you didn't call him? Entice him away somehow?"

Dr. Li let my self-pity hang in the air. When it dissipated she said, "I'm going to take him to my house in an hour. He's never met my son. We are both looking forward to that." I must have made a face of some sort. Dr. Li said, "Jameson was afraid you'd pressure him to go back to you. We were discussing it when admissions called me to say someone was looking for a person who fit Jameson's description. He doesn't know you're here."

"I'd like to see him."

"I don't know if that's a good idea."

"Not your call, Doctor. You're holding him without having admitted him to the hospital."

"No. He is here on his own accord."

"That's not the story I'm going to tell. Now let me see him so I can decide for myself if he's okay. You say no, and I'll have LAPD and the FBI here in minutes. You think health insurance red tape is a pain in the ass, wait until you deal with law enforcement." My threat was complete bullshit, but Dr. Li didn't know that.

She stared at me, sighed, and said, "You may see him. For five minutes. No more."

Dr. Li led me to a closed door. She paused then opened it. Jameson White sat at her desk. He'd disassembled a model of a baby in a uterus and was having a hell of a time getting it back together. I followed Dr. Li into her office. Jameson looked up and said, "I had a feeling you'd find me. Just didn't think you'd start looking so fast. It's like I owe you money or something, which I do not."

I said, "You could have told us where you were going."

"I would have if I'd known where I was going. Just needed a little space." Jameson returned to assembling the baby in the uterus. "And I ended up here."

I said, "You knew where you were going. And I know why you really came to Los Angeles. I don't blame you. Nothing better than an old friend." Jameson finished reassembling the model and looked up at me. I said, "I got to go back to Minnesota. You coming with me?"

Jameson shook his head. "I want to stay here for a while."

"How long is a while?"

He shrugged.

"All right. Well, your ticket is fully changeable. I'll text you the confirmation number and you can come home whenever you want."

Jameson didn't say a word. He looked at me with eyes of gratitude and sadness, as if his friendships with Dr. Li and me were
mutually exclusive. I'd helped him through the last year, but now
it felt like he was leaving me for her. I walked over and offered
my hand. He took it. I said, "So this is where you want to be
right now?"

He hesitated then nodded.

"Well, then this is where you should be." He said nothing. I
thought he might cry. "Take your time. Do what you got to do."

He forced a smile. "Appreciate it."

Jameson White dug into a pocket, pulled out his house keys,
and handed them to me. "Here's my condo keys. Take in my
mail once in a while?"

"How long are you staying in L.A.?"

"I don't know. I really don't."

I took the keys. "Should I let you know if you get any coupons
for the big and tall man shop?"

Jameson forced a sad smile. "Yeah. Thanks, man. I'll keep the
rental car a day or two then return it, if that's okay."

"Sure, buddy." I gave him a hug, turned away, and wondered
when I'd see my friend again. I threw one last look at Dr. Li then
left the room.

19

August, Ebben, and I walked to the parking ramp. August tried to recall Dr. Li from his days at UCLA, but came up with nothing.

Four o'clock and Ebben and I inched through traffic in the rental Land Rover. The setting sun gilded the hills and buildings of Los Angeles. I'd not seen sunlight so soft and golden—its warmth morphed the city into a place more kind and forgiving. Palm trees shot up like too tall telephone poles topped with bad haircuts. Buildings shined bright on one side and hid in shadow on the adjacent side, as if a grade-school art student had painted them. Ebben didn't mention the change in light. He was used to it. But you notice things when you first see a place, whether they're ugly or beautiful. Signage and clean cars and stucco-sided mini-malls and the battle between green and concrete.

I conference-called Gabriella and Ellegaard and filled them in on the short-term future of Jameson and that I'd never make it to LAX in time for the six-something flight so I'd catch the red-eye back to Minnesota.

We returned to Ebben's. Bunion Brit waited for us in the living room. She wore black jeans and a vintage P.F. Flyer on her good foot and a T-shirt that said, *If you're not having fun you're not doing it right.* Her mouth had shrunk to a dash, and her eyebrows V'd like those of a child not getting her way. Apparently, she wasn't doing it right. She said, "That freak beat him up."

I said, "Which freak beat who up?"

"The Russian guy with the eye patch knocked on Thom's door and punched Thom in the face. He's a mess. There's blood all over his front step. It soaked into the concrete. It's fucking impossible to clean up."

Ebben said, "Is Thom okay?"

"I think so. He's upstairs resting. I cleaned him up and bought a few bags of instant cold packs. I'm making him move in here with us. And I'm not going anywhere without this." She reached to the floor and removed a black canister from her purse, taller and thinner than a soda can but not by much.

I said, "Pepper spray?"

"Bear spray. I can blast the fucker from thirty feet away. They make you buy it when you hike in Yellowstone. Didn't run into any grizzlies and I wasn't sure what to do with it, but now I'm glad I have it."

My instinct was to dissuade Brit from carrying bear spray. I guessed it was illegal to use on people, but it wasn't a half bad idea. If it's designed to stop a bear it would probably stop a person. And if it's designed to not kill a bear, it probably wouldn't kill a person.

Ebben said, "Did you take Thom to the hospital?"

"I wanted to but thought they might have to report it to the police, and I know you don't want the police involved in anything having to do with the production." She removed a pill bottle from her purse, opened it, and threw one in her mouth. "Ativan. Anyone want one?"

We didn't. Her mouth grew back to its normal size and her eyebrows lifted like a drawbridge. "Oh! Guess what?! My fucking Twitter is blowing up over Ava St. Clair. I got like three hundred new followers. Plus Sebastiano called and said Disney offered me a rewrite on *Momma Mia! The Lost Verse*. I don't even have to go in and pitch a take. Straight offer. Hey, where's Jameson? We need him with us at all times."

I said, "Jameson is no longer with us," and headed up the stairs as Ebben clarified what I'd meant. I found Thom Burke in the bedroom Brit had slept in last night, laid out on the bed like a hospital patient, his back propped against the headboard with a few pillows, his right eye swollen shut, the lid purple and shiny. Both lips puffed, and cotton protruded from each nostril. A pair of butterfly bandages over a cut on his right cheek. A bottle of Perrier on the nightstand, a bendy straw sticking out of it. Bendy straws are a favorite of the infirm. A spent cold pack rested next to the Perrier. Bottles of herbal and homeopathic remedies on the other nightstand. I walked toward the bed, and he opened his good eye.

I said, "That cut on your cheek might leave a scar if you don't get a few stitches."

A crooked smile formed on the non-swollen portions of his lips. "I'll take a scar. I could use more of a tough-guy reputation in this town."

"Really? The sweaters tied over the shoulder aren't earning it for you?"

He winced. Maybe from my joke. Maybe from pain.

"Tell me what happened."

He sighed, reached over to the nightstand, grabbed his Perrier, and took a hit from the bendy straw. "I'm in my house. Doorbell rings. I open it and the guy with the eye patch is standing there. I ask if I can help him. He punches me right in the mouth. I said, 'What the fuck was that for?' Then he punched me right here." Thom pointed to his cheek. "He told me to drop Kate Lennon from our movie or else. I wasn't thinking too clearly at that point so I said, 'Or else what?' Then he socks me in the eye and says or else my other eye's getting it. And my ribs. And my kidneys. And my throat. Then he turned around and walked to the street, got in his SUV, and drove away."

"What did the SUV look like?"

"Gray. Boxy. I think it was a Mercedes."

"What hand did he hit you with?"

"What?"

"Did he hit you with his left hand or right hand?"

Thom thought for a second. "His left hand."

"Does your head hurt?"

"He hit me in the face three times. Yes, my head hurts. Nils, there's nothing we can do about this."

That was a weird thing to say. I wasn't suggesting we do something about it. I just asked if his face hurt. Maybe he wasn't thinking clearly. That can happen after you take a few to the noggin. I bent down and removed a flashlight that was plugged into an outlet. Every room in the house had one. They'd go on if the power failed. Earthquake preparedness, Ebben had told me. I said, "I'm going to check you for a concussion. Don't close your eye." I shined the light into Thom's good eye. The pupil shrunk to a pinhole. The old dude could take a punch.

"You're going to live. If you want to keep it that way, call the police. Press charges. The man who hit you is named Vasily Zaytzev. I have his address."

Thom shook his swollen head. "Can't do it. We'd have to disclose a police report to the insurance company. They might pull out of the movie. That would be a disaster."

"I had lunch with Sebastiano. He said there's no such thing as a disaster in show business. Worse thing that happens is a project gets pulled and it happens all the time. Isn't your life more valuable than a movie? Isn't Ebben's life? And Brit's?"

Thom responded by taking another sip from his bendy straw.

I went back downstairs to find Debra, the manager, her pretty face furious behind pink octagonal glasses, her dangly earrings swinging back and forth. She tried to melt me with her laser-beam eyes and said, "This bullshit has got to stop."

I said, "Then please stop it."

"I would like a minute of your time."

"You want to drive me to the airport? You can have more than a minute."

"The airport and back is three hours. I don't have three hours. Call an Uber. Can we step out back?"

I used a loud exhale to think about that, then looked at Brit, who'd resumed her role as the petulant child. I said, "Did Thom tell you about his run-in with Vasily or did you see it?"

Brit pulled her knees into her chest like a Christmas ornament elf. "I was in Thom's kitchen when the doorbell rang. I heard Vasily yelling. By the time I got out there, he'd already hit Thom twice. I saw Vasily hit Thom one more time and I saw the blood on the front step. Thom's not making it up, if that's what you're implying."

"Which hand did Vasily use to hit Thom?"

"What?"

"Did he punch with his left hand or right hand?"

Brit's eyes looked up into her head then said, "Left. Why?"

20

I followed Debra out to the backyard. The air had cooled and smelled of jasmine. The sky glowed, reflecting city light back to all who sent it. Debra turned on a heat lamp. Its internal flame burned blue and hissed, and we sat on patio furniture that looked like big loaves of shredded wheat. A square of strung lights burned yellow over the patio, making everything look candlelit.

Debra said, "So you're leaving."

"Yes."

She looked dubious. "Why did you come out here?"

"Ebben's grandparents asked me to check in on him. They're old and weren't up for the trip."

"They asked a private investigator to check in on their grandson?"

"Yes. Today's private investigator is about more than damsels in distress and telephoto lenses."

She flashed me a courtesy smile then took it back. Debra said, "I'd like Ebben to drive you to the airport."

"I'd like that, too. But apparently, getting a ride to the airport in Los Angeles is harder than getting a ride to the moon."

"I'm going to insist he drive you. And during that drive, I'd like you to convince him to drop *For the People*." A helicopter circled overhead, sweeping its spotlight through the air. "We have to take these threats seriously. Making a movie is not worth jeopardizing anyone's safety."

The helicopter stopped and hovered and fixed its spotlight on whatever or whomever it had found, which seemed to be a couple blocks away. I said, "I agree. But what makes you think Ebben will listen to me?"

"You're from Minnesota. He trusts you. You have nothing vested in the movie, so he knows you have no ulterior motive."

"Do you?"

Debra looked to the side, her dangly earrings swung back and forth like fishing lures. She swung her head back toward me. "Of course I don't have an ulterior motive. Don't be insolent. I lose money if this movie doesn't get made. Not only in fees but in the hundreds of hours I've spent helping to put it together. Movies don't just happen. This isn't fucking *Entourage*. The Creative Collective's first film has to be a commercial *and* critical success. It has to make money to attract more investors. It has to be critically acclaimed to attract the best talent. There are no guarantees. In fact, this business fails most of the time. Drive by a multiplex and look at the titles. Ninety percent of those movies will be shit. But we have to at least try to make something good by eliminating all potential stumbling blocks, and a Russian thug committing battery against one of our producers while making verbal threats against the film is one big-ass stumbling block."

"Then why don't you call the police? They'll either stop Vasily or, according to all of you, force the insurance company to cancel the film's policy."

Debra said, "I can't call the police. My name would be on the report. My reputation would be shot, and I'd never work in this town again. I'd be wearing a blue vest at Walmart."

"I find that hard to believe. All the misbehaving that goes on in this business and they'd bounce you out for filing a police report?"

"Talent can misbehave because they're considered a limited resource. Writers, actors, directors, DPs, some on the business side who've built first-place networks and money-printing companies. But most of us work our asses off to make our monthly nut. We're inside the circle, sure, but if we step out or, worse, get pushed out, it's almost impossible to get back in."

"Sounds like a friendly business."

"It's a cruel business. Fucking horrible to almost everyone in it. It's sexist, racist, ageist. Do you know how hard it is for me to be a woman of a certain size? For every size twenty-two like me there are a hundred size twos and another hundred size zeros. Lane Bryant sends me a dozen cupcakes on my birthday. But I get the small chopped salad at La Scala hold the fucking dressing and everyone looks at me with expressions like, *How dare you eat?*

"Do you know what everyone says to me? *You have such a pretty face.* But what they're really saying is it's not my face's fault. It's mine. My lack of self-control. My laziness because they think

I don't exercise. My freezer full of Ben & Jerry's which, by the way, does not exist."

Debra dug a pack of cigarettes from her purse, stuck one in her mouth, and lit it with a gold Zippo. She sucked the tip orange, held the smoke a few seconds, exhaled it skyward, and said, "You think I wear these earrings because I think they're beautiful? No. I wear dangly shiny pendulums so that's what people focus on. Not my waistline or lack thereof. It's not run-of-the-mill fat shaming. Not in Hollywood. It's an image-based business. Success is perception. Thin is power. Rich is power. Sex is power. Fat is weak. Fat is dumb. Fat is incompetent. I have to fucking bleed just to exist in this business. And one fuckup can mean death."

Sounded a little over-the-top, but people under stress with no vision for a way out can get a little crazy. I said, "If this business is so horrible, then why are you in it? There must be something good about it."

Another inhale. She ashed on the patio. Another exhale. "It's what I know. It's what I'm good at. It's what the world talks about. Once in a while, it's incredibly rewarding. Your name gets on the screen, people you haven't seen since third grade tweet you congratulations. Everyone back home follows your career. It's a fucking ego boost and, honestly, anything else would bore me to death." Debra smiled for the first time since I'd met her, and her suit of armor fell off. "I speak at events for young actors. Acting classes and cold-reading classes, showcases, things like that. Couple times a year, I let a desperate young actor pick me up. I take him home. Not that I'm horny or lonely or have any interest in seeing the guy again. But you know why I do it?"

I said, "I can think of a lot of reasons why you'd do it."

"Well, you probably can't think of my reason. I do it so rumors spread. I do it for the affectation. Ironically, even my weight is an affectation. You need something to make you stand out in this town. I'm five feet eleven. I weigh 220 pounds. I wear shiny earrings. I pick up young men. I make an impression. The men don't really want to fuck me but they tell their friends they did because they think having done so ups their chances in this business. Then I get all sorts of attention, which I don't even want. But they remember me. They all remember me. That's why I'm successful."

"I thought you bled to survive in this business."

"I do. I'm just saying you need more than that. You need to have your thing that makes you stick out. I've found it and I'm not going to lose it when a Russian thug kills someone to stop our movie. It'll come out that we all knew about the threats then our careers are over. That's why you're going to convince Ebben to drop the Kate Lennon film."

The helicopter hovered straight overhead, its spotlight shining east if I had my bearings straight. I said, "You sure are spouting a lot of information. Sounds to me like a sales job, and I hate sales jobs."

"Of course it's a sales job. I want you to convince Ebben—"

"Yeah, yeah. I know. But I bet you're more interested in playing the long game. And your long game is to either prevent The Creative Collective from taking off so you can produce Ebben's movies or to step in and run the operation if it succeeds. That would also make you a producer. You've made it clear that standing out from the crowd is what it's all about, and you can't stand out from the crowd on just commissions. You have to produce. That's what I've learned in the thirty goddamn hours I've been in this town. And FYI, you got competition when it comes to running The Creative Collective. Sebastiano's gunning for the job, too."

Debra smirked. "Sebastiano. He's out of the business."

"Really? I had lunch in his office today. Had a couple of assistants sitting out front. Another one waiting on him. Seemed like he was in the business to me."

"I hear otherwise."

I stood. "Well, I'll ask if Ebben will drive me to the airport. For what it's worth, if you didn't live in this town, if you lived in Minneapolis or Boston or Chicago or Atlanta or Denver or anywhere else in the world, most men would love a date with you. A real date."

She stared at me and said nothing. I took a couple steps toward the house then stopped, turned around, and said, "By the way, when I was outside Sebastiano's office today, one of his assistants used her phone to photograph her computer screen. Do you know what that's about?"

Debra's front teeth sucked in her lower lip. She shut her eyes and let out a long "Fffffuck." She looked at me and said, "Fuck, fuck, fuck!"

21

Ebben did not want me to leave. He offered me my daily rate just to stay and do nothing. I politely declined and suggested he hire a bodyguard. He said he'd think about it and agreed to drive me to LAX. Said he wouldn't mind a chat on the way there and he could catch up on Marc Maron's podcast on the drive back home.

Eight o'clock P.M. and rush hour was still strong, clogging the city to a standstill. We were backed up behind a long line of red taillights running straight and long up a hill into nothing. The mini-malls and their signs pushed hard toward the street. Sidewalks served as boundaries between building and roadway but that seemed to be their only purpose. No one walked on them. A few people clumped up at bus stops. Human beings close off when using public transportation. But the Los Angeles bus riders appeared to have vacated their bodies. Their spirits would float along and rejoin their hosts when they got off the bus.

Despite the miles of mini-malls and endless signage and flood of light in pinks and blues and yellows and reds, despite the cars and helicopters and pedestrian-free streets, as if the city was run and occupied by only machines, Los Angeles felt like the Wild West. Ugly and brutal and exciting and beautiful and rife with opportunity. Abject poverty juxtaposed with in-your-face money. Beggars and Bentleys. A cardboard sign: *pregnant and homeless* held below a billboard: *Emirates Airlines First Class Suites.* Show up with nothing and this town will give you a chance to have everything. The rules were different here or maybe there were no rules. The Wild West.

I called The Line Hotel and checked out, then we drove in silence for fifteen minutes, covering a mile at most, then Ebben said out of the blue, "I'll double your daily rate if you stay."

"Stay and do what?"

"This. Hang with me. Live at the house. Maybe carry a gun in case Vasily shows up."

"I understand why you want a bodyguard, but I'm far from that. I'm sure if you call Sebastiano, he'll have one at the house within the hour. Seems like a guy who knows how to get things done."

"Triple your rate?"

"Tempting, but I want to get back to my fiancée."

"Yeah . . ." said Ebben. His voice shook soft and weak.

I felt like the biggest asshole on the planet telling a guy who had just lost his fiancée that I had one to get home to. Everything the guy was looking forward to washed away, and I'd just thrown the dirty water right back in his face. "I'm sorry. That was a terrible thing to say."

"I know you didn't mean it like that."

I was eager to change the subject. "Just before we left, Debra pressured me to pressure you into dropping the *For the People*."

"I'm not dropping the movie. I'm not telling Kate Lennon and Ava St. Clair thanks for taking a chance on me but I've changed my mind. I'm trying to attract talent, not scare it away."

"I get it."

"Why would she even suggest that? It makes me question why I hired her."

"She's taking Vasily's threats seriously. She doesn't want anyone else to get hurt. At least that's what she's saying. My gut is her motivation is more complicated than that."

"I'll talk to her tomorrow. This is such a weird business. The crap you go through to make a movie. Even when you're funding it yourself. It's like a house of cards. One wrong move and the whole thing falls down."

Ebben's phone rang. He took the call on speaker. The screen on the dash said it was from ACI.

A woman's voice said, "I have Jay Rosenstein calling for Ebben Mayer."

"This is Ebben."

"Jay will be with you in a moment. Hold, please."

Ebben said, "I wonder what this is about."

"Who's Jay Rosenstein?"

"The head of ACI. Founded the agency when he was twenty-eight."

"Oh, I think I saw a thing on him on *60 Minutes*. Left Ukraine when he was a kid."

"That's him. Moved here with nothing. Went to Santa Monica Community College. Talked himself into a mailroom job at CAA and—"

"Ebben Mayer! It's been too long. How are you?" Jay Rosenstein had a good phone voice. Bright and light and young. He spoke fast yet somehow sounded like he meant what he said.

"I'm well, Jay. How are you?"

"Fantastic! Just great. Hey, I was looking over our roster of extraordinarily talented clients and when I saw your name I thought we have got to get Ebben Mayer in our big conference room for a general. I need all of my top agents to meet you and hear your thoughts then go back to their client lists and see how they can help you get to where you want to go."

"Great," said Ebben. "Anytime."

"How about tomorrow? Ten A.M. My department heads are buzzing about it. Could not be more excited."

"I'll see you at ten."

"Fantastic! And hey, so sorry about your loss. I stopped by the celebration the other night. You were surrounded by Juliana's family—didn't want to interrupt. You spoke beautifully. Just wanted to let you know I'm thinking of you."

"Thanks, Jay."

"And we'll see you in the morning. Can't wait. Have a great night!"

The phone call ended. Ebben said, "That was weird."

"Not business as usual?"

"I've never met the man."

"He certainly sounds exuberant."

"I wonder why Sebastiano didn't call about the meeting."

The traffic at LAX was worse than the traffic getting there. It took twenty minutes to crawl from Terminal 1 to Terminal 5 in a horseshoe of red taillights. When we arrived, Ebben shook my hand and said, "I'll be back in Minny next month for my grandfather's birthday. Dinner?"

"Absolutely."

"And bring Gabriella. I'd love to meet her."

We said a few more pleasantries, I grabbed my bag out of the back seat and headed into the terminal.

I'd come to Los Angeles to learn whether or not Ebben Mayer was investing in show business. By that measure, I'd done my job. But by any other measure, I'd failed. I suspected someone had murdered Juliana Marquez—but I had no idea who. I also didn't know if that person would try to kill Ebben. And I'd come to Los Angeles with Jameson White. I was going home without him. Leaving him in the care of a tiny doctor with a big attitude.

I knew I wasn't the only person who could help Jameson, although I'll admit I wanted to be the only person. I had a lot of acquaintances but only a few friends. One friend was my business partner. One friend was my fiancée. The other was Jameson White. At first he healed my body, then my heart and mind. He was the rare friend who could call me on my bullshit and make me laugh while he was doing it. I did not want to lose him but maybe I'd have to. Maybe Dr. Li was the only person who could help Jameson, and Jameson's well-being was the only condition on which I'd let him go.

I was headed back to Minnesota in January. Ice and snow and sunsets at 4:30 P.M. People who don't live in Minnesota think we're crazy for enduring winter. They don't understand we get acclimated one day at a time, going from hot and humid August to tolerable September to perfect October to chilly November to the beautiful first snowfalls of December. January and February can be hell but we've waded in—it's not nearly as bad as if we'd jumped straight from summer into the deep freeze. And yet, that's what I was going to do when I got off the plane. I started to understand why everyone else thought we were insane.

The red-eye from Los Angeles to Minneapolis was short in duration and short on sleep. Just under three hours. I walked into the condo before seven. Gabriella had just returned from her run, sweat frozen on her hat and balaclava. I crawled into bed, and she stepped into the shower. Fifteen minutes later, we made love. She left for work. I woke at 10:30, made myself pretty, then fired up my Volvo and headed east to visit Beverly and Arthur Mayer.

22

Beverly and Arthur Mayer sat on the same couch in the same spots. Beverly wore a wool suit, sage green and festooned with a brooch that looked like a twisted mess of gold and silver left over after a jeweler had crafted something recognizable. Arthur wore the same herringbone suit. It was probably his smallest so it fit his shrunken body the best.

"I want you to tell me everything," said Beverly, straight-backed and smiling, more at ease and cheerful than at our first meeting two days ago.

I wasn't going to tell her everything. But I'd tell her everything she hired me to find out. Most of that I'd already told her on the phone, but she took great delight in hearing it again.

"Did you hear that, Arthur?"

Arthur said, "Huh?"

"Ebben raised a $100 million fund and has only invested $1 million himself!" she said, repeating what I'd just told her. "And he's making art. Not all that nonsense with monsters and explosions. We can hold our heads high when the Mayer name is on the screen. Oh, that's a relief."

Arthur Mayer, his chin pressed against his chest, swung his eyes toward his wife. He would never hold his head high again. His neck was too bent. But he grunted a nod, the top of his head still thick with perfect hair. It hadn't receded in front—it hadn't thinned on top. The man was a genetic marvel. Beverly Mayer reached over and took her husband's frail hand. Maybe that was all my errand to the West Coast had been about, to learn whether or not Ebben Mayer would shame the family out there in Hollyweird. Now that the Mayers knew he wouldn't, they seemed more relaxed, more upbeat. At least Beverly did.

"Now," said Beverly, "what I haven't heard much about is that memorial service or celebration or whatever cockamamie thing Ebben called it. I want to know every last detail."

I told her about the house in Hancock Park and the people in attendance, including Ebben's business associates and Juliana's large family. I did not mention Vasily. I told her about the catering and Ebben's speech, saying he had planned to bring Juliana back to Minnesota in the spring to canoe the Boundary Waters and to meet his family. I even relayed a half-honest version of what Ebben had said about Beverly Mayer. What he actually said was she probably wouldn't find anything nice to say about Juliana, but it would be impossible to say something negative.

I altered that into Ebben having said even his tough-as-nails grandmother would have liked Juliana. She seemed pleased with the characterization.

"And what about Ebben's emotional state?" she said. "I've spoken to him, and he seems to be holding up. But how did he seem to you, Nils? I'm concerned." Her smile stayed put. I found it unnerving.

I said, "He loved Juliana. He's hurting. He's keeping himself in motion, taking meetings, having people at the house, but he's hurting."

"Well, that's as it should be. He loved that girl. But you said he's active, continuing his business, having people to the house. That seems like a good sign."

"I think so."

Arthur Mayer grunted a nod.

Beverly Mayer said, "Ebben's coming home next month for Arthur's ninetieth birthday. I'd like to introduce him to one of the governor's staffers, a terribly bright and attractive young woman from Washington, D.C. She moved to Minnesota last year, is single, and hardly knows a soul outside the capital. Do you think Ebben's ready for that?"

It was Beverly Mayer's twinkly smile that undid me. Her oh-so-gracious pushing aside of Juliana's death. Her gentle sweeping aside of Ebben's grief. Clearing the way for *this is what I want. I'm used to getting my way. Do you think everyone else is finished with their obstructive nonsense so I can get what I want?* I said, "Well, he's your grandson. You've known him thirty-five years. Does he usually fall in line when you order him to do so?"

Her twinkly smile vanished. "I beg your pardon?"

"What do you think, Arthur? Is one month of mourning sufficient for Ebben before Beverly shoves her handpicked bride down his throat?"

Beverly Mayer's fingers dug into the soft wool covering her lap. "Mr. Shapiro, there is no need to be rude. I will not tolerate rude."

I stood. "Is that why you sent me to Los Angeles, Mrs. Mayer? You couldn't believe your stroke of luck that Juliana Marquez dropped dead and you wanted to know if Ebben was over her? Hell, if him working in show business would sully the family name, just imagine what Ebben marrying a Mexican would do?"

"That is quite enough, Mr. Shapiro."

"You did your homework on me, Mrs. Mayer, talked to all of your esteemed contacts. The St. Paul chief of police, I'm sure he didn't sugarcoat it. You knew who you were hiring. Hope I lived up to my reputation. I look forward to your Yelp review." Her outrage morphed into confusion. "Don't get up. I can show myself out."

"Wait," said Arthur, his voice small. His eyes lifted toward me and, with effort, his head followed. He had a new Band-Aid on his chin. I don't know if he cut himself shaving or the skin had worn thin in a new spot. "The answer is no."

Beverly said, "What are you talking about, Arthur?"

"Mr. Shapiro asked me if one month is enough time for Ebben to mourn. My answer is no. One month is not enough time." Arthur Mayer turned his head toward his wife. I don't remember if his spine actually creaked or if I just imagined the sound effect because it fit the picture. "What do you think, Beverly?"

"I think it's time for Mr. Shapiro to leave."

I said, "Adios, amigos."

I found my coat, opened the ten-foot-tall mahogany doors, and stepped onto the stone veranda. Minus five degrees and I counted half a dozen pedestrians and a fat-tire cyclist pedaling east on Summit Avenue, his or her face hidden behind ski goggles and a balaclava. Plenty of people born here leave as soon as they're able. They move to Florida or North Carolina, Arizona or California. But most of us stay. Are we crazy? No. Just a little chilly five or six months a year.

23

Stone Arch Investigations is in the Saint Anthony Main Building on a cobblestone street along the Mississippi River. Downtown Minneapolis sits on the other side of the river and, in winter, naked trees offer a clear view of our small but expanding city of tall glass buildings juxtaposed against repurposed grain silos and vintage signs for Gold Medal Flour and Pillsbury.

Our assistant Kenji Thao greeted me with, "Mr. First Class is back to slum it with the rest of us."

"I missed you too much, Kenji. Had to give it up."

"Where's Jameson? I like *that* guy."

"As far as I know, he's still in Los Angeles."

"That's what you say about lost luggage. Not your friend."

I found Anders Ellegaard in his office, working to the whispery exhale of forced-air heat. I never know what he's doing at his desk, but I don't ask because he'd tell me and then he'd get way too excited about accounts receivable or health insurance coverage or his new marketing plan. I'd have to listen because I'd asked, and for that I could never forgive myself.

Ellegaard wore a Brooks Brothers suit, charcoal with a light blue shirt and royal blue tie. Suit-wearing was a habit he couldn't break from his fifteen years as a detective for Edina PD. It was his uniform and, still mourning the loss of his shield, he was reluctant to let it go.

I said, "How was your phone call with Beverly Mayer?"

"Welcome home, Shap."

"How pissed was she?"

"Pretty pissed."

"I was feeling a bit protective of Ebben."

"Ebben's a big boy. He can protect himself." I sat down. Ellegaard looked up. "I hear you did well out there."

"From Mrs. Mayer?"

"Yes. She didn't appreciate your attitude this morning, but said you did an excellent job in Los Angeles."

"Well, I didn't tell her the whole story." Then I told Ellegaard the whole story. About Vasily threatening me and assaulting Thom. About my turkey sandwich with Sebastiano and Debra's freak-out when hearing about Sebastiano's assistant photographing her computer screen. About Ebben refusing to get the police involved and refusing to drop the project. I explained how The Creative Collective worked, how Ebben funded it and hoped to profit from it. And I told him about Jameson leaving me for Dr. Li.

Ellegaard said, "What's Dr. Li's first name?"

"I don't know."

"Seems like an odd detail to overlook for an investigator of your caliber."

"Yeah, well. I may have an emotional block in that area."

"Understandable. You had a busy thirty-six hours, Shap." I must have made a face or something because Ellegaard said, "What?"

"It felt different."

"Different than what?"

"Different than before Gabriella and Evelyn. I've worked cases since those two came into my life. Mostly routine stuff. That insurance fraud case and some background checks and what's-her-face's adultery thing. But Los Angeles was the first murky, dangerous, twisted bundle of lies and liars. Those kinds of cases have always sucked me in. And I've always stayed in regardless of personal safety or just plain common sense."

"That you have."

"And I don't come out until I have answers. But not in Los Angeles. I mean, I think Juliana was murdered. Accidentally, but that's almost worse because Ebben was the intended target, which means he could still be a target. I don't trust his agent. I don't trust his manager. This Vasily character is nuts and may or may not be working for someone else. Maybe even working for one of the people on Ebben's team. All that and I couldn't wait to get home. To sit in that boring condo with Gabriella and Evelyn when she's with us. I used to have nothing to lose. Now I have too much."

Ellegaard shut his laptop. "Sounds like I might be getting the Nils Shapiro I've always dreamed of."

I shrugged. "At your service." He looked down at nothing and shook his head. Now it was my turn to say, "What?"

"It won't work, Shap."

"What won't work?"

"You playing by the rules. Playing it safe."

"It's worked for you."

"Because I'm me. But even with me, it's relative. I didn't choose to be a cop in a sleepy suburb. I sent my résumé all over the state. Edina is the municipality that hired me. Dumb luck. But when I wore the uniform, I still had to deal with potentially dangerous situations. Calls to domestic disputes. And traffic stops. Edina is one of the safer places but you never know who's driving through and who might have a gun in the car. You don't know their state of mind. Every time I pulled someone over I thought of Molly and the girls. Then a couple years into the job—I've never told you this story—Target built its first SuperTarget. I worked the grand opening. Huge event. Press from all over. I got assigned to shadow Target's CEO. He liked me and at the end of the day, asked me to come work security for Target. Not store security. Corporate. First thing that popped into my head was no more traffic stops. No more domestic disputes. Pretty much a nine-to-fiver. Better pay. Better benefits. Better long-term career outlook. I talked to Molly. She said she'd support whatever I wanted to do."

"I'd be trembling with suspense but I know what you did."

"You know what I ultimately did. But first, I called Robert Stanley and asked if I could buy him dinner."

Robert Stanley was one of the Minneapolis cops who trained Ellegaard, Gabriella, and me at the academy. He supplemented our education far beyond the manuals and exercises and operating procedures. To Robert Stanley, the job wasn't just about right versus wrong or good versus bad. The job was about people and their humanity and the importance of not ignoring that humanity even in the most inhumane scenarios. At the most brutal crime scenes committed by the most heinous criminals against the most vulnerable victims. Don't let people's humanity fall through the cracks just because you're chasing a monster.

Robert Stanley was one of the few Minneapolis cops who didn't resent Ellegaard and me for not coming back to Minneapolis PD after we were laid off. We stayed in touch with him, even hired his daughter, Leah, as our receptionist during her gap year before law school. Leah will graduate next year and has threatened to return to Stone Arch as an investigator.

Robert Stanley died in my arms a couple years ago. Ellegaard was there.

Ellegaard said, "I took Robert to Murray's."

"Murray's. Home of the butter knife steak."

Ellegaard smiled. "I told him about the offer I'd received to work corporate security for Target. He asked me a few questions. I answered. Then he asked me why I became a cop. Was it because of the money? Was it because of my personal safety? I said of course not to both. He pointed out that if I sacrificed my principles for my family, I'd resent them. Maybe not right away, but eventually, as impossible as it sounded, I'd hold it against Molly and the girls even though they had nothing to do with it. So better to take a few risks than to resent my family."

The forced-air heat breathed hot and heavy. I said, "So why'd you leave Edina PD for Stone Arch Investigations?"

"I became a cop to pursue justice. And I get more of that working with you than I did for a suburban police department."

"You're welcome."

Ellegaard laughed. "Yeah, well, it certainly wasn't for the money or job security."

Ebben Mayer's name popped up on my cell phone. I answered the call.

He said, "Nils, they can't find him. They can't find him anywhere."

24

Ebben said, "I called Sebastiano last night on the drive home from LAX to tell him about Jay Rosenstein wanting me to meet with all the agents. He didn't answer his cell. I texted. No response. When I woke up this morning, I still hadn't heard from him. That doesn't happen in this town. Agents return calls. At least, they return mine. I called Debra, and she said she'd heard Sebastiano had gone AWOL. No one can find him. I'm at ACI for the big agency meeting right now. I went to Sebastiano's office and his assistants told me they have no idea where he is."

I said, "Do you think now's the time to call the police?"

"I don't know. Maybe. Hey, I got to go into the meeting. I'll call you when I get out."

I hung up and told Ellegaard about Ebben's call. He said

someone should look into whether Sebastiano has a history of taking off without telling anyone—some people do.

I said, "Or Vasily has him. He is going after Ebben and his associates one by one. He ran Ebben off the road. He tailed Brit. He threatened me. He beat up Thom."

"Anything happen to the manager?"

"Debra? Not that I know of. Had a nice chat with her in Ebben's backyard last night. She wants Ebben to pull the project. She didn't mention any direct threats against her."

Ellegaard nodded and thought for a moment and said, "When Ebben calls back after his meeting, ask if he still keeps a residence in Minnesota, and if he does, whether or not he has a Minnesota driver's license."

"You think I should accept his offer if we can rationalize we're licensed to work for a Minnesotan?"

"It's an option, but it's up to you. It's one thing to follow your calling. It's another to work two thousand miles from Gabriella and Evelyn. Ebben can hire someone there. I can get some names if he wants."

I nodded. "Any more business to discuss? Because we're not going to get away with it at dinner."

"I think that's it. Spoon and Stable at seven. And leave your wallet at home. This is our engagement present to you and Gabriella."

"Do we have to write a thank-you note?"

"That would be polite, but you don't have to."

"Check with Molly. Because I won't accept if we have to write a thank-you note. Unless we can write it on the receipt or something at the table. I just don't want to have it weighing on me."

"That's kind of a weird thing to say. Maybe you should talk to

Gabriella. She might like to write thank-you notes. It's possible she even has special stationery with matching envelopes."

"Don't talk that way about the woman I love. She doesn't have those things. You take that back." I stood. "See you at seven. I'm wearing jeans. Don't make me look bad."

I left the office for Linden Hills. Micaela had bought an old firehouse and converted it into an office. She left the pole, but no one used it to get from the second floor to the first except me. She'd turned one of her conference rooms into a nursery where her full-time nanny watched Evelyn while Micaela worked. Micaela took breaks to nurse Evelyn and to stroll her down to Lake Harriet when the weather permitted.

Micaela was out at a meeting when I got there. I told the nanny she could take off for a couple hours. She said Evelyn's cold had grown worse, and that I may have to use the miniature turkey baster to clear her nose. I fed Evelyn lunch. Sweet potatoes and bananas and some other squished mash that contained turkey, spinach, and apple. Micaela insisted Evelyn eat a certain brand of organic free-trade zero-carbon-footprint food. It tasted just like the supermarket stuff. I know. I tried both.

I crawled around on the floor mat with Evelyn, got her to laugh at a few of my best faces, changed her diaper (organic, free-trade food doesn't make that any more pleasant), read a few books to her, and shut the blinds. She lay on my chest as we rocked to *Nirvana Unplugged*. Something about the simple 4/4 rhythm of acoustic rock calmed my baby girl and would hopefully give her excellent taste in music and spare me from ever having to hear Radio Disney. She sang along for bit, saying, "Ba ba ba ba ba ba . . ." until she fell asleep. I didn't feel like transferring her to her crib, so I napped with her. I'd had little sleep in the past forty-eight hours and had breathed six hours of airplane air. The nap did me good.

Twenty minutes later my phone buzzed on the side table. I let the call go to voicemail, transferred Evelyn to her crib, kissed her perfect-smelling head, tiptoed out of the nursery, and found Micaela working at a desk just outside the door.

"Good daddy-daughter time?"

"She asked a lot of questions. We had to have *the talk*."

Micaela's strawberry blond frizz fell just past her shoulders. She wore a white wool jumper thing and black leggings, an outfit a giant toddler might wear. But it suited her. Motherhood suited her. She looked tired and content and peaceful. She said, "I'm glad you got some extra time with her. She kind of likes you."

"Good. I kind of like her."

"I have a week of meetings in London and Paris next month. I'm happy to take Evelyn with me, but if you and Gabriella want, I can leave her with you and not put her through all that travel."

"We'd love to have her." That's how it had gone the last ten months. A casual take it as it comes custody arrangement. Not a lawyer in sight. We chitchatted a bit more, then I hugged the firepole and made my exit.

I got in the Volvo and returned Ebben Mayer's call. He answered on the first ring.

He said, "It's a shit show here, Nils. Sebastiano's disappearance has nothing to do with Vasily. He left to start his own agency. It's a free-for-all for his clients. I just got off the phone with him."

"That's it?"

"What do you mean, 'that's it'? It's a huge deal. Everyone's filing lawsuits. It's all over Deadline. That's what the meeting was about. Jay Rosenstein must have suspected it last night. Half of Sebastiano's clients were there. It looked like the Golden Globes in that room, and they were blowing smoke up everyone's ass."

"I saw Sebastiano's assistants photographing their computer screens. Does that have anything to do with it?"

"Probably. One of the other clients told me Sebastiano can't copy any files that are property of the agency, otherwise he's vulnerable to a huge lawsuit. But if the assistants photograph everything on personal devices, it's hard to prove. Sebastiano's assistants must have been photographing files for weeks. I guess they showed up this morning to make everything look as normal as possible then they just took off during the big meeting. You'd think the United States government was taken over by a coup the way people are reacting around here."

"So all is good?"

"Yeah. Everything's fine."

"Any sign of Vasily?"

"None."

"Okay. Be safe. Let me know if anything feels weird."

"Oh, dude. I'd be calling you every five minutes."

Spoon and Stable is a nationally ranked restaurant by whoever is in charge of ranking things. The place is booked months out, which is why Molly Ellegaard made a reservation months ago after learning of our engagement. It's in an old building on North First Street, just blocks from my former residence in a coat factory. The restaurant had white walls and exposed brick and soft light and was full of the kind of people who make reservations months in advance.

We sat at a table for four in the middle of the dining room. Ellegaard, the son of a bitch, wore a suit. I kept my promise to wear jeans, though I did wear a collared shirt under my sweater and a pair of oxblood wingtips I kept on reserve for special occasions. Gabriella wore her hair down and straight and had wrapped herself in a cashmere thing that looked like a sweater but wasn't. Molly Ellegaard looked lovely in her black dress with long sleeves. She wore her dark hair pulled back, highlighting her heart-shaped face and warm brown eyes.

A waiter brought a bottle of champagne I wasn't aware we'd ordered. Ellegaard said, "Close your mouth, Shap. We're celebrating."

"Now," said Molly, "we want to hear all the details about the wedding."

"Details?" said Gabriella.

"Have you locked the date? Where are you getting married? Who's officiating? How many guests? Have you chosen a cake? Where's the reception? Who's doing the flowers? Will there be live music or a DJ? Where are you registered?" Gabriella and I looked at each other. "It's okay if you don't want to tell us. It's fun to keep it a surprise. It's romantic."

"Uh, no," said Gabriella. "It's not that we're keeping anything a surprise. Our plan is just, well, more simple than most weddings."

"Simple's good."

I said, "Extremely simple."

"Uh oh," said Ellegaard.

Molly caught on. "Oh come on, you two. Don't tell me you're eloping. Or going to the courthouse."

"We were going to elope," said Gabriella, "but we realized our mothers would never forgive us. So . . . You tell them, Nils."

"Our wedding is on the second Sunday in March. That's prime blizzard season so we didn't have to compete with a lot of other weddings."

"Practical," said Ellegaard.

"And the potential for bad weather will discourage out-of-towners we're obligated to invite from coming. We rented out a small restaurant. The guests will be my immediate family, Gabriella's immediate family, and a handful of friends, including the Ellegaards and their daughters."

"Really?" said Molly, disappointment all over her face. "Why do you want to keep it so small?"

I said, "Because we just want to enjoy our wedding with the people we love. We don't need anyone else there."

Molly said, "But more people is more festive. And you'd get more gifts."

"That's another thing," said Gabriella, "no gifts."

"No gifts?!" said Molly. "That's not fair. We want to buy you gifts. To commemorate the best day of your lives."

Gabriella said, "Best day of our lives? Have you been to a wedding before?"

Ellegaard laughed so hard champagne came out his nose, and I fell more deeply in love with Gabriella than I'd thought possible.

I said, "But we're making a kind-of-sort-of exception for the Ellegaard family when it comes to gifts."

Molly said, "Thank God."

"We want Emma and Olivia and Maisy to make our wedding cake."

"Oh, they can't—"

"Yes, they can. Emma loves those baking shows. The girls can make whatever they want, decorate it any way they want. The only requirement is there's enough cake for thirty-five people."

"And Molly," said Gabriella, "we'd like you to pick out the flowers. We'll give you a budget and let you surprise us."

"Okay," said Molly. "At least the flowers will be festive. I can guarantee that. Now, what about invitations?"

I said, "Yeah, we're not doing those. This is your invitation. And Ellie, we'd like you to officiate."

"Me? How do I do that?"

"I've signed you up to be a reverend with the Church of the Latter Day Dude. You got to register with Hennepin County and that's about it."

"Who's going to write the service?"

I said, "I don't know. We'll figure it out."

"So see?" said Gabriella. "The cake, flowers, presiding over the wedding. The Ellegaards have plenty of gifts to give."

Molly deflated and said, "Are you sure you want a tiny, wing-it-by-the-seat-of-your-pants wedding? You might regret it someday."

"We're sure," said Gabriella. "But we appreciate you looking out for us."

Molly emptied her flute of champagne.

Halfway through the meal my phone buzzed. I ignored it, but whoever it was called back. Then called back again. Persistent callers are never calling with good news. I didn't want to ruin a perfect evening, so I excused myself to take the call.

It was Ebben Mayer. Thom Burke was dead.

25

A neighbor found Thom Burke facedown on his driveway in the middle of the afternoon. The neighbor called 911 assuming Thom had had a heart attack or aneurism. The neighbor hadn't noticed the garage door was damaged from impact. Or that Thom's chest had been crushed. An LAPD officer from Robbery-Homicide had called Brit, she being the most frequent contact in Thom's phone, and asked to set up a time to talk with her. Ebben told her she'd have to tell them about Vasily's threats and to let go of *For the People*—the movie was as dead as Thom Burke. Ebben expected the police would want to question him, too. He asked me to come back to Los Angeles and help navigate the fallout of Thom's death. No, not asked—he begged me to come back. I told him I'd call him back in the next few hours.

I had to return to Los Angeles. A client died on my watch last year. It would haunt me forever—I didn't want a repeat.

I returned to the dinner table and Molly trying to convince Gabriella we had to move into a house so Evelyn would have a yard. With a swing set and a sandbox. I jumped into the conversation saying we'd never have a sandbox because every cat within a one-mile radius would make an appearance just to shit in it and kill every songbird that happened to be singing its sweet melody.

Molly said, "Well, what about that?"

"What about what?" said Gabriella.

"Do you want pets?"

"We've talked about getting a dog. We both love dogs."

I said, "I had a big golden retriever when I was a kid. Sheila. Saw her get hit by a car."

Molly said, "Ugh. I'm sorry."

"Yeah. Swore I'd never get another. But I'm ready to give it a shot."

Gabriella said, "We've had such busy, unpredictable schedules as single people but now that we're together we think we can make it work."

Molly said, "Does that mean you're going to give Evelyn a little brother or sister?"

"Molly," said Ellegaard.

"Oh, come on. Nils knows everything about us. He lived with us for six months."

The Ebben Mayer news could wait. The restaurant, the champagne, the four of us together—it was perfect, despite the direction the conversation had turned.

Gabriella said, "That's right. I had forgotten Nils lived in your basement." She looked at me as if she were reevaluating her decision to marry me. Then she broke, a big smile on her beautiful face. She leaned over and kissed me and said, "I'd wish you would've come to me back then. I could have spared you a lot of heartache."

"You didn't have a basement."

My life had fallen apart. No work. No money. I turned to Ellegaard. He and Molly took me in and Ellegaard changed my life when he convinced a friend with the Duluth Police Department to hire me as a consultant. Duluth had suffered a rash of murders. The victims were found out in the open, naked, their bodies spotless as if half their skin had been scrubbed away. Even their fingerprints were gone. The public was scared. The police had no leads. They hired me out of desperation. I threw myself into the case as an escape from myself more than anything. I worked to exhaustion, but solved the case, which is now what people call the Duluth Murders. That case turned my life around.

I had two friends from the police academy. Ellegaard and Gabriella. If I had gone to Gabriella, if she had taken me in instead of the Ellegaards, the last twelve years would have been completely different. Maybe better. Maybe worse. It didn't much matter. The only thing I think about now is I love my life. I love my daughter. I love Gabriella. It doesn't matter how I got here—I'm just grateful I did.

"Have you had enough time with the menus?" said our waiter. He had a booming voice and blond crew cut and a big smile over realigned teeth and used them all to kindly push us along so our table would turn over for the next reservation.

We ordered. Then Gabriella said, "To answer your question, Molly, I've never wanted babies. I love Evelyn in a way I didn't know was possible. But I'm happy it's just the two or three of us depending on the day. Really happy."

I said, "Me, too."

Molly smiled and said, "I'm glad you're happy." She sipped her champagne. "But you could be even happier."

We laughed. We talked. We ate. And, over coffee and dessert, I told them about dead Thom Burke.

26

Ebben Mayer and Bunion Brit waited for me in baggage claim at LAX among the throng of carts and luggage and people of the world. They didn't hide their disappointment when they learned I had brought only a small carry-on and no checked bags. Fifteen minutes later, we exited the parking ramp and started our crawl back to Hancock Park, me riding shotgun and Brit in back. It was 9:30 A.M. and they seemed in no rush—it didn't take long to find out why.

LAPD detectives were scheduled to interview Brit at eleven o'clock and Ebben at noon.

"So like," said Brit, "like what should we say and what should we not say?"

"You should say the truth," I said. "And you should not lie."

"Like the whole truth?" said Brit.

"Yes, the whole truth. What were you thinking of hiding?"

"Well, for one, Vasily's threatening us to drop Kate Lennon. Because as soon as we mention her name, the police will go to talk to Kate Lennon and she'll freak and quit the movie."

"I thought *For the People* was dead."

"Not yet," said Ebben, "but it will be."

"But maybe not if you and me and Sebastiano and Debra agree to never mention the Kate Lennon part. We can just say Vasily threatened us. We can even say he told us to pull the movie. But why bring Kate Lennon into it? Or Ava St. Clair? We need to protect our reputations."

I said, "Have you discussed this with Sebastiano and Debra?"

"Not yet, but—"

"Don't. What you're talking about is conspiracy, and the cops will sniff it out in a minute and then you'll have a lot more to worry about than your reputation with Kate Lennon. Tell the truth. You don't need any advice other than that."

The car got quiet. We passed a couple more mini-malls then Ebben said, "Thank you. That's exactly the kind of thing we need to hear."

"Have you two discussed what you're going to say?"

"A little."

"Undo it. I can't stress that enough. If your interviews sound coordinated, the police will stop focusing on Vasily and start focusing on you."

Brit burst into tears. I glanced at Ebben. He shrugged.

"Hey, Brit. Sorry. Didn't mean to be so harsh. Just trying to get the message across."

She said, "It's not that. I miss Thom. I can't believe he's dead. Dead! Just like Juliana! What is happening? This is insane!"

Brit wailed as if she'd lost a great love, but whenever I'd referred to Thom as her boyfriend, she corrected me. Thom was a guy she was seeing. Wasn't even a guy she was dating. She'd made that clear. She said she missed Thom, but I wondered if what she really missed was her movie script getting produced.

We dropped Brit at the Hollywood police station on Wilcox then drove up to Sunset Boulevard and found a meter. Ebben and I sat in Groundwork Coffee and picked at scones.

I said, "If it was Vasily, why do you think he went after Thom? Why not you or Brit?"

"What do you mean *if* it was Vasily. Who else would have killed Thom?"

"I don't know. I don't know much about Thom. Did he owe anyone money? Did he sleep with anyone's wife? The police will look into all that. But for now, I'm wondering if it was Vasily, why Thom?"

Ebben Mayer shook his head. "I have no idea. Thom was a gun for hire. No disrespect, but he was the least important person on board. He broke down the script."

"What does that mean?"

"Breaking down a script means figuring out how many actors you need. How many locations. How many effects shots. How many days it'll take to shoot. Stuff like that. Then he makes a schedule and budget. Thom's job was largely done."

I said, "Do you think it's possible that if Vasily killed you or Brit or Sebastiano or Debra, it would draw too much attention to the movie?"

"What do you mean?"

"Do you think if Vasily had killed someone with more visibility it could actually ensure the movie would get made because the publicity would help it at the box office?"

Ebben sat back and sipped his coffee and said, "Maybe. I suppose that's possible."

"Ebben, you need to get out of town after you talk to the police. That is, if they're okay with it. Because I can't protect you here."

He nodded. "You're right. It's best if I leave until all this blows over."

Then Ebben filled me in on the adventures of Sebastiano and Debra. Jay Rosenstein and the ACI Agency were caught off guard. Sebastiano had orchestrated his exit perfectly, filling his schedule, smoothing over internal conflicts he'd had with other agents, which implied he wasn't going anywhere, recruiting new agents to ACI, even putting in a request to refurnish his office. He'd built a smoke screen of trust and then blindsided his partners by disappearing. Only his three assistants were in the know—he'd bought their loyalty with promises of quick promotions. Sebastiano had kept his word. He'd promoted all three to agent.

The other mini bombshell of news was that Debra had dissolved her management company to become an agent in Sebastiano's new company. Rumors were flying around town that Debra somehow found out about Sebastiano's intention to leave and blackmailed him into a lucrative job. I did not share with Ebben that it was me who'd inadvertently tipped off Debra.

Bunion Brit texted that she was done. We told her where we were, and she said it was no problem to walk a couple blocks in her boot cast. Fifteen minutes later, she took Ebben's seat, and Ebben walked down to the police station for his interview. Brit got up to order and returned with a latte and a muffin. She pinched off a piece of muffin, looked at it, then set it down on her napkin. I thought she might throw up.

I said, "Tough conversation with the police?"

She shook her head and said, "I'm fine." She changed her mind and ate the piece of muffin. "Do you know if you get murdered, the police can ask a judge for a court order to open your safe-deposit box?"

"I do know that. Did Thom have a safe-deposit box?"

"Oh yeah," she said. "He sure as fuck did."

"Did they tell you what they found?"

Brit nodded then pinched off another piece of muffin and shoved it in her mouth. She took her time chewing, peeled the plastic lid off her latte, blew on the foam, took a sip, and said, "Thom Burke, the guy I was seeing, the guy I was sleeping with, had a safe-deposit box with $15 million in it. A little odd, don't you think, for a guy who was too cheap to valet park?"

27

No one who legitimately acquires $15 million keeps it in a safe-deposit box. The police may or may not have shared that with Brit. I didn't know if they suspected her of being mixed up in however Thom acquired the fifteen million. I didn't know anything. But Brit sure acted as if the money was news to her. She seemed surprised, maybe even in shock.

I said, "Plenty of wealthy people are infamously cheap. Did Thom have money?"

"I don't think so. He bought his house in 2000 for $300,000. That's nothing in Los Angeles. It's worth $1.5 million now. Can you fucking believe that? All that equity and he didn't put a dime into it. The dishwasher broke ten years ago. He did dishes by hand ever since. He drove a 1990-something Nissan until a few weeks ago. He finally got a new car and guess what it was. A Subaru Outback. How utilitarian is that? He hustled for work, going from one freelance project to the next. For fuck's sake, he didn't even belong to a gym. He lived like a pauper."

"Again, that doesn't mean he was without means. What did the police say?"

"They asked if I knew where he might have got that kind of money. I said I had no idea. It makes no sense. None of this makes sense."

I said, "It doesn't make sense right now. But chances are it will. You just didn't know the guy you were seeing as well as you thought you did."

"Well, duh." Brit shut her eyes. I said nothing. She kept her eyes closed and fell asleep, sitting straight up in a hardbacked chair. Her head fell forward. She must have been up all night and have eaten Ativan for breakfast.

No one in the coffee shop seemed to notice. Some looked like professionals treating themselves to a coffee break. Others looked like the intentionally unemployed, pursuing their dreams on laptops and in journals, their noggins sandwiched between headphones. Others looked like full-time personified first amendments. A man with turquoise hair, Day-Glo orange beard, and yellow tights under a leather red kilt read *Joan Collins—Passion for Life*. Sort of. The book was upside down. A woman wearing a heavy and soiled full-length wool coat, her head wrapped in a throw, spoke to the ceiling. A person of no distinct gender sat staring at nothing, a dirty paper coffee cup on the table before them, most likely lifted from the garbage can outside as if it were a discarded ticket to the theater.

This town was world famous for its creative output. It attracted talented people from all over the world. They and those who came before them appeared to have built a sandbox where play isn't governed by rules. It's play, which creates more play, which pushes away boundaries. And that has to attract those who feel constrained elsewhere.

I understand this from what's true in my work. I'm a better investigator outside the rules and operating procedures of a police department. Not because the rules are bad or wrong, but because of who I am. The rules are not one-size-fits-all. They fit Ellegaard. They don't fit me. Los Angeles seemed to be a town that not only tolerates outliers but celebrates them.

Brit jerked herself awake and said, "Holy fuck. Did I fall asleep?"

"Just for a little bit."

"How long is a little bit?"

"Fifty-five minutes."

She felt her coffee cup, which was no doubt cold. "Dammit. Why didn't you wake me up?"

"You seemed to need the rest."

"I'm so fucking embarrassed."

"In this town? Is embarrassment even a thing?"

Ebben Mayer returned. On the drive back to Hancock Park, he told us about his interview with police which seemed less friendly than Brit's. They kept asking Ebben where he thought the money in Thom's safe-deposit box could have come from. They knew Ebben had millions. To the police, Thom and Ebben's business relationship might explain how Thom ended up with a safe-deposit box filled with $15 million.

We pulled into Ebben's driveway and Brit said, "Where is it?"

Ebben said, "Where is what?"

"My car. My brand-new Audi."

"Was it on the street?"

"No! I parked it in the driveway. It was there when we left to pick up Nils at the airport. Dammit!"

I said, "Were you behind on payments?"

"No!" said Brit. "Of course I wasn't behind on my payments!"

"All right. You don't have to scream. It was just a question."

We got out of Ebben's rental and walked up the driveway. It was the kind of driveway you don't see in Minnesota. Two parallel concrete strips ran from the street to the garage with a strip of green grass between them. Not a snowplow-friendly driveway.

"What is that?" said Ebben, pointing toward the grass between the concrete strips.

"Oh my God," said Bunion Brit. "Oh my fucking God."

For a second I thought it was a pair of thong underwear. But then I realized the black piece of fabric was meant to cover something else—a socket where an eye used to be.

"Vasily," said Ebben. "Why would he leave his eye patch?"

"Gross," said Brit.

I said, "Don't touch it. Ebben, did the detectives give you a card?"

"Yes."

"Call them. They'll want to see this."

An hour and fifteen minutes later, two LAPD plainclothes officers knocked on Ebben's front door. Detective Mariana Montanio was small and dark and wiry with brown eyes and dark hair pulled back into a ponytail. She wore jeans and a Rams jersey, which I guessed wasn't her usual on-the-job outfit. She must have been working undercover, which would have explained why it took so long for the detectives to arrive.

Her partner was Detective Dennis Hall, a heavier-than-he-should-be African American who stood about five feet ten and didn't have a hair on his head. He wore jeans and a leather sport coat over a white T-shirt.

When Detective Montanio saw the three of us she pointed at me and said, "Who's this?"

"I'm a friend of Ebben's from Minnesota. My name is Nils Shapiro."

"Bullshit," said Detective Hall. "That's not a real name."

"I'm a licensed private detective in Minnesota, but I'm here as a family friend. I am not working, nor am I in possession of a firearm or any other kind of weapon."

Detective Montanio said, "You talk more like a cop than a private detective."

"I was a cop for a short time."

"What happened?"

"I got laid off. My whole academy class did."

Detective Montanio chuckled. "And they didn't rehire you?"

"They tried, but I'd found other employment."

"Bet they loved that."

"We've made up."

There was an awkward silence, then Detective Montanio reached into her pocket and pulled out a business card. She handed it to me and said, "You know the drill." I nodded and put the card in my pocket. "So Ms. Dawsey's car got stolen?"

We walked the detectives outside and showed them the spot where Brit's car had been.

Detective Hall said, "You marked the spot with a stockpot?"

I said, "Not exactly," and lifted the upside-down pot to reveal the eye patch. "The thief left it as a calling card."

Detective Montanio said, "This belong to that Vasily character you told us about?"

"That's our guess," said Brit.

"Anyone touch it?" said Detective Hall.

I said, "No. It's exactly where we found it. We just covered it to keep it from blowing away."

Detective Hall went back to their car and returned with a ziplock bag. He used a pen to pick up and bag the eye patch.

The detectives looked at each other and Detective Montanio said, "Shapiro, can we talk to you in private for a moment?"

28

I led Detectives Hall and Montanio to the patio furniture in the backyard. I selected a chair. The LAPD detectives chose a love seat. Hall put his feet up on the coffee table and said, "This is nice back here. I could get used to this."

Detective Montanio said, "You just get used to that ninety-minute commute to and from Lancaster because that's where you can afford to live."

"Yeah. That's what grown-ups do. Get a place of their own. We can't all live with mommy back in the hood."

Detective Montanio looked at me and said, "My mother has the diabetes. I'm her caregiver. She can't even put on or take off her own shoes by herself."

Detective Hall said, "Shoe duty gets her free room and board. Must be nice."

Montanio looked at me and said, "You believe I got to put up with this shit all day?"

I said, "Interesting technique. Bickering partners. They didn't teach us that at the Minneapolis Police Academy."

"Well, you know. Pressures of the job."

"I do know."

Detective Montanio said, "So why did you say you're visiting Los Angeles?"

"I first came out to attend the celebration of Juliana Marquez's life."

"Because you're a family friend of the Mayers?"

"Yes. And the matriarch of the family hired my firm to investigate what Ebben was doing with his trust fund."

Detective Montanio said, "So it is business?"

"At first, yes. But it took five minutes to learn what Ebben was doing with his trust fund. I can show you text messages with dates and times to back up my story."

"And after that," said Detective Hall, "you just decided to be a good friend."

"More or less."

Detective Hall said, "Yet we hear you've had direct contact with this Vasily character. What's that about?"

"Wrong place, wrong time."

"Tell us about that."

I told them everything that had happened the last few days. Mostly.

The detectives looked at each other the way partners do. They had a conversation without saying a word. I heard a gurgle, then black spikes popped out of the lawn and sprayed water onto the grass. A hiss of white noise. A baby rainbow in the mist. I felt tiny droplets of cool water in the air. The detectives didn't seem to notice.

Hall said, "Sounds to us like you're working. Cut it out and head home."

I said, "I can be here if I'm working for a Minnesotan. Ebben Mayer is a Minnesotan. He's just renting a house here temporarily for business."

"All the same," said Montanio, "get lost."

"I've violated no laws. I've violated no ethical standards. I'm not in your way. What's the problem?"

Hall said, "The problem is this town is full of private dicks. They fuck us up every day. Now we got a homicide, a stolen vehicle, and an APB out on Vasily Zaytzev. Your direct involvement in all three of these is a serious problem for us. So go back home to the ice and snow and your shit sports teams. Understood?"

"I know you have to say what you're saying. That's your job." I handed Detective Montanio my business card. "But we all know we can help each other. You can do what I can't do. I can do what you shouldn't do. That said, with your permission, I'll take Ebben Mayer back to Minnesota and never come back."

The sprinklers stopped hissing and disappeared back into the lawn, then taller sprinkler heads spread their love to flowers in planting beds. Flowers in January. It was unnatural.

Detective Montanio said, "Sorry, Nils Shapiro. Ebben Mayer

needs to stay in town for a while. You'll be okay flying alone. The pilot might even invite you into the cockpit and give you some plastic wings."

LAPD found Brit's car less than six blocks away from the house. Brit said she never wanted to drive her Audi again because Vasily had contaminated it. Sounded kind of second grade to me but I went to get it, then the three of us met Sebastiano and Debra for dinner.

The conversation pendulated between comparing police interviews and shared excitement over Sebastiano's new talent agency. Debra's demeanor had changed. Her desperate less-than-ness seemed to have vanished now that she had the credibility of working in the top tier of Sebastiano's new agency, which he'd named Enchant. She wouldn't have to hustle twenty-four/seven. Her phone, apparently, hadn't stopped ringing since Sebastiano announced Debra's position at Enchant.

Even Brit had lightened up. The strange thing was that, despite their fears, *For the People* was moving forward. Sebastiano sat down with Kate Lennon and her representatives. Same with the esteemed director Ava St. Clair and her reps. The great salesman and dealmaker tied the fifteen million in Thom Burke's safe-deposit box to Vasily's threats and Thom's murder. He implied there was a separate story between Thom and Vasily that had nothing to do with *For the People*. They bought it. One rep even said if they were lucky, Vasily's trial would coincide with the release of the movie. The dynamics that Ebben worried might kill The Creative Collective's first project morphed into dynamics that might make it a hit.

The food and wine were excellent. I saw a couple of movie stars at the next table. And I enjoyed watching Ebben celebrate the elusive and rare win in show business. This is what they all struggled for, apparently, these brief moments when all was good.

The moment didn't last long, at least for me. My phone buzzed with a text.

Buddy! How you do, buddy? It was from the same number Vasily had called from a few days ago.

I responded. *Doing okay, Vasily. Having a nice dinner. How are you?*

You be funny, buddy. Always funny. Why police look for me? You know?

I do know. They told me. They will tell you too when you talk to them.

Ha ha ha ha. I not talk to police. Tell me what you know, buddy.

They want to talk to you. That's what I know.

Why they do?

Thom Burke is dead. Someone killed him in his driveway.

No response. No dots on my phone to indicate Vasily was typing. Nothing. A couple minutes passed. Ebben, Sebastiano, Debra, and Brit talked about all the trouble between the big agencies and the Writers Guild. I understood none of it. Then:

I no kill Thom. Police think I did?

You followed people, Vasily. You threatened people. You punched Thom.

What they know about Thom? Did they look in house like they look in my house? They make big mess, buddy. Who will clean?

I'd told Vasily all I could tell him. I couldn't risk giving him new information that might help him evade apprehension. My hope was that he'd keep asking questions and maybe reveal something he hadn't intended.

I'll clean your house, Vasily. Is that all right with you?

You are not maid, buddy. You private detective. I know about you. I do not want detective in my house.

Why did you ask if the police searched Thom's house? Is there something you think they might find?

You make me bummed, buddy. You tell nothing.

Vasily, do you want to meet and talk?

"You setting up a hot date, Shapiro?" I looked up from my phone. Debra swirled her glass of wine and had cranked her face up to full smirk. "Find some local action? Invite her over. We'd love to meet her."

"Excuse me. I need to make a call." I left the table and stepped outside and onto a far less famous strip of Sunset Boulevard. I saw pedestrians going in and out of bars, restaurants, a convenience store with barred windows. I dug the business card out of my front pocket and placed the call.

29

I took Brit's Audi and half an hour later I sat in the Hollywood Police Station, Robbery-Homicide division, in a small conference room with Detective Dennis Hall and Detective Mariana Montanio. They both seemed torn between the good fortune of me giving them a break in the case and the bad fortune of having to work late.

The room had a glass wall. The blinds were open, and the police station was busier than any I'd seen, like what you'd see in a TV show set in New York City. A parade of homeless people, sex workers, young people who looked like central casting shoo-ins for runaways or gang members, though I have no idea if they were either. Everyone in the police station, cops and robbers and lawyers and complaint filers—they all acted as if the activity was ho-hum business as usual.

I said, "You got a lot of customers tonight."

Detective Montanio said, "This is nothing. You should come here on a Saturday night. Or on Halloween."

"No," said Detective Hall, "come on New Year's Eve. Perps got to take a number." He laughed at his joke. Montanio and I did not.

Montanio said, "So who else knows about these texts you got?"

"Just you two. I didn't tell my fellow diners. Didn't want to ruin their evening."

"We appreciate that. And who again were your dining companions?"

"You trying to trip me up with hard questions?"

"Maybe," said Detective Hall. "Who were they?"

"Sebastiano. Debra. Brit. Ebben."

"Correct," said Detective Montanio. "Now for the bonus question. Have—"

A uniform walked in, handed Detective Montanio a piece of paper, and left. Montanio read it then handed it to Detective Hall.

Hall said, "Interesting."

Montanio said, "Sure is."

I said, "What was the bonus question? I'm really hoping to walk out of here with a new dinette set."

"We're going to share a piece of information with you. See what the great private detective, Nils Shapiro, thinks."

"Uh huh . . ."

Hall said, "We Googled your ass. You solved those murders in Duluth. And the dust one in Ed-eena."

"Eee-DIE-nah."

"Big fucking difference. The newspapers love you. Producers are always eating up shit like that. Surprised we haven't seen a TV show based on your adventures."

"You just might. Hollywood's all over me. Hey, who do you think should play me?"

I wasn't expecting an answer, but they each gave it a good think, then Detective Mariana Montanio said, "Harry Potter."

"Yeah," said Detective Hall. "Harry Potter would be perfect."

I said, "You mean the kid who plays Harry Potter? Daniel Radcliffe?"

"That's him," said Montanio. "But he's not a kid anymore. He's growed up."

I said, "Really? I was thinking more like Joseph Gordon-Levitt."

"What?" said Detective Hall. "Joseph Gordon-Levitt doesn't do TV. He's movies only. Everyone knows that."

"And you ain't no Joseph Gordon-Levitt," said Montanio. "Think much of yourself, Shapiro?"

The detectives laughed.

I said, "You're welcome."

"Welcome for what?" said Montanio.

"I've cured your incessant bickering."

"Fuck you. Do you know what this is?" She held up the scrap of paper the uniform had just walked into the room.

"The LAPD Code of Conduct?"

Detective Hall said, "No, smart ass. Same time you got those texts from Vasily Zaytzev, his phone pinged a tower in Las Vegas. He ain't even in town."

"So what? How far away is Vegas?"

"Four-hour drive. Forty-five-minute flight. And yes, we're

checking passenger lists at McCarren, LAX, Burbank, John Wayne, Long Beach, Ontario, and San Diego. And that brings us back to the bonus question."

"Oh, good. I'd forgotten about that."

Detective Montanio said, "The bonus question is this: You make any plans to take Ebben Mayer out of town?"

"Not yet. Awaiting permission, Detectives."

Hall said, "Permission denied. Is that clear?"

"Yeah, I understand what a two-word sentence means. But just like Harry Potter, Ebben is all growed up. If you want him to stay, you'll have to tell him yourself."

"We will. In fact, we called him after you left him at dinner. Said we wanted to see him tonight."

"You got to be fucking kidding me."

Detective Montanio said, "Oh, look. We've insulted his hometown pride."

"You're seriously looking at Ebben Mayer for the murder of Thom Burke?"

"That 15 mil in Thom's safe-deposit box had to come from somewhere. Ebben Mayer is a man of means. Kind of logical, don't you think?"

"Look at Ebben's financials. Every dime of income and expenditure. You think you're going to find $15 million that isn't accounted for?"

"We considered that," said Detective Hall. "And we think his financials will be spotless. Hell, all them fancy schools he went to and big financial firms he worked for. He knows how to hide money."

"Not to mention," said Detective Montanio, "all those trips he took overseas to raise funds for The Creative Collective. Who's to say he didn't find a cash investor? Everything under the table. Always good to have a little cash on hand."

"Wow. This town really is full of creative imaginations."

"Why are you protecting Ebben Mayer?" said Detective Hall. "What makes you think he's not involved? If you know something, now's the time to tell us."

I knew nothing. I liked Ebben, but that didn't mean he was innocent. I doubted he squished Thom Burke. If he had, why would he call me in Minnesota to tell me Thom was dead? But I had to admit Ebben may have had something going on under the table with Thom Burke.

I felt protective of Ebben. But he might have been in a jam. And even the best people can stray from the good path when they're in a jam. Maybe they're even more likely to stray from the good path because they're not used to being in a jam—their lack of experience can lead to panic. But I wasn't going to share that with Detectives Hall and Montanio. I said, "I don't think Ebben's involved. I don't have proof, but you ever have a gut feeling?"

"Yeah," said Hall. "I had a gut feeling once. It led to an expensive engagement ring and an even more expensive divorce. Haven't trusted my gut since."

"Well, you're going to do what you're going to do. If Ebben had anything to do with Thom's murder, I hope you nail him." I stood.

"Sit down, Shapiro. We got two more questions for you."

I sat down.

Detective Montanio said, "What's your gut tell you about the death of Juliana Marquez?"

The same uniform poked her head into the conference room and said, "Ebben Mayer is here."

"Give us a minute," said Hall.

The uniform nodded, pulled her head out of the room, and shut the door. I saw Ebben through the glass. The horror on his face gave away his fine breeding and top-tier education and fat net worth as it sat in juxtaposition to the chaos of the police station. The jonesing addicts and half-out-of-their-clothes sex workers and spillover of mental illness.

Hall said, "So, Shapiro? What do you think?"

"About what?"

"About Juliana Marquez's caffeine overdose. How does that sit with you?"

"Why are you asking me?"

"Because," said Detective Montanio, "like you said, we can help each other out."

I thought the chances of LAPD helping me were slim, but it was worth a swing. I said, "Doesn't make sense to me that Juliana Marquez would accidentally consume a lethal dose of caffeine."

"You know about her heart defect?"

"Yeah, I know about it. Still. From what I heard, she was intentional about what she did and didn't put in her body. She'd take diet pills, but not on a regular basis. Only during periods when she didn't have time to exercise."

Hall said, "And you don't think Ebben would have slipped caffeine powder into her drink or food."

"You want my real gut?"

"That's why we're asking you."

"I think someone was trying to kill Ebben. He buys energy drinks by the case. Ebben accidentally overdosing on caffeine makes sense. Whatever Juliana ingested was intended for Ebben."

Montanio said, "Why would someone want to kill Ebben Mayer?"

"I have no idea. Maybe you can ask him since you've brought him in for a second round of questioning in twelve hours." I picked up my phone and started texting . . .

"You think that's excessive?"

"My opinion doesn't really matter. But you can ask Ebben's lawyers. They should be here soon."

Hall said, "Your texting Ebben's lawyers?"

"Oh, way worse than that. I'm texting his agent."

Hall and Montanio shared a look then Hall said, "One last question. Ever hear of a movie called *Veins of Gold*?"

"I don't get to the theater much."

"It never was in theaters," said Montanio, "because it hasn't been made yet."

"Then how would I have heard of it?"

"Thought maybe some of your new friends might be involved."

"Not that I know of. But if they mention *Veins of Gold*, I'll suggest they create parts for a man-woman cop team who overcome their insatiable physical attraction to solve the impossible-to-solve cases."

Hall said, "Get the fuck out of here, Shapiro."

30

I picked up Bunion Brit at Ebben's then we swung by her place to get more clothes and toiletries. Her house above the Sunset Strip looked tiny from the street but it was huge inside. Built on the wall of a canyon, it dropped three stories and included a living room with a twenty-foot ceiling, a kitchen with a ten-stool island, and four bedrooms. The view out the back showed rows of houses built around the canyon like terraced rice paddies. The view looked far different than what most people picture when they hear the word *city*.

I said, "Nice place. Do all writers do this well?"

"Not even close, but if you work on network shows for fifteen years, the money adds up. Most of your friends don't watch the shows you write for. Filling your résumé with network procedurals won't get you a gig on anything critically acclaimed, but it more than pays the bills. There are some great shows on the broadcast networks, but a lot are like paint by numbers for storytellers. Millions of people watch them. And writers buy nice houses. But no one's making art."

"That's why you wrote *For the People*?"

"That's exactly why I wrote *For the People*. Some writers see themselves as manufacturers who make whatever the customer orders. They're not in it for the art. They're not even in it for the craft. Just the money. I'm not judging. I'm really not. There's nothing wrong with delivering what the customer ordered. There's nothing wrong with making money and taking care of your family and having security while wearing a T-shirt all day."

"But . . ."

"But some of us are cursed with a need to make something we're proud of. Something our peers would watch. Something *The New Yorker* might rave about."

Brit asked me to check each room, convinced Vasily may have transformed her house into his secret lair. I did, then she disappeared downstairs and made three trips back upstairs, each with a filled bag of Tumi luggage that matched the one before it.

I grabbed two of Brit's three bags and carried them out to her car. I returned for the third. She said, "Thank you. I can't wait until I get this stupid boot off my foot. It's really bothering me. Do you mind driving?"

We returned to Ebben's house in Hancock Park. One thing I'd begun to appreciate about Southern California: your house was your house but your outdoor space was just as livable. You could put nice furniture out there and use it year-round. I went outside and kicked back in a comfy chair, pushed a button and blue flames licked up in a firepit of crushed lava. I'd have to check the house for marshmallows right after I got off the phone with Ellegaard.

I told him about *For the People*'s resilience to controversy, my text exchange with Vasily and subsequent conversation with LAPD, and Detectives Hall and Montanio bringing Ebben Mayer in for a second round of questioning.

Ellegaard said, "Do you think the texts were actually from Vasily or possibly just from someone using his phone?"

"I don't know, but it sure looked like Vasily. He referred to me as 'buddy' about every other word."

"Someone who knows Vasily could imitate him in texts."

"That is true."

"And the Russians probably know how to mask or falsify a cell tower ping."

"That could be."

"So be careful, Nils. And—"

My call waiting beeped in. "Shit."

"What?"

"Beverly Mayer is calling. I'd better take it."

"Call me back."

I answered Beverly Mayer's call. She said, "What on God's green earth is going on in Los Angeles, Mr. Shapiro? Why are the police holding Ebben in custody overnight? And why are you still there?"

I said, "I hadn't heard the police are holding Ebben overnight. I doubt it's true. Who told you that?"

"I'm surprised you don't know since you're sticking your nose everywhere it doesn't belong."

"I'm doing my job, Mrs. Mayer. Just like I did for you and Arthur."

"But you're not working for us anymore. That is quite clear. So who are you working for, Mr. Shapiro?"

"I'm afraid I can't tell you that, Mrs. Mayer. I value my client's privacy just as I valued yours."

"Oh, do not give me that nonsense. Did Ebben hire you? Did his attorneys? The parents of that dead girl? I insist that you tell me."

"Who told you Ebben's at the police station?"

"You answer my question, Mr. Shapiro, and perhaps I shall answer yours."

"Not tonight, but thanks for the call." I hung up, called back Ellegaard, and gave him the news.

"Sheesh," said Ellegaard. "I'll call her in the morning. See if I can smooth things over. In the meantime, I'm concerned about those texts. Maybe you should stay somewhere else tonight."

"I'll be okay."

"Uh huh."

I hung up and went inside to look for marshmallows. Brit was in the kitchen pouring herself a glass of wine. She said, "You like wine? Ebben's got a shitload in the wine fridge."

"Not tonight, thanks." I walked into the pantry. It was stocked for a doomsday scenario. "Holy shit. Dude's got marshmallows, graham crackers, and chocolate. I'm making s'mores out back if you want to join me."

"Mmm, too cold for me."

"It's sixty degrees. And I got a fire going. I used my survival skills and pushed a button."

"I should probably soak my foot." She filled her tumbler with red wine. "You want to join me in the tub?"

I opened a drawer in search of barbecue tools. Nothing. "No thank you." I went to the next drawer. Nothing.

She sipped from her tumbler of red then set it down. "It's just you and me here tonight. No one would know. I mean, you're cute and you seem like a good guy. You're not overly obsessed with yourself. You're smart and funny and I haven't noticed your eyes landing on twenty-five-year-olds. Guys like that are rare in this town."

I went to a third drawer and pulled out a long metal skewer. "You're very kind. I'm just—"

"Married." She took another sip of red.

"Engaged." I pulled out another long skewer. "Sure you don't want to join me?"

"I prefer a different kind of dessert."

"You're a writer. You can come up with a better line than that. And I'm glad to see you're over Thom."

"Shut up. He was a guy I was seeing. He was nothing more. A guy I was fucking. Does that make you happy?" She smiled. "Engaged is not married. Engaged is . . . engaged. Vows not yet spoken. Don't you want one last fling?" She laughed. "Come on, I'm not good with rejection."

"I'm madly in love with Gabriella. I have no interest in anyone else. Zero. Don't take it personally."

"Ugh."

I returned the second skewer to the drawer, then placed the graham crackers, marshmallows, and an oven mitt on a plate. "I don't want one last fling. With anyone."

"All right, but now I might have to drown myself in the tub." She smiled a sad smile.

I said, "Wait until you get the boot cast off. See what life is like when you're bunion free. Plus, *For the People* is getting made. You'll have men throwing themselves at you. Like your buddy who snuck us out the back of the bar the other night."

Brit's easy, flirty way disappeared. "Why'd you bring him up?"

"I don't know. You two just seemed to have a little spark."

"He's an actor. I cast him in a three-episode arc of *CSI: New York*. Now he kisses my ass hoping I'll cast him again. That's all it is."

"All right. I believe you. Hey, want me to slip a s'more under the bathroom door?"

"I'm good with wine. Thanks."

Brit hobbled out of the kitchen. I headed out the back door to the patio, took my seat, and skewered two marshmallows and held them above the fire. The blue flames burned hotter than a campfire, so my decades of marshmallow roasting experience had to be recalibrated. I was not the type of man who let my marshmallows catch on fire. Where's the skill in that? I kept the oven mitt on my lap in case the metal skewer got too hot.

He emerged from the driveway and walked straight at me, pistol pointed at my chest. Black jeans and a black turtleneck under a black leather jacket. The stringed patio lights, landscape lighting, and ambient city light rendered his stealthy outfit useless. My phone was in my front jeans pocket. If I reached for it I might look like I was reaching for something else. Not a risk I could take with a pistol pointed at me. His one eye locked on my two eyes.

I said, "Hello, Vasily."

31

Vasily Zaytzev said nothing and pulled up a chair on the other side of the firepit.

I said, "I heard you were in Las Vegas."

He stuck a finger under his eye patch and scratched. "I was, buddy. Then fly back to Los Angeles."

"That's interesting."

"Why you say that?"

"Just thinking out loud."

"Thinking out loud? That American saying?"

"Is it a saying? The words kind of stand on their own. Either way, it's something we say in America. Did you come to talk about American sayings?"

"No ha ha, buddy. Not tonight. Do you know my house has

the yellow police tape around it? With big yellow X over door? And man sits in car. Not police car. Plain car. The man in plain car watches my house."

"If you go around threatening people and punching one and then that one turns up dead, the police are going to wonder if you killed him."

"I not kill Thom. I would never kill Thom. It be stupid thing to do."

"But you did punch him, right? You made him bleed on his front step."

Vasily thought for a moment then said, "You know this gun, buddy?"

"Not personally but it looks like a .22."

"Yes, buddy. Yes. .22. It not make big hole. It not take off head. It make little hole and bullet bounces—bing, bing, bing—bounces inside body and make what you call, like in Fryman Canyon . . ."

"A path?"

"Buddy! That good! A path. In stomach and lungs and heart. Blood comes out on inside. From little hole. And little noise. When bullet comes out. Only *pop*. Helicopter flies or siren make *woo-woo* or car make *vroom-vroom* then little *pop*, no one hears. No gun noise, and bullet go bing, bing, bing." Vasily used the index finger on his left hand to draw the path of a ricocheting bullet. "You go to house with me, buddy. To talk to man in car and I go in back of house. You say no, and I make hole in body. They find you tomorrow. But they don't find me. They never find me."

I rotated the marshmallows brown side up. The air smelled of toasted sugar and vanilla. I raised the marshmallows higher to slow the process. I tried not to think of Evelyn and Gabriella but they were the only thoughts I had. The only images my mind could conjure. I'd been in a handful of life-threatening situations. Not more than that. I was a private detective in Minneapolis, Minnesota, not James Bond. And in each of those life-threatening situations I felt the outcome, in a way, could only be good. I didn't have a death wish but if I died in pursuit of my disproportionate sense of justice, well then, that wouldn't be a terrible way to go.

But that had changed. How could I have put myself in this situation? Gabriella and Evelyn helped me love my life the way life should be loved.

I said, "Go to the police, Vasily. Tell them you didn't kill Thom. This is America. They have to prove it. If you didn't do it, they can't prove it."

"Ha ha, buddy. That is not truth."

"Are you afraid of the police?"

"I want to stay in America. Now, get up. We go to my house."

A helicopter approached in the distance, getting louder by the second.

I said, "Do you have a green card, Vasily? Are you here legally?"

"On feet, buddy." He glanced up at the sky. "I not wait for the next loud noise."

"This helicopter might be looking for you, Vasily."

He raised the pistol and pointed it at my head.

I stood. "They might have found your car."

"I am not stupid."

The helicopter circled overhead, its spotlight fixed on something close. The machine in the sky rattled Vasily. Or maybe it was just the moment. Whatever he wanted from me, whether it was to help him break into his own house or do something he hadn't mentioned, the time had come when I'd yield to his threat or not.

Then I saw something Vasily didn't see. The helicopter he'd hoped for to drown out the *pop-pop-pop* of a .22 drowned out more than that. I'd been gifted a window of opportunity. I lowered the marshmallows. The blue flames burst into orange on the end of the skewer. I lifted the flaming stick and pointed it at Vasily. My move wasn't a legitimate threat. Flaming marshmallows were no match for a gun. They were nothing other than ridiculous. But the circling helicopter and Vasily's nerves and my audacity to raise flaming marshmallows in his direction were enough to confuse Vasily. Just for a moment. But a moment was all I needed. All *we* needed.

I don't know if Vasily saw the shadow or felt it. Either way he noticed too late. Just as he turned, a right arm smashed down on the pistol as the left arm squeezed Vasily's neck between biceps and forearm. The pistol hit the pavement. Vasily opened his mouth and bit.

Jameson White howled, and Vasily twisted out of the big man's grasp. He dropped to the pavement. I leapt over the fire pit. Vasily picked up the gun, pointed it at Jameson, and squeezed the trigger.

32

Jameson grabbed his thigh. Vasily pulled the flaming skewer from the back of his neck and screamed like a chihuahua giving birth to a Saint Bernard. I reached forward with my right hand, slapped it over Vasily's right eye, and pressed hard. Jameson let go of his thigh, blood on his hands, and wrenched Vasily's right wrist. Vasily dropped the pistol a second time. I let go of his good eye. He hadn't regained his vision.

When he did, he saw me pointing the .22 at his chest. I said, "Jameson, how bad is it?"

"The bullet went clean through. Seen enough gunshot wounds. Always wondered what this felt like. Ha! Now I know."

"Sit down, Vasily. Jameson, if you can, go inside and find something to secure our friend to the chair."

Jameson started for the house. Vasily's one eye looked at me. Not in anger or betrayal or fear. He looked at me with a plea for mercy. With a plea for help.

I said, "You came here with a loaded gun, Vasily. Not just a threat. Not a prop. You came with a weapon to kill."

"Buddy . . ." His voice was hoarse. "Not to kill. To protect. They kill me if they find me."

"Who will kill you?"

His eye blinked. And blinked again. His shoulders offered an apologetic shrug. Then he turned and ran toward the driveway. I aimed the pistol at his back, then lowered it to his legs. He neared the edge of the house. I lifted my finger off the trigger. Vasily Zaytzev disappeared around the corner.

Jameson White came out a minute later, his thigh wrapped in duct tape. He carried the roll in one hand and a beer in the other. "What the hell happened? Where's the one-eyed Russian?"

"He ran."

"And you didn't shoot him?"

"Didn't feel right."

"Didn't feel right? Didn't feel right?! He would have shot you! I know 'cause he shot me. Might have killed me if you didn't give him a hot marshmallow in the neck. Didn't feel right. Man, Shap, when you see a black widow spider in your house you squash it. You don't put a jar over it and slip a piece of paper underneath so you can take it out and let it go free. A black widow is a deadly spider and you need to kill it or it will come back and kill you. Stomp on it, twist foot, clean shoe. Why the hell is that grin on your face?! I'm saying you did something stupid. Something that could get you killed. Or worse, get me killed. What is that stupid grin doing there?!"

The helicopter flew off. The yard was quiet. I said, "You're back."

"'Course I'm back. Ellegaard called and said you were being stupid. Said I'd better check on you. And good thing I did. Trying to fight a gunman with a roasted marshmallow. What the hell has got into you?"

What I had meant was the Jameson I know and love had returned. Not completely but he was on his way. The sprinklers erupted in the neighbor's yard, hissing white noise behind an eight-foot wall. I said, "Let's not talk about it. I don't want to wreck it."

"What?"

"So two choices. We take you to the emergency room or we call Dr. Li and have her come over to take a look first while we drink whiskey and eat s'mores."

Dr. Li arrived ten minutes later. She examined Jameson in the kitchen, first cutting the duct tape off his sweats. A couple years ago Jameson cleaned and bandaged my arrow wound three times a day. He'd just done the same for himself. When he'd gone inside to get something to tie up Vasily, he'd cleaned the wound with vodka and used a clean white T-shirt from Ebben's dresser to wrap the wound under his sweats, which he secured with duct tape to maintain pressure. Dr. Li recleaned the wound and said Jameson would need stitches. She insisted he go to the emergency room at Cedars-Sinai hospital and warned us hospital personnel would have to report the gunshot wound to police.

Jameson looked at me. "What do we tell the police?"

"We tell them exactly what happened. I'll make the call. I can handle the two I've met."

Brit heard none of what happened in the backyard thanks to her lounging in the tub with noise-canceling headphones blasting her daily meditation podcast. But she was hardly centered and relaxed. She refused to stay at the house alone with Vasily running loose so the four of us got into Dr. Li's Prius and headed to Cedars-Sinai. I called Detectives Hall and Montanio and relayed the night's events. Hall said they'd meet us in the ER and thanked me for the overtime.

At the emergency room, they took Jameson in back. Brit had gone to the cafeteria because she didn't like being around sick people. Dr. Li and I sat in the waiting area.

I said, "How come you're not back there with Jameson?"

Dr. Li said, "I don't want him to focus on me. I want him to focus on people who are doing what he used to do. It will help remind him how valuable he is from the patient's point of view."

Huh. That was nothing less than thoughtful, but I kept up my guard. "Thank you for that."

"I can get Jameson a job as a nurse practitioner in Los Angeles. They are much in demand here."

And there it was. I said, "Nurse practitioners are much in demand everywhere. And it's not like he's unemployed by circumstance. He's unemployed by choice. His hospital in Minnesota is begging him to come back to work."

"I see that you are upset, Shap. May I call you Shap? That's how Jameson refers to you."

"Sure. You can call me Shap. And may I call you something other than Dr. Li?"

"Yes. Nikki."

Jameson had seemed to improve since reconnecting with Nikki, so I said, "Well, Nikki, Jameson's not worse since I last saw him."

"Except for getting shot."

"Yeah. Except for that."

"He and I have had long talks. Our history helps. I've always told him he spends too much time alone. Not when he's working, of course. But in his free time. You don't know how good it has been for him to have met you and Ellegaard and Annika. And he loves Gabriella. Jameson says she's too good for you. You are a lucky man."

"I am. Looks like Jameson might be, too." Dr. Li dropped her eyes and half-smiled. I said, "So, what exactly is your history with Jameson?"

"I met Jameson at UCLA when the athletic department assigned me to be his tutor. He didn't go to the most academically rigorous high school and never would have been admitted to UCLA if not for football. He needed help."

"You did well."

"That is kind of you to say. He and I spent a great deal of time together. We were both freshmen when we met. By his sophomore year, Jameson didn't need my help anymore. He's quite gifted intellectually—he just needed to learn good study habits. I gave him a jump start, and maybe sparked his interest in health science, but he did the rest."

"And you remained friends."

"Neither of us wanted to end our tutoring sessions, so we continued for the duration of Jameson's athletic eligibility. That was five years. The last year, I was in medical school, but we still met under the guise of tutoring."

"Sounds like romance."

Dr. Li smiled. Her eyes shined. "Yes, I think it might have been. But there were obstacles. I was a different person then, very much under the influence of my family. My father had a highly visible position with the Chinese government. I couldn't disgrace him by dating a non-Chinese person. So I showed no romantic interest toward Jameson. He had plenty of that from other young women so he didn't pursue it with me."

"What about after UCLA?"

"Jameson moved to Montreal. I stayed in California and married a Chinese man I met in medical school. Jameson fell in love with Joline then followed her to Minneapolis and went to nursing school there. I'd just had my son when Joline passed away. Jameson's life has been in Minnesota. My life has been here." I glanced at Dr. Li's left hand. No ring. Maybe she lost it in a patient. She caught my wandering eye and said, "I divorced my husband three years ago when I learned he had a habit of paying blondes to have sex with him."

"Sorry the marriage didn't work out."

"I used to be sorry. Not now."

"Because Jameson's back in your life?"

She didn't respond.

I said, "Well, I don't know how long Jameson will stay with you, but if you haven't noticed, he's six foot seven and big-boned. Your grocery bill will go up—you should probably budget for that."

"There he is." It was Detective Hall. "The trouble magnet. If it's bullshit, it sticks to Shapiro."

"I was worried you weren't going to make it, Detective."

"Where is Mr. White?"

"They're stitching him up. He can talk."

Detective Montanio walked in. Hall said, "The vic can talk. Which one do you want?"

Montanio chose me. We found a couple of seats on the opposite side of the room and I described the events that led to Jameson White getting shot in the thigh. She commended me on not putting one in Vasily's back as he ran off.

When Detective Montanio seemed satisfied I'd told her all I could tell, I said, "Are you going to hold Ebben Mayer overnight?"

Detective Montanio said, "No. We cut him loose just before we left."

"Huh. You sounded pretty sure he was tied to Thom Burke's fifteen million."

"Yeah. We still are. But his agent sent Elisabeth fucking Gottlieb to the precinct." I didn't register the name. "Seriously? Elisabeth Gottlieb is *the* criminal defense attorney in Los Angeles. You got to front a retainer of 50 grand just to look at her. And she's got a reality show in development called *Until Proven Guilty*. It's gonna be huge."

"How do you know that?"

"Everyone knows it. Where have you been? Now where's the gun?"

I told her it was at the house. I would have brought it but I wasn't licensed to carry in California. I also mentioned they might find a .22 slug in the stucco which would corroborate my story. She said they'd pick up the gun in the morning. Enough was enough for one day.

Detective Hall returned to the waiting area holding his notebook in one hand. "Shapiro, you're free to take Mr. White home, but we don't want either of you leaving town. Understood?"

I nodded and returned to Dr. Li. She said, "I am so sorry."

"For what?"

A nurse approached and asked who would be driving Jameson home. Dr. Li took the clipboard and pen and signed the form. The nurse said Jameson would be ready to go in a few minutes, and walked away.

I stood. "I'll go find Brit. Can I get you anything from the cafeteria?"

"Please stay a moment." I sat. Dr. Li said, "I spoke to the head of administration at Jameson's hospital in Minneapolis to tell her Jameson is doing better. The woman got very excited and asked when they could expect Jameson's return. I told her I didn't know yet but would call her again soon. Then I got calls from four doctors and seven nurses asking about Jameson. They really love him there."

I said, "Everyone who meets Jameson loves him. But he can't be two places at once. And he seems to be doing better here."

"Jameson and I were foolish when we were younger. Too proud or idealistic or ashamed to acknowledge how we felt for each other. Then life got in the way. Different cities and different partners and even different countries. But we reconnected after the school shooting. We grew close again on the phone."

I said, "You saved him."

"I don't know if that's true. But after his first night with me, we talked of marriage." She smiled a sad smile. "But he talks so much about Minnesota. About you and Ellegaard and Annika. And he likes the assistant Kenji because Kenji gives you a hard time. Jameson talks about the doctors and nurses he works with at the hospital and still communicates with survivors of the shooting. Did you know that?" I shook my head. "Jameson loves me, Nils. I know he does. But he loves Minnesota. I can't ask him to give that up for me." Her eyes shined.

I said, "No."

"No?"

"Jameson will love it here, too. He'll go see the Minnesota Twins play in Anaheim instead of in Minneapolis. He'll talk about the weather in Minnesota because there is no weather here. It may bore you senseless, but you'll get through it. He'll find an NP job in Los Angeles and there will be a whole new crop of doctors and nurses and patients who love him."

She said, "But it will not be the same."

"It doesn't have to be the same and it doesn't have to be perfect. Everyone gives up something for the big picture. It could be stinky sponges left in the sink or an insomniac who likes to discuss their insomnia in the middle of the night or having to move out of your beloved coat factory and into a cookie-cutter condo. Take it from me, when the right person comes back into your life, someone you've known since you were practically a kid, you can't throw that away because it's not perfect. You got to—"

"Whoa, Nelson! Twenty-four stitches in the meat of my leg and another eighteen on top. Good thing it wasn't a nine mil or I'd have more thread in me than a pair of Levi's. And five in my hand where the bald dude bit me. Thank the Lord the dentistry in Russia is lagging, otherwise it could have been worse. Ha!" Jameson White sat in a wheelchair, pushed by a woman the size of Jameson's thumb.

Brit returned from the cafeteria. She and Dr. Li left to pull up the car. The nurse handed me a slip of paper and said, "This is for his painkillers. We've also listed what else he needs to redress the wound."

I said, "We've been down this road before, huh pal?"

Jameson said, "This ain't no role reversal, Shap. You ain't changing my bandages unless you became a nurse practitioner in the last few days, which I am certain you did not. Now walk behind us. We hit an incline, my tiny nurse won't have the horsepower to push me up it."

33

We drove back to Hancock Park and found Ebben in his living room sucking down an energy drink. He'd just returned home and looked wiped by the hours-long police interrogation. He had lived his life insulated from the big bad world. Even being Beverly Mayer's grandson hadn't prepared him for it.

Ebben said, "They kept asking me about a movie called *Veins of Gold*. Anyone hear of it?" No one had other than me. Ebben grabbed a second energy drink and headed to bed. I don't know how that works. Brit also headed upstairs to watch some Netflix, then Jameson and I left with Dr. Li. When we pulled into her driveway, I promised I'd have Jameson home by midnight then we got in the rented Land Rover.

I drove, and Jameson complained about my driving. First stop was picking up August in Westwood. Jameson told August how he got shot, embellishing here and there to emphasize how he'd saved my life and that Vasily only escaped because Jameson had gone inside to get duct tape.

Second stop was Target on Santa Monica Boulevard to buy flashlights, red cellophane, rubber bands, latex gloves, and an overgrown Swiss Army knife.

Third stop was Thom Burke's house in Nichols Canyon, a dark road with houses only on one side. The property was still wrapped in police tape, but not enough to prevent us from slipping behind it and picking the lock on the back door.

"What are we looking for?" said August.

"I'm not sure."

Jameson said, "We can find that, no problem."

"A home office would be a good start. Or at least a file cabinet."

Jameson said, "Can we get in trouble for this?"

"So much trouble. A patrol car probably drives by every hour or two, but we parked a few hundred feet away and, as long as we keep the red cellophane over our flashlights, it should appear dark from the outside."

"It's good to be wearing latex gloves again. I've missed the feeling."

"Don't say that in public."

We found Thom's home office in the second bedroom of the two-bedroom house. Two metal filing cabinets held up an old door to create a desk. No computer in sight. The police probably took it. I opened a filing cabinet drawer. Empty. Same with the others.

August said, "How's the leg feeling, Jameson?"

"Like a 350-pound nose tackle just landed on it. But I'm all right."

I opened the closet and found a bookshelf. The bottom half was filled with scripts, their titles written on their sides just like I'd seen in Ebben's home office. The top half was empty. I shined my red light on the spines. I found *Veins of Gold* on the second shelf. I pulled out the script. Only it wasn't a script. The header said *Veins of Gold—Production Budget*. It was dated June of last year. I saw categories for Actors from leads to background. Another category for Director, including First Assistant Director and Second Assistant Director. Another category for Director of Photography, including Best Boy and Grips and Gaffers. More categories including Hair and Makeup, Wardrobe, Sound, Transportation, Special Effects, Digital Effects, and Postproduction. I didn't understand any of it. Except for one thing—the total. Fifteen million dollars.

I said, "I'll be back in a few minutes," then went into the closet and closed the door, removed the red cellophane from my flashlight, sat on the floor, and used my phone to scan the pages one by one. I got about ten pages in when Jameson opened the door and said, "Kill the light." I did and the door shut me inside the closet with Jameson and August. Two three-hundred-pound men. Jameson whispered. "Cops in the house."

A moment later, I heard voices, but no urgency. Two men spoke in a lackadaisical tone. A going-through-the-motions conversation.

"Nah, Beth's busting my ass about the job. Said Jacob is home for dinner every night, is at home Saturday and Sunday, and takes Jen on two vacations a year."

"Who the hell is Jacob?"

A flashlight beam swept under the closet door. The voices grew more clear. They were in the office.

"Jacob is my son of a bitch brother-in-law. Beth and Jen talk eight times a day, and Beth's always comparing herself to her sister, who lives in a bigger house in a nicer neighborhood and has a lawyer husband and, worst of all, the fuck talks about his feelings and wants to listen to her talk about hers."

"That's bullshit."

The voices grew more muffled, then: "Wait a minute."

Footsteps walked back into the room. The flashlight beam returned. It held on the closet, its beam bouncing off the hardwood floor, illuminating inside the closet enough for me to look up and see Jameson and August looking down at me.

A cop said, "What is it?"

"Was that open or closed last time we were here?"

"Can't remember."

The footsteps grew closer. I stared at the doorknob. I looked up at my closet-mates and held my hands up and implored them to do the same. They did.

"I think it was open."

"Then open it."

"All right. Don't bust my balls."

The floorboards creaked with another step, then I heard the sound of a metal filing cabinet drawer being pulled open.

"Come on. Let's hit that taco truck on Vine and Melrose."

They walked out of the office and out of the house. A car started and drove off. I waited five minutes then finished photographing the budget of *Veins of Gold*.

We went out the way we'd come in. When we got in the car I said, "That was fun. You boys up for one more?"

We twisted our way up Nichols Canyon, Jameson complaining about how the tight curves banged around his freshly stitched-up thigh. We turned, and August said we were on Mulholland. A road called Laurel Canyon dropped us into the San Fernando Valley, and fifteen minutes later, we drove by Vasily Zaytzev's house in Sherman Oaks.

The warm glow of a cigarette gave away the stakeout in front of Vasily's house. But it wasn't a police stakeout. At least I doubted any cop would drive a Fiat 500 on the job. If a bicycle ran a red light he couldn't catch it. That meant the car belonged to a private detective. Or worse. Far worse. That would explain Vasily's desperation.

The house next door had been leveled and half rebuilt. The framing for the first floor had been completed, and the second story looked half done. Lumber sat stacked inside a chain-link fence, waiting to be hammered into its rightful place. A big dumpster sat on the curb.

I pulled up Google Maps on my phone for an aerial view of our location and asked Jameson to drive around and drop me on the opposite side of the block. The properties were large and flat. They didn't look like much from the front, but they had resort-style features in back.

Most had a tennis court and swimming pool and at least one outbuilding. I climbed a chain-link fence to enter the construction site and felt my forty-one years on the way up and the way down. Ambient light lit the way, but I stayed close to the fence to minimize the chance of banging my shin on a rusty piece of rebar or stepping on a nail. I climbed and dropped one more time to get into Vasily's backyard.

The police must have used a battering ram on Vasily's back door. It was boarded up and crisscrossed with police tape. The first-story windows were locked. A pergola shaded the patio adjacent to the house. I pulled over a chest of pool equipment, climbed onto it, and pulled myself on top of the pergola. One second-floor window was open six inches. I pushed it up, crawled inside and turned on my red-cellophane-covered flashlight.

Someone had beaten me there. I found dresser drawers pulled open, their contents dumped on the floor. Furniture cushions ripped open. HVAC vent covers removed and tossed aside. Tables overturned. Mattresses lifted off their platforms and pushed against the wall. The refrigerator door open. Every room in the house had been turned inside out.

The mess gave me a pretty good idea how Vasily was tied to Thom Burke. It also explained Vasily's fear. But the big picture had pieces missing. Chunks, really.

I knew of one person who might be able to enlighten me. I texted Jameson. He said he and August would get in position. Then I went out the way I'd come in, climbed into the construction site, crossed the lot, and wedged open the gate enough to push out two four-by-four posts, each about eight feet long. I climbed the fence again and dropped into what would one day be the house's front yard. I walked all the way around the big block so I could approach the Fiat 500 from the rear. I tapped on the driver's window, and it rolled down a few inches.

"Excuse me," I said, "I'm with neighborhood watch. Some of

us are concerned you're parked out here. I called the police, and they suggested I go out and talk to you, so here I am."

A man with a stubbly head and face lowered his cigarette to the ashtray. He spoke in a heavy Eastern European accent. "I am friend of man who live in house. I wait for him to come home."

"Vasily?"

"Yes. He is my friend."

"I have his phone number. Can I call him for you?"

"I made call and send text. He not answer. So I wait."

"All right. I'll tell the police what you said. They may come out and talk to you. Sorry about that. We've had some trouble lately with break-ins and car thefts around here and we're all a bit jumpy."

He took another drag off his cigarette and said in a smoky exhale, "Do not call police. I not cause trouble. Just wait for friend."

"Well, it's a free country. I can't make you leave. But I'll have to photograph your license plate and send it to the police. No hard feelings."

"Do not call police. It will not be good for you."

"No kidding? Are you threatening me?"

He rolled his window down all the way. The streetlight showed a fifty-year-old face, scarred around cold dead eyes. He said, "I not harm you. But must wait for friend. You will understand and go away."

"I don't understand. But I will go away and call the police."

The man cracked open his door. I heard grunts, the creaking of metal, and the Fiat tipped toward me. The man in the car screamed something in his native language. I jumped back, and the car rolled onto its driver's side.

Jameson and August stood, still holding the four-by-four

posts they'd used to lever the car onto its side. They dwarfed the tipped-over Fiat. Jameson popped the handle on the passenger side door and held it open. August bent over the car, reached in, grabbed the man by the collar, and lifted him out of the car. He threw the man down hard. Jameson held his four-by-four post over the man. Just dropping it would cause serious injury.

"Stop, stop, stop!" said the man. "No drop!"

I said, "What do you want with Vasily?"

The man thought through his options then said, "He owe money. Much money."

"To you?"

"To people not to fuck with."

"What people?"

The man said, "Drop wood. I not tell you. Drop wood now."

34

The man wouldn't tell us who "people not to fuck with" were, and we'd pushed our luck tipping over a car in a public street, so we left the man with his broken English and upended car but not his keys.

Jameson, August, and I drove to Jerry's Famous Deli on Ventura Boulevard. It's a large restaurant with a deli case full of whitefish, a full bar, and an attached bowling alley. We cut through it to get to the restaurant. They had a massive air hockey table in case you were in the mood to visit 1974.

I worked my way through a big bowl of matzo ball soup that was served with enough bagel chips to shingle a roof. Jameson and August couldn't stop laughing about how easy it was to lever over the Fiat, even though Jameson lifted with only one leg.

When they settled down, August said, "So just because Vasily's house is torn apart, you're sure the $15 million in Thom's safe-deposit box was from him?"

"Pretty sure," I said. "Vasily either borrowed the 15 million or acted as a front for someone else to invest it. That someone else wanted it back and searched his house for it."

"That means the investor gave Vasily 15 million in cash?"

"I think so. Whoever used Vasily to invest the money wanted to cloak the transaction."

Jameson said, "And then Thom stole the money so Vasily killed him?"

"Thom was working on another movie in addition to Ebben's. It's called *Veins of Gold*. LAPD asked me about *Veins of Gold* and they asked Ebben about it, too. The *Veins of Gold* budget is what I scanned into my phone in the closet back at Vasily's. It must have been a duplicate, otherwise the police would have bagged it. I haven't had a chance to look at it and probably wouldn't understand it if I did, but one thing I do understand is the total budget is $15 million."

"I'm confused," said August.

"Get used to it," said Jameson. "That's what happens when you're in the company of Nils Shapiro."

"Why wouldn't Vasily kill Thom for stealing the 15 million?"

I said, "Because Thom didn't steal it. He was going to use it to make *Veins of Gold*. But something must have gone wrong. The investor wanted their money back. If Vasily killed Thom he'd kill his chance of getting back the money. Vasily just wanted to scare Thom. He assaulted Thom, but he didn't want to kill him."

Jameson said, "Maybe he killed Thom by accident. Pressed

him up against that garage door with his car and things got out of control."

"Yeah, that's a possibility. That's definitely a possibility."

August said, "So why did Vasily give the money to Thom and not to the producer?"

"You can be confused about that because I am, too."

Jameson said, "So who ran the 15 mil through Vasily?"

My matzo ball was so big I couldn't tell if it was a floater or a sinker. My mother made floaters. My paternal grandmother made sinkers. I was partial to floaters. I spooned off a section to see what it was. Floater. First good news of the night.

I said, "I can think of three possible people who ran the 15 million through Vasily: Arthur and/or Beverly Mayer. They have well over $15 million. Ebben. He does, too. The police are looking into that. And then Sebastiano. I don't know if he has 15 million but he could raise it. Of course, the money could be from Eastern Europe and the source used a go-between to stay anonymous. Maybe the individual has been sanctioned or maybe the individual doesn't want the Russian government to get their share of the profit."

Jameson said, "Maybe you should stop talking and we should order some dessert."

35

We headed out of the Jerry's Famous Deli parking lot and took some other canyon through the hills toward Westwood. I saw the backs of homes propped up on stilts, the structures jutting out and over the abyss. It looked like perilous construction in the land of earthquakes and mudslides. We exited the canyon and moments later dropped August at his high-rise on Wilshire. Then Jameson and I drove back toward Hancock Park.

I said, "I'll drop you at Dr. Li's and bring the car back to you in the morning."

"'Bout time you started chauffeuring me around." Jameson turned on the radio. "Wonder if KROQ still exists. 106.7." He messed with the controls.

I said, "This thing with Nikki. Is it serious?"

"Might be."

"Spoke to her a bit while you were getting sewn back together. Sounds like she's ready to make an honest man out of you."

"Could be the direction we're headed."

"How do you feel about moving back here?"

Jameson said, "You want to get in the right lane to turn on Beverly."

I slid into the right lane. "Maybe we can meet up at the Final Four every year."

Jameson changed the radio to an AM station. "KNX still exists. Wonder if they still do traffic reports even with everyone using map apps."

"All right. You don't want to talk about Dr. Nikki Li."

"You are a brilliant detective."

"Something I did?"

"Yeah, man. Something you did."

"You know, I don't have this issue with Gabriella. She has a problem with me, she tells me. None of this pouting and silent treatment and making me guess what's bothering her. Guess I'll get my quota of that bullshit from you."

Jameson looked out the passenger-side window at high-end furniture stores, the kind that sell $25,000 couches and $10,000 doorknobs. He said, "Keep being a pint-sized asshole, Shap. You'll make this easy for me."

I thought I knew what he meant but didn't want to push it. I said, "The police want me to stay in Los Angeles, but I got to get home. I'm going to talk to a few more people, see if it helps Ebben, then I'm gone. Hear there's a polar vortex coming. Thirty degrees below zero without windchill. If I miss it I won't be able to complain about it and I'll feel left out."

Jameson said, "Thirty below *without* windchill?"

"Sixty below with windchill."

"That's going to be a tough night in the ER. Hey, take a right two blocks up on Arden."

I signaled for a right turn. "There's only one fixed variable in the equation. And somewhere in that big body of yours, you've known it since you were eighteen years old."

Jameson White didn't respond. I turned onto Arden.

He said, "Fourth house on the left. The one with the garbage and recycling still out front. Damn kid. Why doesn't he take those in?"

I stopped in front of Dr. Li's house, a stucco-sided Mediterranean with a huge window looking into the living room and kitchen. Dr. Li's son did his homework at the kitchen island. Dr. Li sat in the living room reading. I said, "Good kid?"

Jameson's voice got small and weak. "Great kid."

"Talk tomorrow?"

"I suppose."

"How's that leg feeling?"

"When you got shot by that arrow, I remember you refused the OxyContin and took a dose of Irish whiskey instead. That numb the pain?"

"No, but it helped me not mind it so much."

I got out of the car, walked around, and opened the door for Jameson.

He said, "What the hell you doing? I ain't your date." He

swung his legs out and stood. The big man winced and put his right hand on my shoulder. I walked him to the front door and handed him over to Dr. Li.

I mapped Ebben's house. It was less than a mile away. I followed the nav's directions across Larchmont Boulevard. My phone rang. The caller ID said Ebben Mayer. I hadn't hooked it up to the car's Bluetooth so I answered it on speaker.

"Nils!" I heard a scuffle followed by a more distant, "Help me!" Then the call dropped. I called back Ebben. Straight to voicemail. I tried again. Same thing.

Forty-five minutes later, three police cars, lights flashing, parked out front of the house in Hancock Park. Brit sat on the couch in her robe talking to four uniformed officers and two detectives: Hall and Montanio. I entered the room, and Brit looked at me as if a puppy had just died.

Detective Montanio said, "We'd like a moment of your time, Mr. Shapiro." I stepped into the back den with Detectives Montanio and Hall.

Detective Hall flipped a page on his notebook and said, "Want to tell us where you've been tonight?"

"Ebben Mayer's been kidnapped and you want to talk about where I've been?"

Montanio said, "That's right. Where were you between eight and nine o'clock this evening, Mr. Shapiro?"

"I was with two men: Jameson White and August Willingham the Third."

Hall said, "The football player?"

"They're both football players. Or were."

Montanio said, "Where did you three go?"

"A few places. Some private. Some public. I can show you a
time and date stamped receipt from Jerry's Famous Deli in Studio City. I'm sure our server will remember us."

"And the private places?"

"I'd rather not say."

"Well," said Hall, "that's a problem for us. See, Ebben was
at home and got a call from his agent, Sebastiano. Apparently,
Sebastiano's having a party up at his place, and he called to
invite Ebben. We know this because Ebben told Ms. Dawsey
and invited her, but she wanted to stay in for the night. Ebben
left. Twenty minutes later a man walking his dog called police
after finding Ebben's vehicle abandoned in a residential neighborhood in West Hollywood, the car running and the door
open."

"Yeah, that's what happens when people are kidnapped."

"We're inclined to agree. The car was running with the keys
in the cup holder. We found drops of blood on the passenger seat
and on the street."

"Maybe he hit his head on the steering wheel or—"

"Maybe," said Montanio, "and we found tire marks right be-
side Ebben's car and no more drops of blood after that spot."

Hall said, "And the tire marks indicate the same exact wheel-
base as Vasily Zaytzev's vehicle."

I shook my head. "I should have shot the son of a bitch."

My phone buzzed. A text from Ellegaard. *Ebben Mayer has*

*been kidnapped. His parents just received a ransom call. Call me
ASAP.*

"Now," said Detective Hall, "where are these private places
you and your friends visited tonight?"

I said, "I'm not going to withhold any information pertinent
to LAPD's investigation of Thom Burke's murder."

"How wise of you," said Montanio.

"Thom Burke was involved with a movie titled *Veins of Gold*.
The budget was $15 million, which is the amount found in his
safe-deposit box."

"Yeah. We know all this," said Hall.

"Good. You're doing your job. What kind of condition was
Vasily's house in when you searched it?"

"That's our business. Not yours."

"Fair enough. But I'm going to take a guess. The moment you
learned Thom Burke was dead you went to Vasily's. He wasn't
home. You got a search warrant and rammed your way through
the back door."

Detectives Hall and Montanio shared a quick glance.

"You didn't find much in the house. Maybe some weapons.
Maybe some drugs for personal use. The only thing you found
of significance was a script or a budget to *Veins of Gold*, the same
project you found evidence of in Thom Burke's house."

The detectives were smart enough not to make eye contact
that time, but their individual looks gave them away.

Hall said, "Where you getting this?"

"We can talk about that in a minute. Now, I'm sure you finding the connection to *Veins of Gold* could be a coincidence in an
industry town like Los Angeles. But a coincidence is unlikely.
Especially when the budget is exactly 15 million."

Hall folded his arms. Montanio scratched behind her ear.

"That pretty much eliminates the possibility of a coincidence. And what you may or may not know is someone else went through Vasily's house after you were there. Ripped the place apart searching for something. And something of size. Envelopes weren't torn open. But whoever was in there took vents off ducts and tipped over furniture. Anyway, it didn't seem like the results of a police search to me. There was something less methodical and more violent about it."

Montanio said, "You were inside Vasily's house?"

"I didn't say that. I'm saying this is the information I've learned. We'll talk about how in a minute. So my theory is Vasily either borrowed the 15 million or fronted it for someone else. Either way, the source of the 15 million changed their minds, maybe because Thom was killed, maybe for some other reason, and wanted the money back. Vasily didn't have it. Thom did. Vasily couldn't get it, and that explains why he's behaving under duress lately."

"Wow. Big theory. Kind of a leap, don't you think?"

"There's more. A man's been staking out Vasily's house. I had a little chat with him and persuaded him to be forthcoming enough to tell me Vasily owes a lot of money to someone. I couldn't persuade him to tell me who, but it backs my theory."

"All right," said Hall. "Now tell us how you know this."

"No, no," said Montanio. "First tell us why you know this."

I said, "That's the better question." Hall rolled his eyes. "The reason I know this is because you leaned on Ebben Mayer. Hard. I felt the need to protect him so I started digging around to learn where else the 15 million in Thom's safe-deposit box might have come from."

"Uh huh," said Hall. "Now how do you know about the inside of Vasily's house and that we may or may not have found a document pertaining to *Veins of Gold* at Thom Burke's house?"

A lie is best preceded by something true. Especially if that truth shames the person you're lying to. I said, "You asked me if I knew anything about a movie called *Veins of Gold*. Ebben and Brit told me you asked them the same thing. You'll talk to anyone about that movie. No discretion whatsoever. So I knew Thom Burke was somehow connected to *Veins of Gold*." Hall and Montanio couldn't deny they'd shared that information and displayed the shame I was looking for in slight head shakes and shifting bodies. "My new friend outside Vasily's house told me the rest. Just a guess, but he's the person who ripped apart Vasily's place. He described it in detail. You can ask him if you find him. Now, if you'll excuse me, I'd like to go look for my friend Ebben."

Detectives Hall and Montanio had a silent conversation with their eyes. Another helicopter made the rounds overhead. Maybe the spotlight on that one was in search of Ebben Mayer. Hall said, "Keep your friend Brit company. We need a minute."

I stepped into the living room and called Ellegaard. I filled him in on what had happened in Los Angeles, and he told me the ransom demand for Ebben Mayer was $20 million. And if he didn't get it soon, he'd put a bullet in Ebben's head. Ebben's parents had been in contact with the FBI and were awaiting further instructions. We talked more about the logistics of our communication, which boiled down to I should respond more quickly to Ellegaard's texts and calls. But I drifted from the conversation because something about $20 million pinged the unreachable part of my brain.

We hung up and I turned to Bunion Brit who cried like a child on the couch. That, too, pinged the unreachable part of my brain. She was behaving far differently than the suave, fast-talking, artsy woman I'd met at the celebration of Juliana Marquez's life. It made perfect sense that she'd be upset by Ebben's kidnapping and Thom's death, but Brit seemed disproportionately devastated and it didn't feel right, especially regarding Thom. She'd been emphatic in her downplaying of their relationship.

Detective Hall poked his head in from the den. "Shapiro, get in here."

I left the sobbing Brit and returned to my two favorite LAPD detectives. Montanio said, "We got to go meet with the FBI. Let us know if you hear anything, all right?" They started toward the living room.

I said, "That's it?"

Hall said, "We appreciate how forthcoming you have been."

Montanio said, "And watch your back. Be safe out there."

I'd seen that before. The "non-ask ask" for help. Kind of a you scratch our back and you'll scratch our back agreement. The only thing I got in return was a little room to work. No threats to get out of their way. No reminders of penalties for me working without a California private investigator's license. Just have a nice night and feed us what you learn. Oh, and don't get caught by good guys or bad guys because either way we will not have your back.

I said, "Thank you, Detectives. I'll let you know if anything comes my way."

They nodded and headed for the front door.

36

I gave Brit a choice. She could stay at Ebben's alone or go to Sebastiano's party with me. She said there was no way she was staying alone, but asked if I could drive because her foot was hurting. She just needed a second to pull herself together. An hour later, Brit played navigator while I drove to Brentwood, home to the Getty museum, movie stars, and Sebastiano.

Brit exhaled hard a few times, either trying to calm herself down or to let me know she just used mouthwash. She said, "Wait until you see Sebastiano's house. Total party pad."

"So crepe paper and confetti everywhere?"

She looked at me with a raised eyebrow. "It's got an infinity pool overlooking the city and coast. And one wall of the pool is glass. There's this long bar at the sublevel."

"You mean basement?"

"Yeah, I guess."

"Son of a bitch. People do have basements."

"Only a few. Anyway, it doesn't feel like a basement. It's this huge room with a huge bar and behind the bar is the other side of the pool's glass wall. So you can sit at the bar and enjoy an underwater view of people swimming and half the time they're naked and about ten percent of the time they're screwing."

"What kind of party are we going to?"

"You never know with Sebastiano. It'll be an inner circle party or an outer circle party. I've seen some shit. Shit I can't unsee."

"Is Ebben in the inner circle?"

Brit said, "I don't know. Sebastiano invited him tonight, so I guess we'll find out when we get there depending on what kind of party it is. That's the way it is with Sebastiano, you eventually find out more about him. He's one of the thousands of open secrets in this town."

"Kind of an oxymoron, isn't it? Open secret."

"That doesn't mean it isn't true. Plenty of people knew Harvey Weinstein was a predatory creep and that a certain comedian exposed himself to women backstage at comedy clubs and which closeted romantic leads hit on young men."

We passed the clump of high-end furniture stores. A window display featured a Lucite toilet. My God. There aren't enough scrubbing bubbles in the world. I said, "Are Sebastiano's open secrets of a sexual nature?"

"Not that I know of," said Brit. "Kind of the opposite. For one, his real name isn't Sebastiano. It's Doug Adams."

"What? Like Douglas Adams as in *Hitchhiker's Guide* Douglas Adams?"

"Yep. Guess he thought there couldn't be two famous Douglas Adamses and being famous was and is at the top of Sebastiano's list. He doesn't have any creative talent so he has to do it on the business side, which is just as effective."

"Wow. Douglas Adams from Danville, Illinois."

"No. He's not from Danville, Illinois. Who told you that?"

"He did. In his office. Told me a big story about being from the wrong side of the tracks."

Brit shook her head. "All bullshit. Sebastiano, aka Doug Adams, is from Covina, California, about thirty miles east of here. Total suburban kid. His dad was an assistant manager at a May Company department store, and his mom was a dental hygienist. He grew up in the middle of the middle class. Went to boring old Covina High and then the University of Illinois because his grandparents lived in Danville and he was somehow able to use their address to get in-state tuition. That's where that bullshit comes from."

We turned left onto Santa Monica Boulevard. I said, "How do you know all this?"

"Once you know Sebastiano's real name and where he's from, you just Google him. You can see old yearbook photos. All sorts of stuff. But it never seems to get out there in the world. It's just the way Hollywood works. Open secrets stay open secrets. A few were busted open by MeToo, but most are still open secrets."

"So how did Doug Adams, University of Illinois student, become Sebastiano, agent at ACI?"

"No one knows for sure. I mean, someone knows, but even people in Sebastiano's inner circle aren't sure. The rumor is Doug got really buff in college. And he's a handsome dude. Tall. Angular features. He was in Chicago with friends and got spotted

by a modeling agent. Even twenty years ago, everyone was looking for diverse models. He did a lot of print work. And there
was another Doug Adams who modeled in Chicago because of
course there was—there's a million Doug Adamses. They asked
if he had a middle name he wanted to use and he said Sebastiano, which is no way his real middle name. Who knows where
that name came from?

"So the newly dubbed Sebastiano starts modeling and soon
realizes gay men love him. They hit on him all the time."

"Now how do you know this?"

"He told me. This is the story he tells his inner circle, and
I think it's true because unlike the name Sebastiano, it actually makes sense. So Doug Adams starts modeling and making
money for the first time. He's not on the cover of magazines or
anything but Chicago's a big market and he does some national
campaigns and he's making a hell of a lot more money than he
did selling shoes at Kinney's. He wants to keep the job, and a lot
of the gay men flirting with him have something to say about
that. Photographers and designers and ad execs and retail CMOs
and basically just everyone. So Doug Adams, now known as Sebastiano in his modeling career, learns how to play that game."

"What do you mean? Is he gay?"

"No. But he's not homophobic either. So he responded to the
flirtations in a kind and non-sexual way. Basically, he acted like
a good friend. When the advances got specific, he politely declined and said he was in a relationship. He did not say whether
it was with a man or a woman. And in the process of modeling
and managing those one-sided relationships of sexual desire, Sebastiano discovered what he's really good at."

"Playing people."

"He's so good at playing people! Yes. If you can make a dozen men, all at the same time and in the same space, think they might have a shot at you and still want to work with you when that shot never materializes, you can make production companies think they might have a shot at casting an actor from your roster of A-list stars and still want to be in business with you when the actor goes to work for someone else."

We turned right onto Wilshire in the direction of August's high-rise. I said, "I'm surprised he didn't want to keep modeling. He could have done it for decades."

"I said that to him once. He said modeling is way harder than it looks. Long hours and brutal travel and all that. And Sebastiano wanted more control. He wanted to be at the center of things. Then one day his modeling agent pulled him aside. She saw what he was doing, how he played the game, and said if he ever wanted a shot at the agenting end of the business, he had an open invitation. And Sebastiano was like fuck that. I'm going to Hollywood. So the minute he graduates Illinois he comes out here and infiltrates the gay mafia."

"The what?"

"It's just a saying. It's the clique of powerful gay people in Hollywood. There are a bunch of those mafias. The Harvard mafia. The Second City mafia. The New York mafia. The USC Film School mafia. The playwright mafia. The Upright Citizens Brigade mafia. It's a long list. He introduces himself as Sebastiano. No last name. And legally changed his name to Sebastiano with no last name."

"I didn't know you could do that."

"Well, he did. Or at least says he did. He gets hired to work the mail room at ACI. Twenty years ago hard copies of all contracts went through the mail room. Sebastiano made photocopies of them, took them home, and studied them. So when he got promoted to work as an agent's assistant, he knew about all the components that go into making a deal."

"What do you mean 'components'? You mean like salary and term of employment?"

"Way more than that. Where does the talent's name appear in the credits? Are they billed above the title or below? How big is their trailer on set? Is it in the contract that no one can have a bigger trailer? Do they have a personal driver? Does the driver drive a limo? Or does it have to be an electric car? How much are they compensated if production runs beyond the scheduled shoot dates? If the actor wears a toupee, who pays for it? If the actor does promotional work, who dresses them to appear on Colbert? It goes on and on."

"So Sebastiano was ready when the time came."

"Everyone thinks this business is about luck and getting your break. In a way it is, but you have to be ready for your lucky break when it comes. You have to put in the hard work. Otherwise you fall flat on your face in a very visible way. And Sebastiano was ready."

When we arrived at Sebastiano's, cars lined both sides of the residential street. My rental Land Rover was the most proletariat car of the bunch. The first parking spot I found was five hundred feet away. I told Brit I'd turn around and drop her off so she wouldn't have to trek so far in her boot.

"Thank you."

"Your foot seemed okay a few days ago. When did it start hurting?"

"Today. I've been overdoing it. My walk from the police station to the coffee shop didn't help. I really got to go easy on it for the next three weeks."

"Not the worst thing in the world for a writer, is it?"

"You'd think."

Sebastian lived above Sunset Boulevard in a two-story modern box with each tree and shrub lit for its close-up. I dropped Brit in front of the gate and drove off to park. She said she'd wait for me—she hated to go into parties alone.

I returned to Brit and checked my phone for news of Ebben. There was none, then we stepped into a foyer decorated with a huge canvas of abstract art. The house was open and modern and inviting. People were everywhere. In the kitchen area. In the living room area. In the dining area. I say area because they weren't rooms—there were no walls. The party reminded me of those we had in high school when someone's parents were out of town. There was an urgency to it, an urgency that obliterated form and function and yielded to chaos. Marijuana smoke hung in the air heavy and pungent. We stepped into the living area. I recognized several famous people and probably would have recognized more if I paid attention to that sort of thing. Servers carried trays of drinks and hors d'oeuvres and drugs—joints and gummy candies, cookies, and caramels. Lines of cocaine and candy dishes of ecstasy. I saw a lot of these drugs in my early days as a private investigator when I chased down runaways and missing persons. Drugs can be magnets for souls in search of a family.

The servers wore nothing but paint. Sebastiano had hired naked servers and an airbrush artist. They were painted in traditional caterer garb: white shirts with black pants.

I said, "Lucky us. Looks like Sebastiano's throwing an inner circle party tonight."

"No, Nils," said Brit. "That's what you don't get about Sebastiano. This is an outer circle party. This is the image he wants to portray. His inner circle parties are a total snooze."

37

"X, thank God," said Brit. She took a purple pill from a naked server and washed it down with a paper cup of water. "Nils, your turn."

"I assume you're familiar with the effects of X."

"Give me a break, Dad. I've had a hard week. I need to take the edge off. You know they use ecstasy in psychotherapy now? Soldiers with PTSD, X just makes it go away."

"Yeah, well, you're not a soldier with PTSD."

"Don't judge me. You don't know what I've been through."

I looked hard at Brit. I didn't know what she'd been through. But I did know the stress one feels can be proportional to one's narcissism. Woe is me because me is so damn important. I'd not only seen it a thousand times, I'd experienced it when I couldn't get out of my own way. I was lucky to have Ellegaard then. He pulled me out of that whirlpool of self. Bunion Brit didn't have an Ellegaard. If she did, the person would have showed up when Thom got killed. Brit was alone, swirling down and around and into herself.

The FBI and LAPD were out looking for Ebben Mayer. They'd search Thom Burke's house again. They'd search Vasily's house and stake it out. I could only get in the way and in trouble in those places. I had one play. Sebastiano invited Ebben to his party. Sebastiano lured Ebben out of his house and onto the road. Talking to Sebastiano might yield something. I had no idea what. Brit's ecstasy wouldn't take full effect for about an hour. I'd have to find Sebastiano and get her out of there by then.

She looked at me like a wounded animal and said, "Please take something. I need a friend tonight."

"I need to keep my head clear for Ebben."

"Yeah, I suppose," said Brit. Then something caught her attention. "Oh shit. There's what's-her-face from CBS. She passes on everything I pitch. Come on. This way. I think she hates women."

Brit led me through the kitchen and into a side entryway and down a wide circular staircase. We stepped into the basement, which was nothing like any basement I'd ever seen. A polished limestone floor. No rugs. The ceiling was ten feet tall. Clumps of casual furniture akin to beanbags made pits of social interaction where personal boundaries buckled. Multiple generations of party attendees clumped in mutually beneficial transactions. Kids who looked fresh out of high school, their faces round with baby fat, tangled with thirtysomethings and fortysomethings and fiftysomethings and beyond. The old wanted youth. The youth wanted money and power. The plain wanted beauty. The beautiful wanted to be wanted. The intelligent wanted recognition.

I saw the bar Brit had told me about. Made of translucent sheets of stone, lit from within to glow browns and pinks and greens. Wide enough for a dozen stools, all taken, each surrounded by people standing. One man and one woman tended the bar, both naked and body painted in the same white shirt as the servers above. The pool glowed blue behind them through its glass wall. Bodies swirled in and out of view. A few in bathing suits but most were not.

The nudity felt cold, forced, benign, and presentational. Nowhere near provocative. Brit and I worked our way through the basement and up another set of stairs that led to the backyard where we found a forest of human beings and heat lamps. A view of the sparkling L.A. basin that turned to black at the coast. Naked torsos in the pool and its adjacent hot tub. And Sebastiano holding court at a round table with Debra and a woman and man wearing business suits.

"Lawyers," said Brit.

"Do you know them?"

"I've seen them before. Mostly around Sebastiano."

"So they're show business lawyers."

"As opposed to?"

"Criminal defense attorneys."

"Why would you say that?"

Sebastiano saw us and waved us to his table. The kid who'd brought us sandwiches in his office appeared out of nowhere with two more chairs. Bunion Brit and I sat. Sebastiano made introductions, and I immediately forgot the lawyers' names. Then he asked if we'd heard any updates on Ebben.

I said, "No. Have you spoken to the police?"

The lawyers took that as their cue to leave. They got up and walked away. Sebastiano said, "Those two come to every party."

"Of course they do," said Debra. "Any excuse to work late and get in a quick fuck before they go home to their spouses."

Sebastiano nodded in agreement. Another open secret among friends and coworkers. Sebastiano said, "The police swung by to see if I was really having a party."

"Because your invitation drew Ebben out of the house."

Sebastiano said, "I feel awful about that, but Vasily was probably camped outside. Ebben would have left eventually. If we'd had any idea this was a possibility—"

"How does that work when the police come up to confirm you're having a party but the party includes illegal molly and cocaine?"

"Do you disapprove of my party, Mr. Shapiro?"

"Not at all. It's a party. People are enjoying themselves. You are, aren't you, Brit?"

"I'm having a lovely time. Thanks for asking, Nils."

I said, "I'm just wondering if the police don't see what's happening or they do and look the other way. Trying to get a feel for how this town works."

"Well, if you must know, I have an assistant parked at the bottom of the street. If a police car is headed up, we have time to hide what needs to be hidden."

"Your assistants do a lot of shitty work."

"Price of admission to the game. And it's just for a year. After that they're on their way."

Debra said, "We all went through it. Besides, how would you

rather pay your dues: a year of personal servitude or four years of medical school or three years of law school?"

"Hey!" said Brit. "There's Carl!"

She got up and disappeared into the crowd, leaving me alone with Sebastiano and Debra. I said, "Ebben's parents received a demand for ransom."

"Wait," said Sebastiano. "What are you saying? The police have confirmed it's a kidnapping?"

"Holy shit," said Debra.

I said, "What did you think happened? Ebben just abandoned his car and leaked blood onto the street?"

Sebastiano said, "I don't know. I guess I just thought Ebben would show up. Why would Vasily kidnap him? It's such an act of desperation."

I said, "Yes. It is. A person feels desperate when they're on the hook for $15 million."

Debra laughed. "You think the 15 million in Thom Burke's safe-deposit box came from Vasily?"

Sebastiano did not laugh. He sipped a martini or what looked like a martini. After learning how the man created himself, I didn't trust that anything was what it appeared to be. I said, "Why is that funny to you? Who do you think the 15 million came from?"

"Ebben Mayer. It had to be Ebben. How else do you keep 15 million off the books and readily available?"

"Why would he have to keep it off the books?"

"I don't know," said Debra. She removed her octagonal pink glasses, blew on the lenses, and returned them to her round, pretty face. "I don't know what it's like to have that kind of money." There it was again, Debra's *I'm not in the club* bitterness.

First it was about her weight, now it was about her bank account. "Thom was working for Ebben, and Ebben is the sole principal of The Creative Collective. He raised a $100 million fund. Plus, with all his personal money, doesn't it make sense that—"

"Easy, darling." Sebastiano reached over and placed a hand on Debra's forearm. "Ebben's a client, remember?"

I said, "Hold on. I'm curious. Is Debra saying Vasily helped fund The Creative Collective and now he wants his money back?"

"I'm not saying anything."

"Maybe Vasily threatened everyone to pull Kate Lennon from *For the People* so it would kill the movie and his investment would revert back to him?"

Debra opened her mouth to say something but Sebastiano caught her eye and she kept quiet. My phone buzzed. Ellegaard. It was 1:00 A.M. in Minnesota. He wasn't calling to say hello. I excused myself from the table and answered.

Ellegaard said, "There's a problem with the ransom."

I watched Brit try to snuggle with a handsome man in his twenties. The man seemed annoyed, as if a stranger in an airplane had fallen asleep on his shoulder. His friends laughed. I had to get her out of there. I said to Ellegaard, "What kind of problem?"

"Ebben's parents don't have $20 million. Not even close. They've given almost everything they had to their foundation."

"Okay. Well, Beverly and Arthur have the money."

"They do, but they refuse to pay it."

"What?"

"I spoke to Beverly Mayer half an hour ago. She said Ebben needs to learn his lesson about show business. She's not paying the ransom."

"And if Ebben gets killed?"

"She said she's willing to take that chance."

"Lovely woman. But Ebben has 20 million, right?"

"The FBI is looking into that. It's not so simple to liquidate assets without a signature. Especially when the owner of the funds is under duress. We don't even have a verbal request."

The handsome man slipped away from Brit, leaving her alone. She looked pathetic. The ecstasy had started to kick in. She was full of love and empathy but had no way to share it. She spotted me and smiled the most compassionate smile.

I said, "Maybe Vasily would make an arrangement so Ebben can sign the necessary documents to liquidate the 20 million."

"Maybe," said Ellegaard.

"One more thing. Can you jump on LexisNexis and run a background on Debra Schmidt. Something's not right about her."

"On it. Stay near your phone." He hung up.

Bunion Brit hobbled toward me. It was her eyes that gave her away. Ecstasy is a stimulant and hallucinogen that doesn't create feelings but brings them out. It tears down the walls behind which we hide our love and empathy. It tears down the walls we've built to protect ourselves.

I got my private investigator's license when I was twenty-five years old and could still pass for a college student and even a high school student. I earned a reputation for infiltrating parties, especially raves where I could move among the pacifier-sucking teens without drawing unwanted attention. This was shortly after 9/11. Law enforcement and parents were concerned raves might become terrorist targets. The whole country was in a state of panic. Security companies hired me to blend into the crowd and keep my eyes open. Parents hired me to search for wayward and missing teens. Shopping malls hired me, too. I spent more time at the Mall of America than any human being should. And though I never saw anything close to terrorism, I saw plenty of young women—no, check that—plenty of girls peddling sex. Girls as young as thirteen.

Ecstasy played a role at both raves and the Mall of America. Some of the girls worked with pimps. But some were just teenagers who wanted a $200 pair of jeans or a ziplock bag full of ecstasy. I saw the drug's effects almost daily for years. Wannabe adults became the children they were. Cool and standoffish yielded to warm and open. Duplicitousness melted away and honesty stepped forward.

I knew how to talk to someone on ecstasy. I knew what I could do with their trust.

Brit said, "Nils. Oh, Nils. I'm so happy we've met. Are you? Happy we've met? I sure hope you are." She leaned against me and placed her hand between my shoulder blades.

I said, "Brit, can we go somewhere and talk?"

"You mean like, just the two of us?"

"If you feel comfortable. You seem calm and relaxed."

"Mmm-hmm. I am. Are you, Nils? Calm and relaxed?"

"Yes. Very much. That's why I thought it might be a nice time to connect. Get to know each other better."

"I'd like that." She used her free hand to take mine. She rubbed her thumb across the back of my hand. "I know a room we can go to. Would you like to see it?"

38

Brit led me through the people and heat lamps, into the house and up to the second floor. We walked hand in hand down a long hall which was open on the right and overhanging the living room below. Doors lined the left side of the hall, some closed, some open offering glimpses into bedrooms and bathrooms. The walls were paper white. Artsy black-and-white photographs hung in the spaces between doorways.

My job was to save Ebben Mayer's life. Sometimes that means blurring ethical lines into smudges. Right and wrong swirl into one. I had a gut feeling about Brit. It wasn't anything more than that. I had no idea what it would yield. Sometimes an investigator gets a break. Mine came from Brit. A double-barreled shotgun of good fortune. Brit invited me to join her in the bath earlier that night. And she took ecstasy. I hadn't facilitated either. In that respect, my ethics were good.

Taking advantage of the situation is where my ethics got hazy.

We entered the last bedroom on the left. I turned on the overhead light, dimmed it to a whisper of gold, shut and locked the door. Brit lay down on the bed, twisting onto her side to look at me. I put my head on the pillow and stared into her eyes. I took both of her hands in mine and said, "You've carried a burden the last few days. It has to be exhausting."

Her eyes smiled. "Yes. It's been terrible."

"I'm here to help. I'm here so you don't have to carry it by yourself."

"You're kind, Nils. And generous. And good. I've felt that. It's attracted me to you." I said nothing. Her whole face smiled, and her eyes teared over. She said, "I want to tell you something, but please don't judge me."

"I'm here to support you. Not judge you."

"You are?"

"Yes."

"That's sweet."

"I'm your friend, Brit. I care about you." She nodded. "You can tell me anything."

She shut her eyes. "You're my friend."

"I'm on your side."

She nodded and opened her eyes. "I'm the one who did it, Nils. I killed Thom." She cried. Not from nerves or fear or guilt but from a rush of sadness, as if an innocent creature had died. But I suspected the innocent creature wasn't Thom. It was her.

I said, "I'm sure you didn't mean to."

"I was so angry."

"Angry at Thom?"

She reached up and cupped my cheek. "Thank you for being my friend."

"I'm honored to be your friend, Brit. Thank you for being mine."

"That's sweet."

"I want to help you."

"I know. I believe you. I trust you, Nils."

"What did Thom do to make you so angry?"

"He said he'd make me lunch if I came over. I told him I'd like lunch. All I'd had that day was a juice which was all vegetables and almost no calories. I was starving. I drove up to Nichols Canyon and parked in his driveway. The empty juice bottle was in my cup holder. It was a glass bottle.

"So when I got out of the car, I took it to the side of the garage where Thom kept a special box for just his glass recyclables. He put plastic and cardboard in the regular recycling container, but the glass he liked to take in himself to get the California refund. I opened the box to throw in my juice bottle, and under the green Perrier bottles, like almost all the way down, I saw a white container. The kind vitamins or supplements come in. And I thought that was weird because it looked plastic, not glass. I was curious about that container. I wondered what Thom had been taking because we'd had some problems in the bedroom. He wanted to take Viagra, but I said no. Thom doesn't put any chemicals in his body, and I didn't want him to start because of me. I didn't want to feel responsible for him taking a pharmaceutical. I knew our sexual relationship was short term."

"I understand. But you weren't ready to end it."

"I didn't know how to because of *For the People*. We were

about to go into preproduction. We'd be together every day. I figured I'd wait until we were done shooting. And the one thing that was good about Thom was the sex. Except when he couldn't do it. But when he could it was really good and so why not continue having sex until we broke up?"

"I understand."

"Aw, you do?"

"It's only human."

"Yes, it's human."

"I understand. You wanted to know if Thom was taking a supplement to help in the bedroom."

She nodded. "So I reached under the empty Perrier bottles and pulled out the white container. And do you know what it was for?"

"Tell me."

"The container was for caffeine powder. Then I knew Thom killed Juliana. He killed her with caffeine powder."

The unreachable part of my brain communicated a feeling—Brit was telling the truth. I let that sink in a moment then said, "After you saw the container, then what happened?"

"I was sad. And angry. I got in my car to leave, and Thom came outside and asked what I was doing. I said I had to go. He asked why, and I started crying and said I knew what he did. He either didn't understand what I was talking about or pretended he didn't understand. He tried to talk to me but I rolled up my window and started the car. Then he got in front of it to look at me through the windshield. I hated him so much then. He banged on the hood of my car and yelled at me. I drove forward to make him back off. I drove forward until he was pinned against the garage door."

Brit squeezed my hands and said, "It was the middle of the day on Nichols Canyon. No one was around. No houses across the street. He yelled. I could hear him through the windshield. He said I was crazy. He said I didn't know what I was talking about. I was crying so hard. I couldn't catch my breath. I couldn't see. Then my boot slipped off the brake. The car moved forward. Thom screamed and I panicked. I slammed my boot down on the brake. But it wasn't the brake. It was the gas."

Brit's soul drifted away from her body. Her eyes went blank.

I said, "Thank you for telling me that, Brit. You're a good friend."

Brit returned to her body. She found my eyes and said, "I'm a bad person. I drove away and didn't tell anyone what I did. Or what Thom did."

"You told me."

"Because you're my friend."

"Yes, Brit. I'm your friend."

39

We walked back downstairs and returned to the party. Brit saw the executive from CBS and proceeded to pitch her the series about the down-and-out actress turned private investigator. I went back outside, found a quiet spot with a multimillion-dollar view, checked my phone to confirm it had recorded Brit's confession, and emailed it from NilsShapiro@gmail.com to NilsShapiro@yahoo.com so it was backed up on two servers. I called Ellegaard to relay what I'd learned then texted him the audio recording of Brit's confession. It wouldn't be admissible in court, but I doubted that, when sober, Brit would change her story.

I left Brit in Sebastiano's care and, half an hour later, parked a couple hundred yards from Thom Burke's house. He'd kept his garbage and recycling on the side of his house. I walked past that and, toward the back corner, saw a wooden box with a hinged lid. I pulled my latex gloves from my front jeans pocket and snapped them on. I lifted the lid on the box. It was still full. The police had gone through Thom's garbage and recycling, but didn't check a wooden box that looked like where you'd keep hoses. If they had, they would have seen a white, plastic container buried under a few layers of Perrier bottles. I removed the bottles one by one until I had a clean look at the plastic container. I stuck my flashlight into the box and turned it on. The white plastic container had a simple, almost generic-looking label: 100,000 milligrams of caffeine powder. That's equal to 1,000 Red Bulls. A teaspoon of the stuff can kill a person.

Brit's story appeared to be true.

I replaced the Perrier bottles, walked back to my car, called Detective Montanio to tell her I had some information she'd want and asked if I could buy her a cup of coffee. Half an hour later, we sat in House of Pies in Los Feliz. The place was old school. Brown vinyl-upholstered booths, a cheap suspended ceiling, a counter with simple stools, a refrigerated glass case of pies. The clientele was a mix of working class and hipster. Montanio looked tired.

I said, "Long day, I know."

"This had better be good, Shapiro."

"It is. I promise. But before I tell you, I'd like to ask you a favor."

"What a surprise."

A too-good-looking server wearing a maroon apron took our order, filled our cups with coffee, and disappeared.

I said, "I'd like you to share a simple piece of information with me in exchange for what I'm about to tell you."

"I don't know if I can do that."

"I'm hoping you can because I'm going to tell you who killed Thom Burke."

"I know who killed Thom Burke. He's got Ebben Mayer and—"

"No."

"No?"

"Vasily Zaytzev did not kill Thom Burke."

Mariana Montanio emptied a tiny plastic cup of cream into her coffee, stirred it, and looked at me with eyes so dead you'd think I'd just told her my five-year goals. She said nothing, hoping I'd elaborate. It's a good technique. I did the same. A full minute went by, then the server dropped a slice of banana cream pie in front of me and one of those fresh strawberry globs in front of Detective Montanio. It looked more like fruit than pie, and I felt sorry for her.

My slice was halfway gone when she gave up and said, "If your story holds up, I'll share what I can."

"That's all I'm asking. You're going to get a murder cleared off your board either way."

Detective Montanio and two crime scene unit investigators met me at Thom Burke's house. The crime scene unit investigators emptied the wooden box one bottle at a time, bagging and tagging each for analysis at the lab. After processing twenty or so green glass bottles, they removed a white, plastic container with a simple, almost generic-looking label.

Detective Montanio nodded, looked at me, and said, "Come talk to me, Shapiro." We walked to the far end of the driveway where it met Nichols Canyon. She said, "What do you want to know?"

"How did you and Hall learn about *Veins of Gold*?"

She looked down, sighed, and looked back up. "We found a budget and script on Thom's computer."

"I bet he had a lot of budgets and scripts on his computer. That was his job, breaking down scripts into budgets and shooting schedules."

She nodded. "You ever see a movie budget?"

I couldn't tell her about the *Veins of Gold* budget I'd found in Thom's home office. "Yeah, at Ebben's. They're thick. I don't understand anything except the final number."

"Well, if you weren't afraid to read the thick part of the budget, you'd see all sorts of interesting things like who's starring in the movie and who's the executive producer."

"Thom Burke was the executive producer?"

"And guess who was supposed to star?"

"Kate Lennon."

"You're a crack detective, Shapiro."

"About time you noticed."

She smiled. "Except for one thing. You said back at the police station that the budget was $15 million. You misread it. Total budget was 20 million."

"For *Veins of Gold*?"

She nodded.

Then I understood everything. Well, almost everything.

I returned to Sebastiano's house a little after 12:30 A.M. The party had not thinned, and Sebastiano and Debra still sat at their round table on the patio.

Sebastiano saw me and put on his best smile. "Nils, you're back. Any word on Ebben?"

"No. Not yet. But I'd like to ask you a favor."

"Ask away."

"I want to talk to Kate Lennon."

40

I woke to an Ellegaard text informing me that Vasily sent Ebben's parents a video of Ebben with C-SPAN on the TV in the background, proving Ebben was alive and well other than he had to watch C-SPAN. Vasily added that if he didn't receive the money by sunrise tomorrow, he'd shoot Ebben in the head.

I hopped in the rental Land Rover, plugged the address into my nav app, and left Hancock Park at 8:00 A.M. It took one hour to drive five miles. After a quick pass through a full parking lot, I circled through an alley to Riverside Drive and parked a block away from the restaurant. In my short time in Los Angeles, I'd learned you could wait for a parking spot for fifteen minutes, or you could park a block away and walk two minutes. It seemed I was the only one who preferred the latter.

Hugo's in Valley Village sits near Riverside and Coldwater on a corner shared by two gas stations and a Whole Foods. It was 9:00 A.M. and crowded. Twenty or so people clumped in twos, threes, and fours waiting for tables. I spotted her in the back corner under a logo-free white baseball cap, her ponytail sticking out the back. She wore a jean jacket over a black T-shirt, khaki pants, and Adidas that looked like they had built-in socks. She already had a hot beverage in an oversized mug. She sipped from it, two handed, while studying the menu.

I walked up to the table and said, "Ms. Lennon?"

She looked up with big brown eyes and spoke in a smoky voice. "Nils Shapiro. Nice to meet you."

We shook hands and I sat across from her. She looked like the person I'd seen in the movies except her head looked too big for her tiny body. Maybe that's what made her photogenic. She said, "Have you been here before? Their breakfast salad is perfect."

"I haven't been anywhere before and I've never heard of a breakfast salad."

"Never been anywhere before? Welcome to the big beautiful world."

"Thank you."

The server came and took our orders then Kate Lennon and I chatted about where we came from and what happened after high school and a few topics in the news then our breakfast salads came and looked delicious and they were. If I had to guess, she was trying to assess whether or not she could trust me. I'd experienced that kind of seemingly idle chitchat with other, if not famous, highly accomplished and well-off people. Every day someone wanted something from them. An acquaintance starting a business or a charity or a down-on-their-luck relative or a private investigator.

Her agent had told her I only wanted answers to a few questions, none personal. That coupled with a thorough deployment of her bullshit detector and she was ready to talk.

"So," she said, "you have a few questions for me?"

"Just a few. I promise."

The server swung by, refilled my coffee, asked Kate if she wanted another bath-sized latte. She declined.

"Did you have any involvement in a movie project called *Veins of Gold*?"

She smiled. "Oh boy."

"You've heard of it."

"Oh yes. I met Thom Burke. He was an associate producer or something on a movie I shot last year. It's not out yet and they keep changing the title so I don't even know what it's called. He seemed like a nice enough guy and told me he was making a movie about the gold rush and asked if he could send me a script. I said sure because what else am I going to say? I figured the script would suck and I'd bow out gracefully. It happens all the time. Have you read the script?"

I said, "No. I haven't seen it."

"Well, shocker—it's pretty good. And the part was great. The story is about a super interesting time in U.S. history and the foundation of today's struggles for equality. Two huge things happened within one year. California was a part of Mexico until 1848 then it became a territory of the United States. So the Mexican nationals, called Californios, who had lived on the land for generations peacefully alongside Native Americans, were all of a sudden shit out of luck because they weren't Mexicans anymore and they weren't Americans. They had no country. Then gold was discovered and white people poured in from all over the world, and within a few years, San Francisco saw its population boom from like 300 to 300,000. The settlers viewed the Californios and Native Americans as obstacles to getting rich. And neither the Californios nor Native Americans had any government representation or power, so the settlers pushed them out and took their land."

"Guns, germs, and steel."

"Exactly. And San Francisco attracted women seeking freedoms that weren't available anywhere else. Like in the eastern United States and Europe, women were second-class citizens. They couldn't own a business or property. But because of San Francisco's huge influx of male fortune hunters, the city of San Francisco enticed women to move West by abolishing the shit that held 'em back. Women were suddenly free to start businesses and own property. It's pretty interesting."

"So you agreed to do the part?"

"Eh, kind of sort of. I gave Thom a window where I was free and said I was inclined to do it. But there were a ton of moving pieces in my schedule, then this fucking fantastic script came my way called *For the People*. Really powerful. And it's the first project of something called The Creative Collective, which I want to be a part of, so I told Thom I couldn't do *Veins of Gold* in that original window and I have like four projects lined up right after *For the People* so it would be at least a few years until I'm free again."

"How did Thom take the news?"

"I had my agent tell him, but the report I got back was Thom begged me to reconsider. Guess he sounded pretty desperate.

But I was super clear with him that I wasn't attached to the movie. We never had a contract. I said don't raise money using my name. But I think he did."

"How do you know?"

"He told me he'd escrowed the entire cost of production. The money was ready to go. He even offered to pay me before principal photography. My whole fee. That never happens. Seemed pretty strange. Have you met Thom?"

"Yes."

"The police told me he died, but they didn't tell me how."

"Hit by a car."

"Oh my God. Where?"

"His driveway."

41

I left Kate Lennon in Hugo's and got in the Land Rover and headed west to Subaru of Sherman Oaks on Van Nuys Boulevard, a street so wide you took a risk crossing it without trail mix and a bottle of water. The dealership was a converted industrial space of red brick with an arched wooden ceiling. It was open and friendly and seemed more appropriate for an ad agency or artists' loft.

A young woman approached and asked if I needed help. I asked if I could speak to a manager.

She said, "Is there a problem?"

"Not at all. Just have a general question about accepted methods of payment."

"I can help you with that."

She seemed like a knowledgeable, responsible sort, so I said, "Can I buy a car with cash?"

"Of course. You don't have to finance. Just write a personal check and—"

"I'm sorry. I meant, can I buy a car with actual cash money? No check."

"Oh. Well, anything more than $10,000 and we have to report it to the IRS, which is kind of a pain. And I'm not implying anything by this, we love to sell cars—that's why we're here—but we'd rather not sell to someone who may have acquired their money illegitimately. That's not a big problem for us. Most drug dealers or what-have-you don't aspire to drive Subarus."

"So you don't take cash?"

"Our finance department suggests instead of cash that the buyer uses a debit card or even prepaid credit cards. One guy bought his Outback on prepaid credit cards. Something like seventy $500 cards. It took the cashier over an hour to process the sale."

"$35,000 in gift cards?"

"Yes. I saw them. Prepaid Visa cards and Mastercards and American Express. You can buy them at CVS. It was crazy."

LAPD detectives Hall and Montanio offered me a deal—I had to buy them lunch in exchange for their time. They suggested some place with a French name near Highland and Melrose, as if I knew where that was. But my phone found it, and I parked at a meter three blocks away and had the sidewalk to myself the entire walk. The restaurant was tiny. It didn't even have tables. Just one counter against the left wall and the bar and kitchen against the right wall.

It was decorated early 1900s with dark wood and wallpaper and light from glass globes. We arrived early enough that we didn't have to wait for a spot. The hostess led us to our seats, and the detectives made a tactical error. They thought they were suckering me into paying for an expensive lunch, but in doing so they chose a restaurant where I could sit between them. There were only three stools available. I stepped forward and took the middle one. Hall sat to my left. Montanio to my right.

The hostess asked if we wanted bread and butter. Hall said, "That's the only reason we're here."

The hostess smiled and left.

Montanio said, "So we're guessing you want to know what happened this morning with Brit."

"Not why I wanted to talk to you but I'm happy to listen."

"She spilled," said Hall. "The whole story just as you relayed it. So thanks for lunch and thanks for that."

"Is the D.A. going to charge it as a homicide?"

"Don't know yet. Don't much care either. A murder was on our board. Now it's not. So why are we gracing you with our presence?"

"Ebben Mayer has eighteen hours to live."

"All the law enforcement in this town is combing the city. We can't find him and that Vasily guy anywhere."

"Yeah, I've noticed. That's why I want you to use the 15 million from Thom Burke's safe-deposit box to pay Ebben Mayer's ransom."

Montanio said, "Are you fucking crazy? Why the hell would we give Vasily $15 million?"

"Because it's his money."

Montanio and Hall tried to communicate but my seat between them got in the way.

Montanio said, "That asshole never had no 15 million. That's why he kidnapped a rich dude."

I said nothing. The server brought the bread and butter. I thought Hall was kidding about it being the only reason we were there, but after one bite I said, "This is the best thing I've ever eaten."

Hall said, "They fly the butter in from Normandy. Fucking France. It don't get better than this."

I ordered a croque monsieur and my detective friends ordered a couple of entrées each and wine and a side of frites for me because Hall said, "You don't go to this joint and not get the motherfucking frites. You just don't."

Montanio said, "How in the hell could the 15 mil be Vasily's? Plus, he's asking for 20 mil. According to my North Hollywood High math, that leaves 5 mil missing."

I swallowed a bite of bread and butter and said, "Here's what I think happened: Vasily invested $20 million with Thom Burke to make *Veins of Gold*. I agree with you that there's no way the 20 million was Vasily's. He was the go-between, investing it for someone else. Could be someone local trying to cover their tracks. Could be a Russian oligarch who's been sanctioned by the U.S. government and can't legally do business in this country. Kind of doesn't matter who it is at this point.

"What does matter is that Vasily probably convinced the person to make the investment. So Vasily's on the hook. The whole deal was predicated on Kate Lennon being cast in the lead role, but Thom never had a contract with her. Kate Lennon was inclinded to start in *Veins of Gold* but dropped out because she fell in love with Brit Dawsey's *For the People* script and she wanted to work with Ebben Mayer and The Creative Collective."

Hall said, "That kind of thing happens every day."

Montanio said, "So no Kate Lennon, no *Veins of Gold*."

"Exactly. Now the investor wants his money back. Vasily goes to Thom and says no *Veins of Gold*, give me the money back. But it's not so simple."

Montanio sipped her wine and said, "And why is that?"

"Thom made two budgets for *Veins of Gold*. One for $20 million, and one for $15 million. He showed Vasily the $20 million budget, but the actual shooting budget was for 15 million."

Montanio said, "The son of a bitch skimmed 5 million."

"That's how it looks to me. And maybe Thom already spent it or part of it or maybe not. Maybe he just didn't want to give it back. Either way, he tells Vasily to hold tight. He's going to get Kate Lennon back for *Veins of Gold*. And how do you think he tries to do that?"

"Kill Ebben Mayer," said Montanio, her mouth full of bread. "Make it look like a caffeine overdose."

"Fucking A," said Hall.

I said, "My guess is Thom gets to Ebben Mayer by saying he'll work for no upfront money, you know, in the spirit of The Creative Collective. Now Thom has access to Ebben. He sees Ebben sucking down energy drinks all day. So he uses his access to slip Ebben caffeine powder—a teaspoon or two of the stuff is lethal—but somehow Ebben's fiancée Juliana ingests it instead."

Hall and Montanio thought it through, both nodding in silence. The tiny restaurant was filled now and loud with conversation and the clatter of forks and knives on plates. I said, "And think about this: since the 15 million was in cash, it seems likely the 5 million Thom skimmed is, too. And how's a guy like Thom Burke going to handle 5 million in cash? How's he going to hide it from the government? He's not a career criminal. He doesn't have the connections to launder that kind of money."

Hall said, "Offshore bank account?"

"Possible. Did you find any paperwork in his files or anything on his computer that referenced an offshore account?"

Hall and Montanio looked at each other. Again, my seat was advantageous, not to block their communication but participate in it.

I said, "I didn't think so. And an offshore account seems too complicated for Thom Burke. He was all about simple. All about practical."

Hall said, "Maybe he bought cryptocurrencies."

"Nah," said Montanio. "Too volatile. Too risky. Too complicated."

I agreed and said, "I think Thom planned on living the rest of his life on the 5 million, dollar by dollar."

Montanio said, "You really think that much money is hidden somewhere in cash?"

"Yes." I buttered another chunk of baguette. "Thom Burke bought a new Subaru. Didn't have license plates yet. But the plate holders were an ad for Subaru of Sherman Oaks. I went there this morning and asked if it was possible to buy a car with actual cash. The salesperson said they try to avoid it. If a customer insists, they suggest a debit card or prepaid credit cards."

"Fuck," said Hall. "That's the way to launder money these days. Gift cards and prepaid credit cards. There's a whole market for 'em online."

"And just out of curiosity I went to a CVS. You can buy a prepaid credit card for up to $500. Cash. You can stop into a CVS, a Target, a Rite Aid, a Von's and pick up a few gift cards at each and launder four, five grand a day that way."

Hall said, "But Thom probably only scratched the surface of that 5 mil."

"I'm guessing 100 grand at the most. Could be half that."

Montanio said, "So there's 4.9 million in his house?"

"It's worth a search."

Hall and Montanio looked at each other a long time. Too long.

Hall said, "You think we should convince our CO to send a platoon of detectives to Thom Burke's house and search it for $5 million?"

"Yes. And to release the original $15 million for Ebben Mayer's ransom. Vasily's desperate. He's dead if he doesn't pay back the 20 million. But paying 15 million would at least buy him a little time."

"Can't do it, Shapiro. Our CO will never go for it, and we ain't sticking our necks out to fight for it. Got to choose your battles. Know what I'm saying?"

"I know exactly what you're saying."

Montanio looked at Hall. I kept my eyes down. I knew what was happening. To confirm it I said, "LAPD all right with me leaving town now?"

"Please do," said Hall. "It was nice knowing you."

Our food came. Croque monsieur for me. An omelet and chicken leg for Montanio. A cheeseburger and escargot for Hall. And three orders of frites. Hall and Montanio each ordered a second glass of wine. As good as our entrées were, nothing could beat the baguette and butter when we first sat down. Too bad I couldn't enjoy any of it.

We chitchatted through the meal then went our separate ways, Hall and Montanio full-bellied and buzzed on French wine, and me with a lunch receipt for $227 that would be reimbursed by Ebben Mayer.

If he lived.

42

I drove back to the big house in Hancock Park, grabbed a few supplies, then texted my best friend in Los Angeles. Jameson White waited for me on the front steps of Dr. Li's house. He got in the Land Rover and said, "You want me to drive?"

"No need. I'm getting the hang of it."

"Oooh, look at you! Minnesota boy driving in La La Land! I sure as hell hope your right foot put on a few pounds because last night you did not keep up with traffic. I'm surprised you didn't get shamed off the road. What in the hell are you looking at?"

"Jameson White. As I know and love him."

"Shut your mouth, Nils Shapiro. You and me, we're friends. That is all."

"Buckle up and tell me where to go."

We drove five minutes to California Surplus Mart on Santa Monica Boulevard and Vine. Shortest drive in L.A. by far. We bought matching navy blue coveralls with color-coordinated caps, two duffel bags, and some equipment. We zipped ourselves into the coveralls then Jameson directed me to drive about a mile to Anawalt Lumber for tools.

When we got back in the Land Rover, the afternoon sun had baked the interior. I lowered the windows. It didn't seem right turning on air-conditioning in January. Jameson sent us north on Highland. We drove in silence. I thought of turning around, going back to Ebben's house, grabbing my stuff and continuing to LAX. I was free to go home. Ebben Mayer's kidnapping shouldn't have been my problem. The problem belonged to his parents and grandparents, to the LAPD and the FBI. But they were in negotiation mode. They didn't understand Vasily had no room to negotiate. He owed someone $20 million. Someone dangerous. Not repaying that money would cost Vasily his life. None of the players understood Vasily's desperation. None of them had seen all that fear concentrated in his one eye.

I didn't want the responsibility. I didn't need it. But the burden had infected me like a virus, and I was stuck with it until it ran its course. I stopped the car and said, "Grab the stuff. I'll meet you around back."

Jameson said, "Why'd you stop at the house? Shouldn't we park far away?"

"I'm dropping you at the house. I'll park down the canyon."

"Oh, I get it. Can't have a black man walking around in broad daylight."

"I was thinking more like can't have a six-foot-seven man walking around in broad daylight."

Jameson White said, "I think we should wait until tonight."

"Too risky. Pretty sure Hall and Montanio will be here to-night."

Jameson shook his head. "You really think two LAPD detectives will try to steal $5 million?"

"I think those two will. Los Angeles isn't different than any-where else. There are honest cops. And there are not-so-honest cops. Montanio and Hall are the latter."

"Why don't we just tell the honest cops? They can stake out the place. Wait for Hall and Montanio to find the money and bust 'em."

"You can't count on cops to bust other cops. Even the good cops. Chances are one would tip off Hall and Montanio and they'd deny the whole thing. And worse, they wouldn't cooper-ate with me anymore. Better for us to do this now."

Jameson grabbed our purchases out of the tailgate and headed around back of Thom Burke's house. He seemed to be in no hurry, like a house inspector or HVAC repairman. And some-thing about brand-new blue coveralls says legit. Nothing suspi-cious. Just a person doing their job.

I parked a few hundred yards away, less for the neighbors and more for the police if they happened to drive by, then met Jameson behind the house. A bistro table under a large umbrella on a patio of fabricated stone. A simple hedge. A bubbling fountain. A tiny patch of lawn. Something about the landscaping made me think Thom Burke had done the work himself. It appeared profession-ally done, but the materials looked like something you'd buy at Home Depot. Maybe he bought the materials and hired the labor.

I picked the garage's service door lock. Jameson said, "You think Thom would have hidden the money in here?"

"Maybe. But right now I'm looking to see what kind of tools he had."

"What for? We brought our own tools."

"That's not what I'm curious about. I want to know if Thom was handy."

The garage had a workbench under a wall of pegboard filled with hand tools. Power tools, stored in their original boxes, filled a shelf underneath.

"Shit," said Jameson. "He was handy like a handyman. That money could be in the walls. Or in the floors."

"I don't think so."

"Then why the hell did we look for tools?"

"To get a feel for Thom's aptitude. I bet he hid the money in a place that's accessible so he could take from it little by little. But accessible doesn't mean obvious, and that's where Thom's aptitude comes in."

"Accessible as in not-buried?"

I said, "Or not buried deeply. And it's probably in a fireproof safe."

We started in the backyard with the new metal detector we'd purchased at California Surplus. We found a few nails and a buried dog collar with tags but no safe. So much for a quick job. We snapped on our latex gloves.

I picked the back door lock. The last time we were in Thom's house we saw only what our red-cellophaned flashlights allowed us to see. In daylight, I learned Thom Burke wasn't the kind of person to get rid of things. His house was clean but cluttered. Too much furniture. None of it appealing. Too much art on the walls. None of it actually art. The kind of stuff you'd see at a flea market. Too many electronics. Even the obsolete machines like square TVs and cassette tape decks. Retro electronics can set a mood, an analog vibe reminiscent of when listening to music was a deliberate act that required physical interaction to select and play music long before Siri or Alexa were born. But Thom's retro electronics weren't that—they just looked like junk. Thom Burke had stuff. He didn't have taste.

We split up and started with the obvious, going from room to room, looking under rugs and behind anything hanging on the wall for an in-floor or in-wall safe. We looked behind pictures. We looked behind wall-mounted flat-screen TVs. Nothing. We removed vent covers and checked the ductwork. Nothing. Outside, the California sunshine softened from blue-white to gold.

Jameson White shook his big head. "Man, we'll have to take this house apart nail by nail. It's almost five o'clock. Shap, you said the money would be in a safe and the safe would be accessible."

"Well, I might have been wrong. It's been known to happen."

"It sure the hell has." Jameson sighed a big sigh and said, "I'd think the dude would take a different approach to hide something he knew people might be looking for than to hide something no one knew existed." I wasn't quite sure what he meant. It must have registered on my face. "Okay, if Thom thought people knew he was hiding 5 million in his house, he'd make it impossible to find, like put it in the bricks of the foundation and you'd have to dismantle the structure to get at it. But Thom thought nobody knew he was hiding 5 million because he skimmed it from the movie budget. Vasily thought that money was going into the production according to the $20 million budget. The production had all the money according to the $15 million budget. Only Thom knew he had $5 million. That means no one would be looking for it, so he could hide it in a jar of cookies or something like that."

"Five million dollars wouldn't fit in a jar of cookies."

"I said or something like that. You definitely wouldn't put it in anything a burglar might steal, which is just about nothing in this house. Haven't seen so much junk since I visited my aunt Clara—I know, *Bewitched* had an Aunt Clara but so did I—and she hoarded shit like she wanted to be the star of that hoarders show. All she did was go to garage sales and bring home more crap and clean it with Q-tips while watching *The Price Is Right* and *Let's Make a Deal*. Visiting her was like— Why you got that stupid grin on your face?"

43

We bought a bag full of tools and the only one we needed was a Phillips screwdriver. The TV was a Sony from the last millennium. Big and deep with a forty-inch screen. We popped the back off and Jameson White said, "Damn you, Nils Shapiro. Of all the shit in this house, how'd you know it was in the TV?"

A steel safe about eighteen inches square filled the inside of the old Sony. Thom Burke had gutted the TV's components to make room for it, even cutting the back off the cathode ray tube. The safe looked like one you'd buy from a discount office supply store. It was probably waterproof and fireproof, but far from high security. Jameson pulled it out of the TV and lifted it. He guessed its weight somewhere around 125 pounds.

I said, "There's a bar in The Line Hotel decorated with analog equipment. Amps, receivers, speakers, turntables, vinyl, tape decks, reel-to-reel machines. Analog is cool. But only in audio. No one misses big, heavy, energy-hogging, shit-picture TVs. There's a flat-screen TV mounted in almost every room of this house. Why would Thom have kept an old, monstrous Sony?"

Half an hour later we were back in Hancock Park. Jameson called Dr. Li to say he'd be late, we watched a few instructional YouTube videos, then headed back to Anawalt Lumber. I returned everything I'd bought earlier and purchased the most powerful electric drill they sold, a few $500 drill bits, and a $1,500 magnetic drill press. We ate burgers on Larchmont, walked across the street and bought a burner phone at Rite Aid, then went back to Ebben's house and started drilling.

By 10:00 P.M., the safe was open and we were looking at almost $5 million in cash, gift cards, and prepaid credit cards.

Jameson said, "You going to call him or text him?"

It took a while typing out text on the disposable flip phone. I had withheld one thing from the police—Vasily's burner number. I had a feeling I might need it. And I did.

Do you miss your .22 that goes pop? I still have it.

Twenty minutes later I got a response. *Buddy?*

The police have 15 mil of your money. I have the other 5. Will you return Ebben for 5?

How you have 5?

Thom skimmed 5 from the 20. Was going to make Veins of Gold for 15. He scammed you.

He lucky he dead.

Return Ebben. I will give you 5 million. You can disappear for 5 million. Start a new life.

I need 20. Fast.

R you safe?

No buddy.

Is Ebben ok?

For now.

I promise you the other 15. After Ebben is back.

Twenty now. Ebben is my only chance.

The police know you didn't kill Thom. They arrested the person who did. She confessed.

It took ten minutes for Vasily to respond. The text came from a different phone. He was switching burners in case anyone was trying to track him. *Need 20. They will find and kill me soon. Even if I have 5 million they find me.*

Who are they?

Twenty million tonight.

Bring Ebben home. No police. Five million will buy you time. Ebben will pay the other 15. Bring him home.

No response.

Vasily?

Nothing.

Jameson said, "Well?"

I showed him the texts. He shook his head. "Now what?"

"I'll go bail out Brit and give the remainder of the 5 million to the police. They'll log it in properly so it'll be safe. Then we wait for the police and FBI to do what they do."

"Hmm." Jameson folded his arms on his chest.

"What?"

"The old Nils Shapiro would have come up with something more clever."

"I'm sorry to disappoint you."

He shook his head. "End of an era."

I loaded the cash and prepaid credit cards into my carry-on luggage and said, "Come on. I'll give you a ride back to Dr. Li's."

I hated lying to Jameson White, but I saw no other way. We stopped at Salt & Straw for ice cream on Larchmont Boulevard, me wheeling my carry-on like a tourist, spot-checking to see if Vasily was following. He was not. There was a line in front of the ice cream shop. I do not line up for food, but I didn't mind because I was with Jameson. Didn't know when I'd see him again. Didn't know *if* I'd see him again. I had to push the thought away or I'd break down right there between the velvet ropes on the sidewalk outside the ice cream shop.

I said, "You ever going to visit me in Minnesota?"

"Let's not talk about that now."

"All right. Can we talk about how typical it is for a nurse to marry a doctor?"

"Nurse practitioner."

"Right."

The conversation went like that until we were inside. Then I saw why the line for ice cream crawled like rush-hour traffic. Every customer was sampling flavors with tiny spoons.

I said, "Sampling flavors is bullshit."

Jameson said, "What wrong with it?"

"You pick a flavor and you stick with it. Yeah, it's a little risky because you might pick . . ." I read the chalkboard above the servers. ". . . Silencio Black Tea & Coconut Stracciatella but wish you'd picked Cupcake Royale's Salted Caramel Cupcake. But that's part of the fun. And why the hell did we wait in line for these flavors? I don't even know what they mean."

"That's why you sample 'em."

"Where's the chocolate and vanilla and cookie dough? I don't have to sample those."

Jameson shook his head. "It's gourmet. They don't insult their clientele with the simple stuff."

We each sampled a few flavors, made our choices, and strolled Larchmont Boulevard toward Dr. Li's house, me pulling the carry-on behind me. Still no sign of Vasily. We walked in silence for a few minutes then I jabbed my spoon into my Smoked Sea Salt and Chocolate Crack and said, "I'm going to hug you goodbye."

"Yeah. I suppose you are."

That's what I did. The big guy hugged me back.

I said, "I'll miss you."

"Yeah."

"We're going to vacation together."

"When's the last time you took a vacation with a guy?"

"Never, because I didn't have one to vacation with."

"I suppose," said Jameson.

We said goodbye. I wheeled my carry-on back to Larchmont Boulevard and got in the car. Ten minutes later, I walked into the police station on Wilcox and bailed out Brit with $20,000 in cash.

I did not give the police the rest of the 5 million. I never intended to.

Brit got into the passenger seat and said, "You fucking saved me, Nils. Damn lawyer said she couldn't post bond until tomorrow morning. I thought I was going to spend the night in there."

"I figured if they hadn't let you go, they must have charged you."

"They did. About three hours ago. Manslaughter. Ugh." She

turned in her seat and looked at me. "Thank you again. I just want to crawl into bed and go to sleep."

"That's what you should do. But not at Ebben's."

"What? Why not?"

"You need to sleep somewhere else tonight. You'll be safe. Vasily has Ebben. He has no incentive to hurt anyone else."

"He knows where I live."

"So stay at a nice hotel. On me."

"No, I want to stay—"

"Brit. It's not happening. You have no choice."

She got small and quiet. We stopped at Ebben's to pick up a bag of her stuff. When she threw it in the car, she saw my carry-on and said, "Are you going home tonight?"

"Yeah."

"Why didn't you just tell me that?"

I didn't tell her that because it wasn't true. But I'd lied to Jameson, I should have had no problem lying to Brit. "I don't know. I don't really want to talk about it."

Brit closed the tailgate and returned to the passenger seat. "Wait a minute. Are you pissed at me because you bailed me out?"

"Not even close. It wasn't my money."

"Whose was it?"

"Vasily's."

"What? How is that possible?"

I said nothing and headed to the Peninsula hotel in Beverly Hills, gave her $3,000 in prepaid credit cards, and told her it would all be over in a day or two so she should relax, eat some good food, and go nuts at the spa.

In front of the hotel, suit-clad men appeared at both driver and passenger door. I rolled down my window and said, "Just dropping her off."

"Of course, sir."

Brit didn't move. She said, "Am I ever going to see you again?"

"Probably not."

"Well, what about my actress turned private investigator idea? Who's going to help me with that?"

I shrugged then got out of the Land Rover and grabbed her bag. The suit-clad man opened her door, and Brit stepped out. A man took the bag from me and wheeled it into the hotel.

Brit looked at me with wet eyes, shook her head, and hugged me hard. She sniffled in my ear and stepped back, gave me one last glance, and disappeared into the hotel. I got back into the car and drove east.

I took a circuitous route to make sure Vasily wasn't following and called Gabriella.

"I'm sorry I woke you."

Gabriella Nuñez said, "I'm glad you did. I miss you."

"I miss you, too. I love you so much." I didn't know who might be listening to this phone call—it's something you have to think about now. I said, "Can't wait until I see you again."

"When might that be?"

"Maybe tomorrow. Maybe the next day."

"Just maybe?"

I said, "You know I love you like I've never loved anyone, right?"

"I've heard rumors to that effect."

"The rumors are true."

"Good. And right back at ya, sailor. You taking care of your-self out there?"

"Trying my best."

Neither of us said anything for ten or fifteen seconds. Then Gabriella broke the silence. "I won't tell you to walk away from your job. I know how I'd respond if someone said that to me. But your lucrative paid vacation to California has changed into you being grossly underpaid to put yourself in harm's way. And dammit, Nils, you had better use your best judgment. You had better keep yourself safe. Not for you. Not even for Evelyn. But for me. Yes, I'm going to be selfish about this. You'd better come back to me. 'Cause it'll fuck me up if you don't. Got it?"

I took a few breaths and said, "Yes, ma'am."

"All right. Good night. Come home soon."

I didn't want to get off the phone with her, but I had one more call to make. I said, "Being grossly underpaid to put myself in harm's way is kind of what cops do."

I could hear her smile. "It's exactly what cops do."

"Good night, beautiful person. I love you."

"I love you, Nils."

I drove a few more blocks, circling back in a haphazard way to check for tails. Nothing. Stopped at a liquor store on Beverly and bought a bottle of Midleton. One hundred and eighty dollars, but the situation called for it, especially since it was Vasily's $180.

When I returned to the car, I called Ellegaard and woke him. He said, "Any word on Ebben?"

"Nothing new. Just wanted to say I should be wrapped up here soon regardless of what happens with Ebben. Only so much I can do."

"Hmm," said Ellegaard.

"Couple more things, then I'm done."

"I don't like the sound of that, Shap. That little talk we had in the office. I may have spoken without thinking things through all the way when I said you'd resent your family if you played it safe."

"You've thought everything through all the way since you were born."

"Nice of you to say. But playing it safe for me is different than playing it safe for you. And I didn't take that into consideration."

I said, "You want it stricken from the record?"

"Yes, please."

"I'll see you soon, Ellie. Go back to sleep."

"Don't call me Ellie. And I don't like the sound in your voice."

"Good night." I hung up before he could say another word. I circled around the block again. Still no tail. A few minutes later I parked in Ebben's driveway, grabbed my carry-on out of the tailgate, and rolled it through the front door. I went to the kitchen, found a solid lowball, and pressed it against a lever in the freezer door. Four ice cubes dropped into the glass. I usually take no ice. Sometimes one cube. But I needed that sound of ice tinkling in a glass of alcohol. Maybe I could have achieved it with water but it's not quite the same sound. I filled the lowball with Midleton. I took it into the living room, sat in a comfy chair, put my feet up, and texted Vasily. *Call me.*

44

LAPD detectives Hall and Montanio showed their true characters when they wouldn't go to their CO about the 5 million I suggested Thom Burke had skimmed and hidden in his house. The detectives were loud and clear. I could not trust them, and they didn't give a shit about me. Or Ebben Mayer. I considered calling my FBI friends at the Minneapolis Field Office so they could relay what I'd learned to the Los Angeles Field Office, but I didn't know the L.A. agents. And a field office, just like a police precinct, is only as good as its officers.

I considered setting a trap for Vasily. Law enforcement hiding in the closet and all that. But if taken into custody, he wouldn't talk. He was far more afraid of whoever invested the 20 million through him than he was of the police or FBI. And if he didn't talk, Ebben Mayer might starve to death wherever he was being held.

I thought of going to the press—maybe if they told my story local law enforcement would act properly. But that would lead to two things: Jameson and I would get arrested for breaking into Thom's house and stealing $5 million, and Vasily would become even more desperate.

Vasily was on the hook for $20 million. Whoever gave him the money wasn't the type to write it off as a bad investment. They were the type to make an example of Vasily one fingernail at a time. One bone at a time. One testicle at a time. Maybe he'd been there before. Maybe with someone who made an example of him one eye at a time.

Vasily was fighting for his life. A rat in a glue trap. He'd chew off his own foot to escape. He'd sacrifice Ebben Mayer.

The eye patch called twelve minutes after I'd texted him. From yet another burner. He said, "Buddy, when does my 20 million come?"

I held the lowball near the microphone of my phone. I swirled the ice. It sounded like a Fairy Godmother had just waved her wand. "Vasily, Ebben's family won't pay. His fiancée is dead. The FBI is trying to raise the money."

"Why FBI?"

"Kidnapping is a feral . . . federal offense . . ." I'd downed a couple ounces of alcohol, just enough to help me feel a slight buzz. The town was full of actors, but I wasn't one of them so I needed a little help. "So that's who you're dealing with. The motherfucking FBI." I slurped a sip of Midleton, held the phone away, and spit it onto my shirt. More ice tinkling in the glass. I could hear him thinking.

"Buddy, why you text me to call?"

"Come on, Vasily. You're being stubborn. Bring me Ebben, and I'll give you $5 million. Think of what you can do with that." I felt a burp rising in my chest. I let it escape. "Five million. You can disappear. Hey, you know where it's supposed to be just awesome now? Colombia. It's safe. And beautiful. And the women. Come on, man. You could live like a king for the rest of your life on 5 million in Colombia. A big house. A live-in maid. A chef. A pool surrounded by bikinis."

Vasily didn't respond. I planted an idea, but he had to cultivate it, make it take root. He said, "I think about it. When could you get money?"

"That's the best part! I have it. Now."

"When bank opens."

"No! I have it. I found it at Thom's. Hidden in a safe that was inside an old TV."

"I don't want safe. I want 5 million."

"No, no, no. Vasily, you don't understand." More tinkling. Another sip. I held the phone away and spit it out. "It wasn't a high-security safe. Average piece of shit you'd buy at Office Universe or one of those kinds of places. I drilled the shit out of it and opened it in less than an hour. I have the 5 mil in cash. Well, 4.9 something of it and 20,000 of it is in prepaid credit cards but those work just like cash. Even better. Because you can buy airline tickets with them."

"Buddy, you have 4.9 million. Right now? In cash and cards?"

"Yes. In Ebben's living room. Come on, Vasily. Bring Ebben home. I'm tired." After a long pause, I said, "Vasily? You still there?"

He said, "Go sleep, buddy. I call in morning." He hung up.

I walked to the kitchen, uncorked the bottle of Midleton, poured some down the sink and some on my clothes, then re-filled my glass. I went to the back door to make sure it was un-locked then returned to the comfy chair in the living room to wait next to my roller bag filled with money.

My phone battery was close to its end-of-day death. I plugged it in, checked my email, sent one to Ellegaard I was sure he wouldn't see until morning, read some news, avoided social me-dia in case anyone was paying attention, drank more whiskey, read some more news.

The back door opened.

I'd left all the lights on, but had drawn the blinds. It was 1:02 A.M. I felt tired but my head was clear. My heart fluttered. My glass was three quarters full. I took one big sip. Footsteps in the kitchen. One set of footsteps. Even if Vasily had brought Ebben, he would have left him bound and gagged in the car. But I doubted he brought Ebben. Ebben was Vasily's ticket to staying alive.

My eyelids felt heavy. I let them droop.

"Buddy."

I looked up. Vasily stood at the other end of the living room.

He said, "You awake. Why no sleep?"

"Thinking of getting in the hot tub. But just thinking about it. What are you doing here? How'd you get in?"

"Door not locked. Walked in. Buddy. You drunk."

"Eh. Long day. Just relaxing."

"I saw bottle in kitchen. Half gone. You little man."

"Join me. There's vodka if you're feeling homesick."

"I not drink tonight. Another time."

"I thought we were friends. Friends drink together."

"You put hot stick in my neck. Not friends."

"You shot Jameson."

"He okay. We make trade now."

"All right. Get Ebben."

"No, buddy. You show money."

"I have the money, Vasily." I belched, rubbed my chest and winced. "I need to see Ebben to make sure he's all right."

"He fine. I promise you. All good. Buddy. Is that money?" He pointed to the roller bag next to my comfy chair. "The 5 million? In there?"

I stood. "You can't have it unless you give me Ebben."

"Just you here, buddy. I see no more cars."

"Bring me Ebben."

"Buddy. I'm going to take money." He stepped closer, kept his eye on my hands, then looked up to my eyes. He walked toward me. Calm and steady.

I feigned drunkenness to legitimize my poor judgment in telling Vasily the money was at the house sitting in the living room all ready to go. Now I had to put up a legitimate fight. At least in appearance. I couldn't hold back. Vasily needed to hear the whiskey's effects in my speech, smell it on my breath and on my clothing. The big wild card had yet to be revealed: whether or not Vasily had brought a gun. Brit's bear spray lay sandwiched between chair and cushion. It would stay there unless I felt he intended to execute me.

I said, "Who fronted the 20 million?"

"Go to sleep, buddy."

"Why would you be the middleman? What's in it for you?" I took another sip of whiskey.

He said, "You Americans can no drink. Why you not learn?

Too many laws. Wait till twenty-one. In Europe kids drink wine and beer. It nothing. When turn twenty-one not care anymore. You stupid drunk now. Like little boy. Why not America learn?"

"Vasily, why are you involved in *Veins of Gold*? There's no writing credit on the screenplay. Did you write it?"

"Buddy. Shut face. I take money now." I stood. He stepped into my personal space. "No big man come save you now. No hot metal stick. Sit down, Nils Shapiro. Sit now or I make you sit."

I did not sit. "Bring Ebben and you can have the money." Vasily said nothing. He put his left hand in the pocket of his leather jacket. I said, "What are you doing? Why didn't you bring Ebben? Did something go wrong? Did Ebben escape? Or is he dead, Vasily? Did something go wrong? Did you kill him?"

Vasily's left arm twitched. I didn't know if he was about to pull out a gun or a knife but this was my chance to put up my best fight. I swung hard with my left hand. Vasily spun away, my fist grazing his chin. When he turned back toward me I saw what was in his left hand. Brass knuckles. Fuck. I lunged at him. He threw a punch into my midsection. It hurt like hell, but I kept my wind and threw another punch, which he ducked. I lost my balance, and Vasily came back at me with an elbow into my chest.

The last time I'd been in a fight was in sparring class at the Minneapolis Police Academy. So never, really. That was eighteen years ago. I was young, quick, and fully padded. And I still stunk at fighting.

I dove back toward the chair, crashed into it, and grabbed my lowball off the end table. I spun around, cocked my arm, and Vasily stepped back. He smiled and said, "Buddy. Put down glass."

I couldn't fight but I could throw. I may have pitched beyond high school if I'd weighed more than 140 pounds. And two-plus decades later, my aim was true. I'd proven it within the last month throwing snowballs at trees while snowshoeing with Gabriella. But Vasily didn't know that. So I threw hard just left of his head. His missing eye robbed him of depth perception, and he lifted his arms to shield his face. He heard the lowball shatter on the wall fifteen feet behind him. He lowered his arms, his eye filled with fury. He rushed at me hard.

This was me playing it safe. Before Gabriella and Evelyn, I would've drawn Vasily to the 5 million, let him take it from an empty house, and followed him back to Ebben. Once there I would've tried to rescue Ebben myself. Maybe I would have called in backup if I knew someone in L.A. I could trust the way I trust Gabriella or Ellegaard or Annika. Jameson was in L.A. but he wasn't trained for a situation like this. Either way, I would've made sure I learned Ebben Mayer's location firsthand.

Instead, I put myself in a minimum amount of danger and hoped it would work out for Ebben. I put my safety above his. And on paper, this was the safest way to play it. But even the safest way meant some risk. Hell, we all take some risk. Every day of our lives. Luck goes our way. Or it doesn't.

Vasily head-butted me. My nose split and, just as the pain started to register, I saw a flash of metal in my right eye. That was the last image I remember.

45

I cannot see but I can hear. Sometimes. Other times I fall asleep inside my sleep. The doctors and nurses talk to me. They tell me what they're doing. I feel something on my arm—a nurse says they're taking my blood pressure. I feel a sting on the back of my hand—a nurse says they're changing my IV. I feel my weight on my right side—a nurse says they're adjusting my position so I don't get bedsores. A different nurse tells a doctor, "This one can hear us. I'm sure of it. Not all of them can, but you can see him twitch when you ask him questions."

A different nurse tells me everything. He says he's wheeling me to imaging. My brain is bleeding and swollen, which puts pressure on my brain stem and that caused the coma. They're going to put me in the MRI and see if things are getting better or worse. He jokes it can be claustrophobic in there but coma patients don't seem to mind. He says after, if I'm good, some visitors want to see me.

I can hear the machine buzz and make clicking noises. I think about Vasily. I trusted him because he didn't kill Jameson when he could have. He shot Jameson in the leg. He had a clear shot. He had time. He seemed more than comfortable and capable with a gun. But he shot Jameson in the leg. Not the head. Not the torso. And Jameson has a huge torso. I think I was right to trust Vasily. He just got in a lucky punch. Or was it unlucky? Happened to hit me in the wrong spot. The brass knuckles helped, but he was not trying to kill me. If he wanted to kill me he would have brought a gun or a knife. He said he could get a Minnesota's driver's license in two hours. He could have gotten a gun in half that time.

Bad luck. It happens. Like good luck. And I've had plenty of that. Like when Brit took the ecstasy and told me she killed Thom. That was good luck. Right place. Right time. You got to take the bad with the good.

I fall asleep within my sleep. I don't know for how long. I wake within my sleep, and a doctor tells a nurse not to get too attached to me—my twitches are nothing more than muscle spasms.

I feel no fear. I'm halfway there, unconscious yet conscious in my cocoon, like I'm in a car waiting in line to cross the border from the United States into Canada. Canada is right in front of me. I can see it. I could get out of my car and walk there in one minute. But you're not allowed to get out of your car. So I wait and inch closer one car at a time. I want to laugh but can't. I want to laugh because I think of how Canadians would feel if they knew I likened entering their country to dying. But I would tell them how much I love Canada because I really do and likening death to Canada must be a message from the part of my brain I can't reach. A message that says death is like going to a place you love.

The nurse says I'm one lucky son of a gun because I have a private room and only lucky people have private rooms 'cause they have the good health insurance. I want to tell him Ellegaard is the one to thank for that. Ellegaard always takes care of me, like I'm part of his family. And there it is again: luck. I'm so lucky to have Ellegaard as a friend. I'm so lucky to have good health insurance. But luck has to balance out over time. The good with the bad. If Vasily had hit me just a quarter of an inch away from where he did, I'd be fine. If he had swung differently. If I had positioned myself differently. If, if, if. It can't go your way all the time.

The nurse says, "Nils, it's your lucky day. You have some visitors." He tells the visitors they should talk to me because he's sure I can hear them. And they should watch my face to see if it twitches because sometimes it does. And they should hold my hand and pay attention because they might feel a slight squeeze. Maybe not but they might. Then the nurse says, "I'm out of here now, Nils. Tawny will be checking on you and I'll see you tomorrow. You have a good rest of your day, and I'll let everyone here introduce themselves."

It's quiet for a moment then I hear, "You don't look so good, Shap." It's Ellegaard. He takes my hand. I try to squeeze it but I don't know if he can feel it. I feel like I can control my body but I can't. I wonder if I'm already dead. But why would people talk to me if I'm dead?

I hear sobbing, but it's not Ellegaard. He's my stoic Scandinavian. Everyone should have one. If Ellegaard ever cries, he probably rows out to the middle of a lake and cries with the loons. Never in public. No, this crier is Gabriella. She hasn't said a word, but I can tell it's her.

This is weird. I don't like this part at all. I'm okay in here. I'm not in pain. I'm not afraid. Yeah, I want to see Gabriella again. I want to see Evelyn. But if I don't, I'm okay to move on or be nothing or whatever. If it doesn't happen now it'll happen sometime in the next forty or fifty years and that's not much more time anyway. Every day is precious, but it was not an enjoyable experience getting in the space I'm in, and now that I'm here I don't mind it. Do I really want to journey back here again?

Gabriella says, "Can you feel my hand, Nils?" She squeezes mine, and I try to squeeze hers. Her tone changes. "Ellie, I felt something. I swear."

"Shap's a fighter. He's hanging in there."

"Remember what the doctor said."

"Yeah." Ellegaard pauses. Is he sniffling? Dammit! He's letting me down. Maybe I should snap out of this coma just to slap him. Ellegaard says, "The doctor said it can be helpful if we tell you stories. I'm going to start by filling you in on what's happened the last couple days."

Gabriella says, "You'll want to hear this, Nils. So, listen."

I'm listening.

Ellegaard says, "I woke up early the morning after we last talked. No reason. Just got up about 4:00 A.M. and was wide awake. I checked my email and saw what you'd sent me and Gabriella. So I called the first number you asked me to call. LAPD Hollywood division. They sent officers over to Ebben's right away. They found you unconscious in the living room. You were on the floor, bleeding badly from the head. And your carry-on was there. Wide open and empty. Vasily had transferred the money into something else to carry it out. So your plan worked."

It's strange how, even in my condition, it feels so satisfying to hear that.

"I also called the second number, the FBI Field Office in Los Angeles. I gave them the tracking information. I don't know where you found a tracker that looks exactly like a credit card, but it was brilliant to hide it among the gift cards and prepaid credit cards."

I want to tell Ellegaard I bought the tracker that looks like a credit card at House of Spies in Hollywood. Jameson told me about it. Said you can buy all sorts of spy-like devices there, and Jameson was right. So when I came up with the idea to bait Vasily into stealing the $5 million, I went to House of Spies and bought the tracker. I paid for it with Vasily's money. I want to tell Ellegaard this, but I can't, so he keeps talking.

Ellegaard says, "Ninety minutes after I called the FBI, they located Vasily and apprehended him. And the best part of the story is Ebben is fine. You were right about Vasily. He wasn't out to hurt anyone. He'd just gotten himself in over his head and was acting out of desperation. And thanks to you, Nils, that desperation didn't last long enough for him to hurt Ebben."

Gabriella squeezed my hand again and says, "Vasily confessed everything to the FBI."

Ellegaard says, "You were right about that, too, Nils. He talked someone into investing 20 million in Thom Burke's *Veins of Gold* movie. He didn't say who that person is, but whoever it is agreed to invest the 20 million because Kate Lennon was in the movie. When Kate Lennon dropped out to be in *For the People*, the investor wanted his money back. Thom wanted more time to save the project, and Vasily thinks he tried to kill Ebben but accidentally killed Juliana in the process. Same as your theory. Vasily's investor threatened him, and Vasily tried to intimidate Thom into giving the money back. That's what the altercation on Thom's front step was about. That's why Vasily threatened the *For the People* production by telling everyone to drop Kate Lennon or else. Your instincts were spot-on, Shap."

Gabriella says in a soft tone, as if I can't hear her, "Should we tell him about yesterday?"

Yes, I think. You should. I'm quite the captive audience at the moment.

Ellegaard says, "Vasily's instincts were right, too. I don't know how you'll feel about this, Shap, but when the feds put him on pretrial in front of the magistrate, a gunman entered the courtroom and shot and killed Vasily. No one knows how the guy got a gun past the metal detector. The FBI thinks someone in organized crime had the gun planted inside before Vasily's court appearance."

I fell asleep within my sleep and now I can hear again and everyone is gone. But I'm not awake. I'm dreaming. I think I'm dreaming. I'm looking down on myself. The me I see is lying on my ratty couch in the coat factory where I live. It's not a factory anymore. The machinery is all gone. It still has old awning windows, a worn wooden floor, a high ceiling, and an eyewash station. But I've made it into a home with furniture and a freestanding kitchen of discarded restaurant fixtures: stainless steel counters and shelving and a sink and an industrial refrigerator-freezer.

The coat factory is where I lived before I moved in with Gabriella. I'm looking down on me lying on my couch, and there's a knock on the door but the lying-down me can't get up to answer it. I tell myself, "Get up. Someone's at the door." But I can't. I just lie there with my eyes open. Then the door opens. I look over to see a boy enter. I guess he's ten years old. He's African American, wears a Los Angeles Rams football jersey, jeans, and Jack Purcell sneakers. He carries a sack lunch in a brown paper bag.

The boy says, "Shap? What's going on? Why didn't you answer the door?"

The lying-down me can't answer. It's frustrating, like watching a movie when you want to scream at the screen and tell a character they're being an idiot. If they'd just make a different choice, the conflict would resolve itself. The choice I wanted the lying-down me to make was to wake up. But he (aka I) would not.

The boy says, "Oh man, Shap. You look like shit, my friend. Good thing I showed up." The boy reaches into his lunch bag and pulls out a roll of gauze and a bandage scissors. He says, "I know just the thing to make you feel better. I'll wrap you from head to toe in gauze and then you'll be a mummy and you can walk around and scare people and damn, that will be funny. Ha! What do you think, Shap? Want to be a mummy?"

The me who is looking down says, "Would I be a mummy forever or just for a little while so I can scare people?" But the boy can't hear the me who is looking down. And the me who is lying down won't talk. He's such an idiot! I want to throw a bucket of water on his face. He's just lying there. So damn frustrating. Then the scene in the coat factory fades to dark and credits roll just like in a movie. The credits are just names but they don't say what jobs the names have. They're all my relatives. My grandparents and great-grandparents and great-aunts and -uncles. All dead. Then the credits end and everything is dark.

I'm back where I was with Ellegaard and Gabriella. I can't see but I can hear. My parents are there with my brother and sister. They're a mess. Always making a big deal about nothing, my family. So much drama.

My little brother, Marty, cries his way through a story about how when we were kids I said I'd sell him my BMX bike for twenty dollars thinking no way he would pay twenty dollars for my BMX bike because he didn't have twenty dollars. Marty was only eight and he always spent his money as soon as he got it. But he said okay he'd buy it and told me he'd have the money the next day. And the next day he gave me a twenty-dollar bill, and I asked where he got it. He told me it was none of my business. I accused him of stealing it from my stash of cash which I kept inside a copy of Howard Pyle's *The Merry Adventures of Robin Hood*.

I'd hollowed out the middle of the book, page by page, so it looked like a regular book when you picked it up. Only when you opened it could you see the middle part of each page had been cut out. I hadn't told anyone about my hollowed-out *The Merry Adventures of Robin Hood* but Marty must have discovered it and that's where he got the twenty dollars. But I had no idea how much money I'd kept in the book so I couldn't prove he stole it and I begrudgingly agreed to sell Marty my bike.

Now Marty's blubbering his eyes out admitting he did steal the twenty dollars from *The Merry Adventures of Robin Hood*. Yeah, now he feels bad about it. When I'm in a coma. What the hell took so long? I want to calculate the interest on twenty dollars over thirty years but I don't know how and even if I did I can't communicate.

My mind is so active. I wonder why I hadn't seen the irony of me having money and Marty having none so he stole some from *The Merry Adventures of Robin Hood*, which was about taking money from the rich and giving it to the poor. And I wonder if not being able to prove Marty stole the money motivated me to go into law enforcement. No. That's ridiculous. And at the same time I think about how strange it is that family stuff just keeps bubbling up. It never stops. Even when one guy's in a coma. Not a big incentive to wake up.

My mother takes one hand and my father takes the other and they tell me they love me and Marty and my sister do the same and then they're gone.

46

I hear a machine beep a steady beep and figure it must be my heart rate but other than that it's quiet. A few minutes ago some nurses replenished my IV and bathed me. The wet sponge felt cool and one nurse said I had gooseflesh and that might mean something or it might not. Then they turned me on my side and propped some pillows behind me to keep me there.

I can tell it's night. I don't know how but I can. I think that means no more visitors but then I must be wrong because I hear, "Shap, you son of a bitch. You wake the hell up right now." It's Jameson. He says, "The only reason you took this case was to bring me to California because you thought it would help me get my shit together."

That's not true, I want to tell him. I would have taken the case anyway. I thought it would be easy work for easy money and this is my fault for not letting go when I could and should have. I want to explain this but I can't.

Jameson says, "I know more about comas than a person should know. I've cared for hundreds of people in comas. And I know some can hear and some can't. I've talked to the doctors and nurses and they think you can hear. So does Gabriella. Ellegaard isn't sure but that's Ellegaard, always taking the conservative approach. So I asked Nikki to get me in after visiting hours so I could have some time alone with you because you and me have some talking to do."

The machine that beeps keeps beeping. "Listen. The way I figure it, you and me are now even. No way you would have survived that arrow wound if I hadn't been chasing you around changing your bandages and making sure you took your antibiotics. See, you got this disease, Shap, where you just got to do what you do like a shark has to keep swimming or some shit like that. But I was there to make sure you got healthy while you kept moving.

"Then I fall apart when those kids got shot and I was there and watched a bunch of 'em die and saw their parents get turned into zombies when the life drained out of them, too. So you took care of me. Even though I was a pain in the ass and had to wallow in my shit for a while you would take me out to ball games and to dinner and I'd just sit there and do nothing, kind of like what you're doing now. But you didn't give up on me and brought me to Los Angeles and I never would've reconnected with Nikki if you hadn't done that. I needed the push, Shap. I needed the push."

God, I wish I could talk to Jameson. But he's been so quiet

over the last year, listening to him ramble is nice. Makes me want to hug him. I wish I could do that, too.

He says, "Something about Nikki you know. Maybe 'cause we were secret friends for five years and she helped me love books and classrooms and I helped her adapt to America. I don't know. Having a secret friend you can count on no matter what is pretty fucking special. You and me, we kind of got that. At least I think we do."

I think we do, too, Jameson. I know we do.

"It's like what you have with Ellegaard and Gabriella. It goes way back, real deep. But you and me, we kind of had it right away. We didn't need all them years for it to ferment and get good and powerful.

"I made a mistake letting Nikki get away. You fixed it by bringing me back to her. You didn't even know you were doing it but you did. I'm never letting her go again, just like you're never letting Gabriella go. So you know what I'm talking about when I say I'm not letting go of you so get the hell out of that coma, Shap. It's up to you. I've seen it. Some people, they just keep hanging on till they get strong enough. Other people, they just don't got the fight in 'em so they let go. Nothing wrong with that if it's their time, but brother, it ain't your time. Not even close."

I feel Jameson take my hand. I concentrate and press as hard as I can. Give it everything I have.

Jameson says, "Well, I didn't expect you to wake up right this minute. These things take time. Weeks. Maybe months. Maybe longer. A little squeeze of the hand would have been nice, but you got to go at your own pace."

Someone else steps into the room and says, "How are you two doing?" It's Dr. Li.

Jameson says, "Tell Nils what we're going to do when he wakes up. Go ahead. He needs to hear it from you."

I hear footsteps, then Dr. Li speaks almost in a whisper, but I can hear her clearly. Her head must be close to mine. She says, "Shap, Jameson and I and my son are going to Minnesota with you."

Jameson says, "Tell him why."

I want to tell Jameson there's no need. I get it. But I can't so I just lie there and listen.

"Jameson and I are going to get married in Minnesota, Nils. And you're going to be Jameson's best man. And then me and my son are going to live there with Jameson. That might seem odd to you, but I love Jameson and would like to live in a quieter place. And my son's had a rough time in middle school and wants a fresh start where no one knows him. He's very excited for the snow and to cheer for the Minnesota Vikings."

I want to say if he thinks middle school is hard, wait until he's a Vikings fan. It's so fraught with anxiety and disappointment it's like being in middle school for the rest of your life.

Jameson says, "Yeah, Nils. We're all moving to Minnesota even though you chose Ellegaard to be your best man and you probably got me slated to be usher or some bullshit like that. Tell you what, I'll be your usher, but I insist on carrying a flashlight with an orange cone on the end 'cause that's what ushers should have."

I want to tell Jameson nothing would make me happier than him seating guests at my wedding while wielding a flashlight with an orange cone on the end. I want to tell him yes, absolutely do that, and then see the surprise on his face when he learns there's only thirty-five people at my wedding and there's no need for an usher. That would be fun.

Jameson says, "And I figure, now that we're even, I'll nurse you back to health so that way you'll owe me again. I like you being in my debt and being beholden to me, Shap. Plus there's the best man inequity so that means you double owe me. And Nikki and her son are moving to Minnesota to live full time. So you owe her, too. That's a lot of personal debt you'll have to carry, Shap, so the sooner you wake up and start repaying your debt the sooner you'll be out from under it. That's all I got to say."

Jameson lets go of my hand. Someone touches my forehead. The touch is soft. I hope it's Dr. Li.

Dr. Li says, "I have to get home to my son, Nils. I will be back in the morning. Good night."

She kisses me on my forehead. I barely know the woman. Not sure how I feel about it.

Jameson says, "All right, Shap. I'm going to sleep in the recliner. Got some blankets. Some snacks in case I get hungry in the middle of the night. Apologize in advance if there's some snoring, but hey, my soft palate has been a little extra soft lately so I can't help it. Might get me one of those CPAP machines but I don't know—I'd look ridiculous and sound like Darth Vader. Oh, and I have a request: No bullshit while I'm asleep. No waking up then falling back to sleep again. And no letting go. You got that? Do not let go. Ellegaard and Gabriella will be here in the morning. I know Micaela wants to fly out with Evelyn but Evelyn's got a bad cold and they're worried it will hurt her ears on the plane."

Oh, that makes me sad. I'd love to hear Evelyn say her gibberish one more time.

Jameson says, "Man, one punch. One punch and you are out. I don't know why I thought you were tougher than that. But clearly, you are not. Kind of embarrassing. All right. Might watch a little SportsCenter to help me fall asleep. You know what I'm talking about."

I hear the television and then I don't and I'm sitting on the bank of a stream where a riffle empties into a pool. A limestone bluff walls the other side of the stream, and trout rise in the pool and take mayflies off the water. But most of the mayflies hatch to freedom and rise above the water's surface slow and steady like helicopters.

It feels like a warm October day. The leaves are near peak color, and the sun's not too high in the sky. It's almost hot, but it's okay because I know it's the last heat of the season. The grasses in the marsh behind me have turned to gold.

A dog I haven't seen in twenty-five years sits next to me. Her name is Sheila. She's a seventy-pound golden retriever, which is a bit of a misnomer because she has dark red fur. She was hit by a car when I was fifteen. It happened right in front of my eyes. The driver didn't stop. I reach over and pet her. Sheila's fur feels warm in the sun.

I say, "Sorry I let you off the leash. I didn't think you'd run away from me."

She says, "I didn't run away. I saw a squirrel on the other side of the street."

"Yeah, well. I should have thought of that possibility."

"Don't be ridiculous, Nils. I'm a dog. I'm hardwired to chase squirrels. It's what I do. Not my fault. Not your fault. When I'm chasing squirrels, I'm at peace. I was in pursuit of a squirrel. It was a delightful way to go."

"Really? I cried for months after you died. I still get sad when I think about you. I've been afraid to get another dog ever since."

"Don't be. I wasn't going to live much longer anyway. I was twelve."

I hear an airplane. I look up. There's one right over our heads. Then another. And another. I say, "Why are there so many airplanes? Are we near an airport?"

Sheila says, "No idea. I'm a dog. Hey, you bring your rod? Maybe you could catch us some fish."

"Remember when you used to try to catch them with your mouth?"

"I was a puppy. I didn't know any better. But I do now. So you got to catch 'em."

"Sorry. I don't have a rod."

"Well." She sighs. It's a dog sigh. The best kind of sigh a person could ever hope to hear. "I suppose we can just sit here. It's kind of pretty."

"It sure is." I pet Sheila behind her ears. She shuts her eyes and tilts her head toward the sun.

47

I recline and look at the sky, and Sheila does the strangest thing. She lies on my chest like she did when we were young. I pet Sheila behind her ears. She feels soft like when she was a puppy. But something's wrong. Her fur doesn't feel like fur. It feels like hair. And the sky is gone. I can't see anymore. All I can do is pet her.

"Ellie." Is that Gabriella? "Ellie, come here." I hear footsteps. Gabriella says, "Look. Oh God, look."

Ellegaard says, "Shap?"

I say, "Ellie, I can't see you." I hear my words in my head but not in my ears. In my ears I hear myself groan.

"Nils!" says Gabriella. She cries. "Nils . . ."

I hear, "Ba ba ba ba ba ba ba ba ba . . ." It's a baby. It's not Sheila's fur I'm touching. It's Evelyn's hair. She wriggles on my chest.

A hand caresses my cheek. Gabriella says, "His eyes are fluttering."

Ellegaard says, "I got Evelyn. Go ahead."

I feel Gabriella's breath near my face. I hear her breathe. She kisses me. I have three thoughts: (1) I can't wake up right when she kisses me because that would be like a fairy tale and thus humiliating. (2) Please don't kiss me. I have coma breath. (3) I came back from the comfortable place. I'm alive.

"Ba ba ba ba ba ba ba ba ba ba ba . . ."

I open my eyes.

I was in a coma for twenty-seven days. When I'd stabilized, Ebben Mayer paid a small country's GDP to fly me to Minnesota on a jet ambulance staffed with a team of doctors and nurses. I came out of the coma at Abbott Northwestern Hospital in Minneapolis.

I'd missed the polar vortex. It got down to minus thirty-one degrees Fahrenheit. People were still talking about it. I was and still am furious I missed it.

The doctors said I recovered from my coma quickly, but I remained in the hospital for five more weeks. Most days I felt better, but other days I couldn't get out of bed. I watched a lot of college basketball and news and read a tall stack of books. My favorite activity was walking the hospital hallways with Gabriella or Ellegaard or Jameson. Annika Brydolf, Stone Arch's junior investigator, visited almost daily. Kenji Thao, our assistant, visited several times a week. Ebben Mayer visited me three times. My parents and siblings didn't miss a day, as if I were still a kid. Micaela visited when she could, and she or Gabriella brought Evelyn every single day. Evelyn took her first steps in pursuit of a Winnie the Pooh in the gift shop window. She sleeps with that Winnie the Pooh every night.

One evening, Ellegaard and Gabriella brought in takeout from a restaurant called Yum which lives up to its name.

We were sharing a chocolate chip cookie the size of a manhole cover when Ellegaard said, "Do you remember when you were in Los Angeles and you said something was weird about Debra and you wanted me to run a background check on her?"

"I do remember that."

"It took some digging, but get this: Debra's grandmother was Beverly Mayer's sister."

Gabriella said, "That's weird."

Ellegaard said, "Frederick Fallhauser had three granddaughters. No grandsons. The oldest married a wealthy talent agent and moved to New York, leaving Beverly with her youngest sister. Her younger sister moved to Beloit, Wisconsin, and married a butcher."

I said, "And that sister is Debra's grandmother?"

"Yes. I spoke to Debra about it when you were in the hospital in Los Angeles. She was not happy I'd looked into her family background. I promised her it would remain our secret if she explained the connection."

Gabriella said, "And did she?"

"Yes. Apparently, Debra's grandmother ran off because Beverly Mayer tormented her constantly. So much so that Debra's grandmother spent two years in an asylum. Debra said Beverly convinced Frederick Fallhauser that her younger sister was mentally ill. When Debra's grandmother got out, she ran away and never returned to the family. When Frederick Fallhauser died, his fortune went to his two oldest granddaughters. He left nothing to his youngest because the way Beverly had spun it, the youngest had turned her back on the family."

I said, "Oh, that Beverly Mayer is a real sweetheart."

"Debra didn't hear the story of her grandmother's family until after she graduated college."

I said, "Does Ebben know Debra's his cousin?"

"No," said Ellegaard. "And she begged me not to tell him."

Gabriella said, "So Debra was already working in Hollywood when Ebben Mayer showed up with his millions of family money?"

"Yes," said Ellegaard. "And according to Debra, she made it her mission to manage Ebben to get some of the family fortune back. She succeeded in getting the job, but when Ebben started The Creative Collective, she felt like her side of the family was losing all over again. But then Sebastiano hired her as a top-level agent at his new agency, and that seemed to make everything right again."

I broke off another piece of the delicious manhole cover and said, "But before Sebastiano hired Debra, when she felt cheated again . . . Is there any chance it was Debra who sent that caffeine overdose Ebben's way? Is she the one who killed Juliana?"

Ellegaard shrugged. "It's possible."

"Thom could have had caffeine powder for another reason. Like he was trying to keep up with a woman twenty years his junior."

Gabriella looked hard at me with her big brown eyes. I smiled. She returned the smile. And we both understood I wouldn't go back to Los Angeles to investigate Debra.

I married Gabriella Nuñez the day I left the hospital. Our wedding, as we'd hoped, coincided with a March blizzard. Luck seemed to have turned in my favor again. Technically it was neither cold nor windy enough to qualify as a blizzard, but seventeen inches of snow fell in less than a day. It made our small wedding feel extra cozy and intimate. Everyone who survived the journey felt fortunate to be there.

Ellegaard officiated. The cake was lopsided, delicious, and topped with figures of me and Gabriella. Olivia Ellegaard had sculpted us out of fondant, Gabriella wearing her dress blues and me wearing a T-shirt and jeans. Molly Ellegaard didn't let seventeen inches of snow stop her from filling the restaurant with flowers. Gabriella's sister took pictures. Jameson walked around carrying a flashlight with an orange cone and wouldn't shut up about being the usher. Dr. Li and her son already felt like family. Gabriella's father walked her down the aisle. Her mother cried as if she'd won the lottery, as if it were a pipe dream that her fiercely independent daughter would marry. Evelyn walked our rings down the aisle, unsteady on her legs like a drunk walking on a boat in rough seas.

A delivery person showed up at the restaurant with a gift. It was a small box, about the size of a book, professionally wrapped in silvers and golds with paper and ribbons and, if I wasn't mistaken, lingonberries.

Gabriella said, "Some jerk broke the no-gift rule."

I said, "Should I throw it out?"

The delivery person looked at us like we were crazy. I tipped him, and he left. I handed the present to Gabriella and said, "Open it. I don't want to put it in the car if we're not going to keep it."

She scrunched up her pretty mouth and ripped the wrapping off the box. It was a decorative box, all silver. She lifted off the lid and said, "It's photographs." She looked more closely. "Oh my God."

Gabriella handed me the top photograph. It was of a litter of puppies. They looked like springer spaniels. I said, "What the hell?"

She looked at the next photograph and said, "This is ridiculous." She handed the photo to me. It was of another litter of puppies. Labs in chocolate, yellow, and black.

Gabriella thumbed through the photos and said, "There's twelve pictures in here and they're all of a different litter of puppies. Doodles and mutts and whoa, these look like foxes."

I said, "Is there a card?"

She pulled out a small note card and read: "All of these puppies will need a home between May 1 and June 1 and all have deposits on them in your names. Pick one or two or three or more. Sorry to break the no-gift rule. But not really. Happy wedding, Nils and Gabriella!"

My wife said, "No signature."

I said, "Huh."

Molly Ellegaard denied the puppies were from her. Micaela denied it, too. We questioned everyone at the wedding. They all denied gifting us puppies. And we believed them.

We'd postponed our honeymoon. Me being out of the hospital was its own honeymoon. We'd go on an official one in April before the summer travel season started. Possible destinations were Patagonia to ride horses in the Chilean autumn, Banff because it's stunning and where we got engaged, and Paris because it's Paris. Or we might just drive up to Minnesota's North Shore of Lake Superior because it's beautiful and the rest of the world doesn't know it exists.

I looked at the clock on the nightstand: 1:34 A.M. Gabriella, my wife of less than eight hours, slept. I could not sleep. It felt like when I'd visit New York. There, the energy of the city keeps me awake. On our wedding night, it was the energy of being out of the hospital for the first time in nine weeks. And the wedding. And my new life.

But was it a new life? Yes, it was. New love. New wife. New baby. New home.

What had remained the same was me. I had changed, but the change preceded falling in love with Gabriella. Me changing is what allowed me to fall in love with her, and her with me.

I was forged in the fires of adversity like everyone else on the planet. Steel can only be reshaped when hot. No one wants an ugly, rusty hunk of steel. But put it in the fire, hammer it when it's vulnerable, and you may just end up with something desirable.

In Los Angeles, Jameson White accused me of going soft, turning my back on justice, burying the person I used to be. And maybe I tried to do all that because, with all I had to lose, pulling back seemed the logical thing to do.

But it didn't work. Instinct took over. Logic and common sense fell dutifully behind.

Gabriella and Evelyn made me stronger, not weaker. For them, I'd be more focused. More deliberate. Bolder. Sharper. Hungrier.

I rolled onto my side and big-spooned my wife. She pressed back into me, and I felt twenty-one years old. Reset. Rewound. Recalibrated.

This wasn't the end. It was . . .

The Beginning

ACKNOWLEDGMENTS

In 1987, I got in my dented Ford Escort with a few hundred dollars and a credit card and drove from Minneapolis to Los Angeles. I'd just turned twenty four and aspired to write television. I spent my days in a tiny Studio City apartment watching videotaped episodes, charting the story beats with a stopwatch, and scripting my own stories of then-popular shows like *It's Garry Shandling's Show*, *Golden Girls*, and *The Wonder Years*. I read books like William Goldman's *Adventures in the Screen Trade* and Lajos Egri's *The Art of Dramatic Writing*. I understood none of them. I made ends meet by telling jokes, raking in $25–$50 a night.

In 1989, Jerry Seinfeld and Larry David invited me and fellow writer/comedian Pat Hazell to write on what was then called *The Seinfeld Chronicles*. That was the beginning of my writing career and an on-the-job learning process that will never end. The people who taught me are writers, producers, directors, and actors. There are some wise executives, agents, and managers, too. But most of my learning happened in writers' rooms where we'd toil through lunch and dinner and often well past midnight before heading home for a few hours of sleep so we could get up and do it again.

Those writers are too many to name, but I thank them all for their minds and spirits, their kindness, generosity, and patience.

One Los Angeles person I will mention by name is my accountant, Susie Neasi. With Hollywood's droughts and deluges, she has kept the farm in business, and for that I will always be grateful.

I lived in Los Angeles full time for eighteen years. I commuted there from Minneapolis for an additional twelve years. That's significant time, and I understand why Los Angeles is such a fertile setting for crime fiction. The town attracts the ambitious and the talented. Yet Los Angeles offers few rules and little structure to achieve success. It is the Wild West.

Writing Nils Shapiro's visit to Los Angeles felt visceral. I backed up in time. Relived my early days there. How strange the place felt to an unworldly Minnesotan. The sun shined differently. The place sounded and smelled like no place I'd known. The trees were different. The grass was different. You could pick oranges and avocados in your back yard. Wonderful and weird. And it took me five years to stop myself from thinking, every time I saw a steep hill, "How do people drive up that in winter?"

Television taught me character and voice, story and series architecture. I hope to write more television. I love and respect the medium. I miss my fellow writers. But I will always write books. Sitting alone in a room is, after all, my natural habitat.

Dead West is my fourth book. I have only scratched the surface of novel writing. Thank you to my agent, Jennifer Weltz, my editor, Kristin Sevick, and to everyone at Forge for making my transition a smooth one. For your support, guidance, hard work, and taste. For helping me up my game.

I feel terribly excited for what's ahead.

And thank you to my wife, Michele, for her love and support. Day after day. Book after book.

—MG